A YEAR OF LESSER

A YEAR OF LESSER

DAVID BERGEN

A Phyllis Bruce Book
HarperCollins*PublishersLtd*

http://www.harpercollins.com

Excerpt from THE GOLD CELL by Sharon Olds. Copyright © 1981 by
Sharon Olds. Reprinted by permission of Alfred A. Knopf Inc.

Two chapters of this novel, "Saved" and "Eggs, New-laid," were first
published in *Prairie Fire*.

*The financial assistance of the Canada Council and
the Manitoba Art Council is gratefully acknowledged.*

First Edition

Canadian Cataloguing in Publication Data

Bergen, David, 1957-
A year of lesser

"A Phyllis Bruce book."
ISBN 0-00-648107-8

I. Title.

PS8553.E665Y43 1996   C813'.54   C95-932434-8
PR9199.3.B47Y43 1996

---

96 97 98 99 ❖ HC 10 9 8 7 6 5 4 3 2 1

Printed and bound in the United States

For Mary

FALL

SAVED

Johnny feels perfectly new. Two months ago when he kneeled before Phil Barkman and Phil laid hands on him, Johnny had felt like an ugly ugly man. "I'm all screwed up," he told Phil that night and Phil had smiled and held him close. Then they'd discussed Johnny's burdens and Phil touched Johnny's head and they'd closed their eyes and Phil asked, "Can you feel it?" But Johnny couldn't feel anything, just the weight of Phil's hands. "It's okay," Phil said. "It'll come, maybe when you're in the car driving home, or tomorrow morning in the shower."

Phil was right. It hit Johnny that night as he climbed into bed. It was like a large wave rolling over him. A warmth pervaded his body, starting at his toes and working past his knees, filling him up. His chest tingled. He thought of explaining this to Charlene who was reading on her side of the bed but her body was turned slightly, telling him she didn't want to be bothered. Still, he lay there, hands at his sides, staring at the cracks in the plaster above him, itching for Charlene to notice. She did turn finally, rolling a leg onto him, her mouth at his ear. "Good night, Johnny." She kissed him, offering the faint echoes of whisky from her evening drink. Then the light clicked and Johnny was lying in darkness. For a long time he did not sleep; he remembered the aquarium he had owned as a boy, dipping his hands into the water and fishing for an elusive and slippery guppy. Salvation was that guppy and that night he had it firmly in his grasp.

And it has been two months already, a sort of record for Johnny Fehr. He's a rock. At work — he is a salesman at OK Feeds — he fairly bounces. The girls in the office smile and he knows they must see a difference in him. He sits beside Leonard Ostnick in the coffee room and he forgives the man for who he is. Everybody knows Leonard is an angry, bitter man who doesn't like Johnny much. But that's okay, Johnny thinks, and an overwhelming sense of rightness springs into his chest.

Johnny knows that his equanimity baffles Charlene. She says it's false and won't last. This has happened before. Johnny becomes a Christian and for three weeks he's an angel. He's so perfect he doesn't even want to have sex with Charlene, and though that's not so bad she will let him know that sometimes she aches for the old Johnny. "But," she says, holding his little finger, "I'll wait, you'll come back." Perhaps Johnny knows too that this is temporary, that he lacks resolve, because he'll stop the car at an intersection and sit there for a long time as if meditating or wondering where or who he is. Then, he drives and his face is not happy, not really new; it is slack and pulled down, as if a tremendous force were yanking him earthward.

On Friday and Saturday nights Johnny runs a drop-in centre. He's borrowed a little place adjoining Herb's Electric; he's put in a pool table, stereo, couches. Pepsi donated a machine. He opened the centre for various reasons: he felt sorry for kids who had nowhere to go, he wants to prove that this time around he's going to succeed at his new life-style, and he's also trying to be a bit of a missionary. Though the centre's been operating for over a month, the grand opening is on Saturday night. The mayor makes an early speech and then runs off, claiming another commitment.

Very few adults show up, they seem embarrassed by Johnny's enthusiasm. Charlene comes for half an hour. She smokes a cigarette and talks to some other women and then they all go for coffee at Chuck's. About fifteen kids straggle in and stand around looking at each other. Then some of them go outside and smoke. Johnny tries to interest a few in pool but it isn't until he pulls out his old record collection that he snags the curiosity of the "heads" who wear big boots and flannel jackets and have just walked in after a joint underneath the glow of the Petro-Canada sign. They pass around Led Zeppelin, Peter Tosh, and Jimi Hendrix. Johnny knows from talking to the kids that in twenty years music has come full circle; this is what the kids like. Their faces are sullen, trying hard not to look impressed. Dennis, one of the skinnier kids — Johnny figures he never eats — says, "My old man had these too, then he hooked up with this Phil Barkman guy and he burned them. Nuts."

Nobody looks at Dennis. One girl grunts in response. Her long brown hair is split down the middle and she pushes it back with a quick nervous movement. Another girl says "Hey" and holds up a picture of Janis Joplin. Johnny feels guilty. He knows he should have burned his records too. But he couldn't, they mean too much. He feels badly now for sharing them with these kids, wonders if he's leading them astray. But he doesn't have to wonder long because suddenly they're gone. They rise as one, clinging to and needing each other, and Johnny, watching from the centre window, sees the group zigzag down the street, their breath rising above their heads and disappearing.

By ten o'clock Johnny is alone. He drinks a cup of coffee and puts on some religious rock and roll that Phil recommended. It doesn't sound any different but for some reason it stirs in Johnny a feeling of something okay. He looks around at his bare walls and says, "Gotta get some posters." A couple of kids with skateboards come in and Johnny recognizes Chris, Loraine's son. Seeing him makes Johnny want to see Loraine. They had something. "Hi ya," Johnny says.

Chris stares, then his head stutters around the room. A kid in the back of the group says, "Fuck all, let's go."

"Streets clean enough to skate?" Johnny asks. He isn't pushing, he's just letting them know he knows.

"Yeah." Chris says this. He looks at Johnny, neither good nor bad, and then he leaves. Johnny wonders if Chris knows about him and Loraine. Kids aren't dumb, Johnny knows that. He often tells Charlene, *Kids are smart.* He finishes his coffee, turns off the lights, and locks the door. Driving home he thinks about kids and about Charlene. First Charlene didn't want babies, then he didn't, and then they both didn't. The problem was they never both did and so they've stayed childless and sometimes Johnny thinks they've done things wrong, that maybe he'd find it easier to be clean if he had kids. Children make you faithful, he figures. Keep you honest. He pulls into the driveway of his farmyard and glides in, no power, in neutral. Johnny doesn't farm. Never will. He rents his land out. He lives here because his father and mother died and left him the property. He sits in the shadow of the trees, door ajar, a slight wind blowing on his neck, and he watches Charlene work at the kitchen window. She doesn't know he's there and he likes that because then what he sees is real.

Charlene is rinsing out the sink. She wrings the rag, touches a hand to her forehead, dips and disappears, then pops up again. Her mouth is slightly open, her tongue touches her lip, dives back inside. Johnny watches her and likes what he sees. Her shoulders round to her arms. Her neck is hidden by hair and a high collar. Johnny likes to unbutton that collar and kiss the bones below her throat. Charlene turns, the light goes out, and Johnny goes in.

Wednesday at supper Johnny says to Charlene, "I'm going to a meeting tonight at Phil's, this faith-healer guy from Arizona. Do you wanna come?"

"Tonight's my book club, we changed it this week, sorry, sweetie." She doesn't seem sorry. In fact she seems pleased not to have to excuse herself in another way.

"What do you do at these book things anyway?" Johnny asks. Though Charlene's participated in them for a long time he's never really asked her about them.

"We sit in a circle and talk about a book," Charlene says. "Simple. Kinda like a Bible study. Only more interesting."

"Oh, that's good. Who's smart?" Johnny says. He stands in the bathroom and runs the electric shaver over his jaw. He pats on some aftershave. Charlene is sitting in panties and bra on the edge of the bed. She's working panty hose up one leg. Johnny watches her through the mirror. Her leg lifts and he can see the softest part of her body just below the crotch, the inside thigh. The leg drops. "When are you leaving?" Johnny asks. He's trying to weigh time and desire.

Charlene concentrates on her stockings. "About half an hour," she says.

"Wanna have sex?" Johnny asks. He's standing in the doorway, just in jeans. His toes curl in anticipation although he can tell by the way Charlene's leg lifts what the answer will be.

"Yaaa?" she says, and her stockings glide on. And that's that.

Johnny knows most everyone at Phil's house. He went to school with a lot of them or he sees them around town. Chuck from the Chicken Shack is there with his wife Dora and their baby daughter. Mr. and Mrs. Bartel, an older couple, are already seated. Mrs. Bartel has a chin that extends like a hammer claw. There are a few basketball buddies, the Penner brothers, and there is little Erwin Heinrichs who is epileptic and once fell foaming at Johnny's feet during silent-reading in Grade Eight. Melissa Emery is there without her husband. He's a truck driver. Johnny remembers Melissa because she has wonderful teeth and a deep widow's peak dropping into a polished forehead. Most of these people, like Johnny, were raised in a Mennonite church and then left because they wanted something bigger, an emotional lift the stoic Mennonite preachers couldn't offer.

The room they are sitting in has been built especially for meetings. It's hall-like, stretching the width of the large unfinished house. There are hard benches, some lawn chairs, and a small lectern at the front. Phil starts the meeting with a lengthy prayer and just as he's wrapping up Melissa Emery shows her teeth and starts to speak in tongues. Johnny, who's seated on the outside of the circle, opens his eyes and watches Melissa's body move. Her hands snake, her body shakes, this alien language bubbles up, and though it makes no sense to Johnny he is taken by the sharpness of Melissa's shoulders, by the poetry of her words. After Melissa sits down, groaning in ecstasy, two more people stand up and recite their own strange versions of rapture until finally Phil Barkman cuts in and says, "Because Mr. Singleton has come a long way to minister to us, we will forgo interpretation tonight. Praise God he can be a part of our small humble group." Applause breaks out and Johnny wonders why, if he has the Holy Spirit — he recalls being smacked by it as he crawled under the quilt — *he* can't speak in tongues too. He wonders if it has to be forced or if a special kind of breathing is required. He bites the inside of his cheek, then he breathes deeply ten times but only succeeds in getting dizzy.

Mr. Singleton is a round man with a small forehead that crinkles every time he pauses to snap a breath. He talks quickly as if trying to catch up to a splendid idea. His hands are all over the place. He gives a talk on the woman at the well and how that woman was immoral and an outcast and how Jesus accepted that woman. Then Mr. Singleton talks about homosexuals and he says they are sinners, "Probably the *worst*." Then he quotes whole chapters of the New Testament.

Johnny's mind wanders. His eye rests on Phil's wife, Eleanor, who is breast-feeding their baby. Eleanor is barefoot, legs crossed, one foot flat on the floor, toes spread. Her face leans into the baby, cooing, she is not really listening to Mr. Singleton. Five children. How prolific Phil is; honey in his throat, honey in his loins. The bustle of supper remains in the air; dishes still on the table, fresh bread, cabbage, beets maybe. Beet jam perhaps, globs of butter. His own mother used to strain beets, boil up the juice into a froth. Drops of crimson on the yellow lino. Sticky underfoot. Phil and Eleanor have to finish this floor. The plywood must produce slivers, stubbed toes. It's like the rest of the house, unfinished. Cabinets without doors. No baseboards. There is a comfort in this. Johnny too has unfinished business at home. A large unmowed lawn, curling shingles, downspouts unhinged. A fallow wife. Eleanor's baby stops sucking and pulls away slowly, leaving a shiny nipple poking out like the end of Johnny's thumb. Johnny aches for a woman like Eleanor who accepts so easily the strife and commotion of children.

Mr. Singleton is in the foreground again. He says a loud "Amen" and is soon praying over Mrs. Bartel for her diabetes. In her excitement, Mrs. Bartel's chin swings dangerously close to Phil Barkman's eye. Then one of the old basketball boys has his bum knee touched. Chuck tries to have his gout cured and, of course, the climax of the evening is the laying on of multiple hands on poor Erwin Heinrich's messed-up head.

At that moment, Johnny is tired and embarrassed for Erwin, whose epilepsy, he's decided, is probably no more a curse than speaking in tongues. Johnny's been on the outside of this group all evening, and decided a while back that these people don't really know how to have fun. He's been horny too, Melissa here, Eleanor there, Johnny's hand in the fish tank, losing his grip. So, when the group throngs around Erwin, who looks like a cornered mouse, Johnny slips out the back door into the night and drives home to Charlene and again he lies beside her in the dark and says, "Melissa Emery can speak in tongues."

Charlene laughs. "Well, then you just stay away from Melissa Emery."

"You still on the pill?"

"Yeah."

"Oh."

"Don't start that, Johnny. I'm sorry."

"Don't be sorry."

"Sometimes I hate this town," Charlene says. "This house. I hate walking around on your father's carpet, eating off those chipped plates, sleeping in your parents' bedroom. I hate that tree out there. I feel so small, everything's so dangerous."

Johnny doesn't answer. He wants to ignore Charlene, pretend she is someone else. But he doesn't, she won't let him tonight. Sometimes he wouldn't be surprised to come home and find her gone. She could run. She's that kind of person. He says, "They healed Erwin Heinrichs tonight."

"Wow." A mocking, bitter tone.

Johnny ignores her. "I'll be curious to see him in a few days, find out what the details are."

"You're too literal, Johnny."

"Yeah, well, that's me, Charlene."

The next morning, before Charlene is awake, Johnny dresses, puts on a jacket and rubber boots, and goes out into the machine shed. Since last fall he's wanted to do this but has never felt right about it. He climbs up onto an oily work shelf and lifts down a thick, hard rope that's tied up in a tight coil with baling wire. He snaps the wire with cutters and smells the rope; this is the one his father used. A pigeon coos and beats a rhythm in the far corner of the empty building. Within the small square of light that falls on Johnny through a dusty top window, he fashions a rudimentary noose in the thick rope. It is not easy and his palms burn. His fingernails break. When he is done he jumps down from his perch and pushes his way out into the morning light and walks, rope in hand, to the back of the house where the tallest elm stands. It's a good climbing tree and about twelve feet up a thick branch extends parallel to the ground. A good swinging tree. Johnny climbs to that branch and sits there with the noose around his neck. The rest of the rope dangles loose so it would be obvious to any onlooker that he has no real intentions here. He thinks about Charlene sleeping inside the house, about how some day he'll chop this tree down, it's just too easy this, about how the land he owns, given to him by his father, stretches for miles all around this farm, but he's never touched it.

He pats his pockets, looking for a cigarette, then remembers he quit. He thinks he'll start again, maybe today. He takes the rope off his neck and throws it to the ground. The grass is wet from a night rain and the water bubbles on the oily rope. It's a harmless piece of string. Not much really, nothing to be afraid of. Johnny climbs down the tree slowly, aware of his age, of the possibility of falling.

He says to Charlene at breakfast, "Terribly easy to kill yourself, really. Easier ways than hanging."

Charlene's in her bright red dress and dark blue stockings with red shoes. Johnny likes the outfit and he watches her stand by the stove. She turns her head to look over at the table and Johnny sees her chin is double, especially when she ducks forward. She grimaces and turns away.

"If I were a poet like you," he says, "I'd write a poem and list the ways. Keep it simple but still make my point. Drowning, gunshot, asphyxiation, gas, overdose, wrists, jumping. That's the easiest, I guess, jump off a twenty-storey building."

There's a pause and then Charlene says, "I'm not a poet."

"Funny," Johnny says, "how we become like our parents. Brushing my teeth this morning I saw my dad's profile in the mirror." He reaches up and strokes his neck. "He had this flesh that pulled off his cheeks when he was older, and his neck had spots. See, I'm getting spots."

Charlene comes over to the table, coffee in hand, and stands beside Johnny. She touches his neck, then leaves her hand lying on his shoulder and says, "You scared the shit out of me this morning. If you're going to be so damned selfish, then do it somewhere else. Not in this yard. Not in this house."

Johnny's eyes lift, imagining Charlene watching him from the upstairs window. "I'm sorry," he says. "I just wanted to get his perspective, see things his way."

"You scared me," Charlene repeats. She's moved over to the window. Then she says, "And what did you see?"

"Not much."

Charlene turns and leans against the edge of the window frame.

Johnny watches her face, looking for the softness that usually comes with forgiveness. It isn't there. Then she says, "We're not doing very well. Maybe we've never done very well, but lately it's been worse. Whether you're here or gone, it's about the same. I miss you when you're away and then you come home and I still miss you."

While Johnny listens he looks at the cloth-covered buttons on Charlene's dress. They have Xs stitched into their centres. Charlene keeps talking. "Everything's a joke, isn't it? This morning, up in the tree? I think about you and I wonder, How many more times is he going to be saved? The girls at the bank? Well, they talk sometimes and they kid around asking if you're still a Christian. I play along because what else can I do? So, my husband's a joke. And then you go and climb that tree like a little monkey and I don't know who you are any more. Oh shit, I'm late." She plucks Kleenex from a box, dabs at her nose, punches her arms into her spring coat, says "I'm late" once more, and walks out of the house, leaving Johnny at the table, spinning an empty coffee mug in his hands. He listens to Charlene's Mustang start up and then she's gone, down the driveway and out onto the mile road turning right, towards town.

Almost a year ago, the day Johnny's father killed himself, Johnny was with Loraine Wallace. They'd talked meat-meal and feed additives out in the yard, the wind blowing leaves around their feet, and then they'd gone in for coffee and sat at the kitchen table that looked out onto the grass and the machine shed. Johnny hadn't visited for a while and Loraine was being shy but soon Johnny was talking nonsense from the back of his throat and Loraine was letting him.

"Missed you, Loraine," he said.

"Not me," she answered. "The sex."

"No, no, you. This kitchen here, the way you push through life, your knuckles there." He took her hands and touched her knuckles, one at a time.

"You know, sometimes, Johnny, I think I should get a different feed salesman. I wait for you and wait for you and you don't come and I have to phone in my order and then the next moment you're here and I don't want to let you go." Loraine came around the table and held Johnny's head. She was a small woman. Johnny liked her tiny nose, her little ears, the size of her bum in his hands. Her arms were muscled from heavy work, her tummy flat. When he undressed her and ran his hands around on her body he thought of her as a young boy who happened to grow breasts. She wore an invisible wreath of oats and Palmolive and the faintest scent of ammonia.

When they were finished touching each other all over and Loraine had bitten into his chest, they lay on her bed and she traced his face and said, "I love your mouth. It's so big. Ugly sometimes. I think of your mouth when you're not here and I wonder what it's doing, the food that's in it, who it's talking to, who it's with. Your voice too. When I first heard your voice on the phone, the time you called about that bad mix, I was surprised because your voice was different, as if disguised, and I didn't recognize you. But then, I just had to think about your lips, your gums, your teeth, your tongue, the way the left side lifts in a kind of happy sneer, and I realized, yeah, that's him." She kissed his ear. "I have to go clean out the barns."

Johnny rolled onto his side. Put a hand on her waist. "Let's just say, you and me, we were together. Okay? Would you want children?"

She nosed his chin. "Sure, anything."

"No, really. You've got a thirteen-year-old. Would you start again?"

Loraine pulled back, her small blue eyes skipping over Johnny's body, then resting on his face. "What are you saying, you'd leave Charlene?"

"I'm not saying that, I'm just wondering what you think."

"Don't play with my head." She pushed him away and sat on the edge of the bed, pulling on a T-shirt, socks, panties, jeans. Her hair bounced as she moved. Johnny watched her shoulder blades, her ribs shine through her back.

He asked, "Do you eat?"

"Yeah, eggs." She left him there to get dressed on his own.

When he walked out into the yard she came out of the barn and met him by his half-ton. Johnny watched her come, her black boots up to her knees, her thin face flattened by the light, and he wondered why he kept hurting people, what there was about him that made him want to see people in pain. Sometimes it worked to will a good feeling, a love for someone, and he tried that now. He lit a cigarette, put an arm around Loraine and squeezed.

"Sorry," she said.

"Me too."

"You'll come again soon. Okay? It gets lonely out here by myself."

"Sure, soon."

"And you know, Johnny?" Loraine pushed in and gripped one of his legs between hers; hot on his thigh. "I could have a baby, really." Her eyes were watery from the wind. She tried to kiss him again. He let her and then put his chin on her head and watched the swallows spin over her barn. He didn't say anything, he just let her hold him.

"Go now," she said finally, pushing him towards his truck.

After leaving Loraine's, Johnny drove a mile south and turned into his father's farmyard. Johnny's mother had died a year earlier and his father lived alone. Turning off the engine he sensed immediately something was wrong. Jack wasn't barking and that was unusual. He watched the house, the barn, the shed, and the yard, looking for movement. He climbed out of the car, leaned on the door and listened. The wind was knocking leaves off the trees. The shed door was off its latch and banging. He found the black Lab dead alongside the west side of the house. Its head was crushed as if it had been hit with a heavy pipe. Nearby he found a baseball bat with Jack's hair on it. Blood too.

He found his father hanging from the branch on the big elm, the branch that stretched out parallel to the ground, twelve feet up. His father was in socks, his shoes lay on the ground below him; Johnny imagined they fell off in the act of death. He didn't look at his father's face. He went into the house and phoned Ike at OK Feeds and then he sat down in the rocker in the middle of the big room and waited. He heard Ike come in and talk to him and ask him if he was okay. Then Ike made some phone calls and took Johnny into town and Charlene was located. Johnny learned later that a grain truck was used to cut his father down. They drove the truck right under his feet and someone, Leonard Ostnick, he thinks, stood on the cab and cut him down.

He knows when he's backsliding. It's happened so many times before he sees the signals before they're there. Except this time he doesn't care as much. The sense of failure isn't quite as acute. After Charlene's Mustang has left that morning, Johnny calls OK Feeds and says he's sick. Then he sits at the kitchen table and pours himself Five Star, one glass after another, and he watches the clock on the wall. He falls asleep, head on the table, and wakes late in the afternoon, his temples aching, his hands light. He shaves sloppily and then leaves the house and drives to his sister Carol's place in town.

Carol has a three-year-old girl and she's also eight months pregnant. She stands, her ankles thick, and tells Johnny that he can stay for supper. Her voice is defensive, impatient. Johnny considers saying, *I'm clean,* but he decides against it, knowing he must smell of alcohol. He finds Erica in the living room and he lies on the rug beside her and pretends to bite her leg. "Alligator," he growls. Erica squeals and jumps away. She runs back at Johnny and lands on his head. She's wearing shorts and her bare legs are soft and cool. Johnny likes the feel of them on his neck and face. He tickles her till she calls out, panicky and breathless. Carol comes into the living room and suggests they read a book. "I hate to see her get all wound up just before supper. Roy does the same thing."

So Johnny reads a book to Erica and from where he sits he catches glimpses of Carol in the kitchen, straining spaghetti, opening a tin of corn, and he thinks how she's changed. She used to like him, a lot, but lately she's more aloof, as if she doesn't trust him any more. He leaves his niece with a lift-the-flap book, goes into the kitchen and leans on the counter. Carol's face is flushed and the windows along the far wall are steamed up. She lifts down three plates from the cabinet and as her arms go up so does her top and Johnny sees perfectly how her stomach looks. Her belly button has popped out into a tiny elephant's trunk. There are narrow red pencil marks creasing her belly. Her top is thin and Johnny can see that her breasts and nipples are bigger. She's wearing big sweat-pants, her hips are wide.

"Roy's going to be late, he's got a meeting."

Johnny gestures at her stomach. "You gonna have more?"

Carol stops, supports her stomach with her hands and says, "This is not a good time to ask. I remember with Erica, right after she was born I wanted six more like her. But now, I just want to get rid of this bun-dle." She dips a spoon into the sauce and lifts it to her mouth. She looks at Johnny and says, "How long you here for?"

Johnny shrugs. "Oh, I don't know. A few nights? I won't bother you, sleep in the basement, eat at Chuck's. It's just Charlene and me, we need a break."

"You're going to lose her." Carol says this softly, as if talking about the spaghetti in the colander, but her meaning is there.

He sleeps on the floor in the basement, wrapped in a thin sleeping bag. Before turning out the light he hears Carol on the phone with Charlene. First they're discussing him and then they're not, and Johnny falls asleep wondering how long it'll take before Charlene misses him or he misses her. He thinks about her walking around alone in the big house, touch-ing walls and light switches with her thick fingers, locking the doors, wishing for the dog Johnny doesn't want, and then climbing the stairs to crawl into the bed, keeping to her side, her hair spread black across the white pillow.

He calls in sick again Friday morning, has breakfast at Chuck's, then goes home for clean clothes. Charlene has left for work. The bed is unmade, dishes lie unrinsed in the sink, a couple of books are spread and lie cover up on the rug beside the bed. There is a sense of haste or anger in the way the house is topsy-turvy. Johnny guesses that Charlene is upset and he's glad for this. He hates indifference. He listens to an oldie-goldie station while he bathes and dresses. He thinks about Loraine and how when she touches him it's like the Holy Spirit tickling his spine. He packs an overnight bag and in the early afternoon he drives to her farm and finds her counting eggs in the barn. She's wearing coveralls and an Expos cap.

She looks up at him standing in the low doorway and she doesn't look surprised. "Go put on the kettle," she says. "I'll be there."

When she comes into the house she's changed into jeans and a black sweater that buttons up the back. She takes off her shoes at the door; she's not wearing socks. She stands on tiptoes and washes her hands at the sink and Johnny sees the bottoms of her bare feet, the insteps like two milky stains. They don't talk for a while, just sit across from each other and clink spoons against saucers. Finally Loraine says, "News has it you're saved."

Johnny pulls at an earlobe and tilts his head. "I guess." He sighs, lights a cigarette and offers Loraine one. Sometimes she smokes, today she takes one. The cigarette sits deep in the crotch of her fingers, unlit until she takes Johnny's hand and guides a match close to her mouth. Her eyes blink and her lips wet the filter and she says, "Thank you." Johnny finds her smallness exhilarating. So tight. She smokes half the cigarette and then puts it out. "Makes me dizzy," she says. Johnny watches her fingers move and thinks she wants to touch his hands. "I sure wish I could be saved sometime," she says.

Johnny searches her face for mockery but knows he won't find it. Loraine doesn't have Charlene's cynicism. He snorts, "What do you mean?"

"Exactly that."

"Aw, you don't know what you're talking about. It's silliness, really.

It's for fools like me who think maybe if they can talk in tongues, they'll be a better person."

Loraine keeps pressing. "And each time you do this you release a few sins, I guess?" This evokes for Johnny the image of a child freeing helium balloons into the sky. He smiles but does not answer. He does not really like to talk about his own salvation, because unless he is in the throes of redemption the entire act seems ridiculous, made up, a poorly told tale.

"I believe in sin," Loraine says, and her face is so bright and cheery that Johnny lets her go on. "Sin is spending your whole life worrying about it." Her nose moves up and her nostrils become black holes.

"That doesn't make sense."

"I saw Charlene this morning. She said hello to me and then I paid my bills and she gave me the three twenties I asked for. We talked about her reading club. She said I should come. I said that sounded nice. Mostly women. Why is it, do you think, that men don't like that kind of thing?"

Johnny has this sense of things not being right. Loraine is too happy, too much in control. Normally by now they'd be holding each other or he'd have said, *Do you want to?* and they'd have laughed and done it. He's breathing through his mouth and watching Loraine's knees, her chin, throat, thighs, hands. White hands, like those perfect eggs she gathers.

Loraine says, "Charlene said you'd left. It was strange her telling me that, sometimes I wonder if she knows about you and me, and for a bit there I felt close to her like we could be friends. I said I hadn't seen you, I mean selling feed, and now here you are."

"I haven't left her." Johnny takes Loraine's hand. He likes her gullibility. She's like him in a way, great intentions but a weak eye for completion. It's the things of the flesh that throw them off and that's why they'd make a poor couple. But that doesn't stop Johnny now. He talks about Chris, Loraine's son, about seeing him at the drop-in centre where they talked about skating, about boards and half-pipes.

"That's so good," Loraine says. She breathes quicker when talking about Chris. She holds Johnny's fingers and they talk about drugs and girls. Her boy is fascinated by both, she says. Johnny promises to help Chris. "The boy's good, he's smart." Then Loraine has her hands on Johnny's head and neck and then they're down his shirt and she's whispering, "Jesus, Johnny, Jesus, you've got me way down deep."

After, when Johnny is playing with her hands, her beautiful hands, Loraine says, "Who are you?" He feels her breath on his cheek and he doesn't answer, he just keeps touching her hands. They are soft considering the heavy work she does. But she wears gloves all the time and in the evenings she pours lotion on her palms and she smooths the lotion around over her knuckles and up her wrists. Then she works carefully at her fingernails with tiny tools and she paints her nails. She paints them the colour of her hands, like the inside of a large seashell, so Johnny, when he holds them close like he's doing now, has a hard time seeing her nails. He takes one of her hands and holds it over his nipple and she pinches him lightly while he thinks about her question.

Johnny doesn't like questions like this. It reminds him of exams and impossible expectations and gnawing on pens. Stupid questions about people long dead, about history. Questions that have nothing to do with those small breasts there that a few minutes before he took into his mouth. "Here," he had said and filled his mouth with one and then the other and measured them with his tongue. Then he smelled them and he was reminded of when he was a boy and he sucked on his arm and laid his nose on the wet spot that was left.

Charlene told him once, *You have no sense of yourself other than what you need.* That may be true, Johnny thought, but not so bad. And now, listening to Loraine breathe, watching her breasts rise, then fall, rise again, knowing she is waiting for an answer, he says, "I've known joy. Not all the time and maybe never for very long, but I've known joy."

The drop-in centre remains closed Friday and Saturday. Johnny doesn't show up. After Loraine tells him he can't spend the night because of

Chris, he drives out to St. Adolphe where he sits in the bar and drinks shooters with guys he knows and some he doesn't. There are a few women present too, women around forty with soft stomachs and last names like Rochelle and Laperriere. There's one younger woman who reminds Johnny of Loraine; she's thin-mouthed and skinny and wears jeans. Johnny knows a guy from St. Adolphe, Ronald Lavallee, and he spends Friday night at Ronald's house. He finds himself back in the bar on Saturday afternoon trying to talk to the girl in jeans.

"Who are you?" Johnny asks.

"The waitress."

"What's your name?" Johnny presses, but the girl ignores him.

Johnny loads himself up and by early evening he is in his half-ton and driving. He tries to remember where he's going but he can't. The road is empty and Johnny figures he's driving slowly down the middle. The trees pass him and he misses the turn to Lesser. Then a curve appears and the Rat River bridge and he feels a jolt as he rubs the guard rail and rolls to a stop on the edge of the grassy embankment. He puts the half-ton in park and falls asleep.

Two fishermen wake Johnny Sunday morning. They are wearing green hats and checked jackets and they're standing outside his truck saying, "Lucky," and "Yeah, one lucky fellow," and then one guy pokes his head in the door and asks, "You okay?"

"Sure, sure."

"You're lucky."

Johnny doesn't answer. After the men have slid down the slope to the river and walked up to the point, Johnny climbs out of the truck and looks at a big hole in the guard rail. "Quite a blow," he mumbles. He stares down at the river which has slowed now in fall and then he looks at the trees and he figures they're poplars but he's never been terribly sure about trees. He sits on the ground with his back up against the wheel of his truck and he watches the men in green jackets still-fishing by the point. His stomach hurts. He has a bruise on his cheek where he hit the steering wheel. His hands shake.

He goes to church that morning. First he drives home to see Charlene but she's not there. The same dirty dishes are still in the sink and this surprises him. He showers and drives to town. He goes to the Mennonite Brethren church, the one he attended as a child. It's a big brick building with a blue rug on the main floor and oak pews with blue cushions. Johnny sits near the back. He hears the songs, the organ, the voices all around him but he doesn't really listen. At one point he considers standing and relating his own personal experience but there is something about the woman in front of him, perhaps the angle of her neck, that stops him. He lifts his eyes once during a prayer and studies the vaulted ceiling. Between the varnished rafters, at their base, run narrow rectangular windows that reveal the blue sky. There are pigeons roosting outside those windows. Johnny watches the pigeons and then the sun flows through the windows and strikes the far wall just above the heads of the people praying. They stop praying and begin to sing. The sunlight reminds Johnny of warm hands, all one colour, and of how, eyes watering in the wind, Loraine squeezed his leg and said long ago, "And you know, Johnny, I could, really." There is a goodness in people, he thinks, that is remarkable.

EGGS, NEW-LAID

Loraine calls Johnny at work on a Friday afternoon to tell him the news but he's not in and she won't give the secretary a message. She doesn't say who's speaking, just hangs up. She phones his house later that evening but Charlene answers and so Loraine has to make small talk; the book club, the bonspiel, work, farming. Just before Loraine hangs up, she says, "Oh, Johnny wouldn't be there, would he? It's about some feed mix."

Charlene's voice is cheery and ignorant. "No," she says, "He's at the centre."

Loraine sits by the phone, pushes a pencil around on a paper, and considers calling the centre. She hesitates because her son Chris might be there and she dislikes giving the impression of meddling in his life. The dog is scratching at the back door so Loraine lets him in. She holds the door open a while and pokes her head out and looks up and breathes the air. She can hear a car passing by on the mile road over by the Loepky farm. It's a cool October night, close to Halloween, and there's a smell of smoke; some farmers are burning stubble.

The generator over by the second barn is faltering; it's been like that for a few months. Loraine figures it'll just go one of these cold nights and then the emergency generator will have to cut in and if it doesn't, she'll have ten thousand dead chickens. Chickens are stupid. She closes the door, rubs her bare arms, and considers that if people were locked in cages, in groups of three and four, they'd be stupid too, or deviants, or homosexuals. She wanders back to the phone and picks it up. She can smell herself on the receiver. She likes that. She curls up in an armchair, folds her small legs under her, and punches at the numbers.

A kid answers. Loraine can hear music in the background. She would like to ask this kid about Chris. Is he there? But instead she says, "I want to talk to Johnny Fehr."

And then, after a few minutes, she hears his voice and for a moment she can't speak. She's been aching to tell him, walking around sucking on this secret for several weeks and now, at this point, she wants the giddiness of telling.

"Johnny?" she says, "It's me."

He seems neither pleased nor concerned. Loraine tries to imagine him, the way he looks standing by the phone. He'll be wearing jeans and she likes that. She knows he's smoking, she can hear him draw, even though he's got a no-smoking rule for the centre.

"We have to talk," she says. She lifts her eyebrows and says, "Is tomorrow okay?"

Johnny hums. The phone crackles as he shifts and stubs his cigarette. "What's wrong?" he asks.

Loraine's mouth is dry. This was supposed to be fun, she thinks. "Nothing," she says, "I got some news."

Johnny's thinking. Loraine can tell. And then he says, "Listen, I'm going up to Sprague tomorrow, talk to a customer. You wanna come? For the morning?"

"Yes," Loraine says, too quickly perhaps. She's holding herself, one palm on her stomach, and she's remembering the way Johnny looks when he stands by the window and puts on his shirt. He rarely tucks in his tails and a couple of buttons are missed and this could be sloppiness to some people but to Loraine it's what and who Johnny Fehr is and she loves him. "Yes," she says again.

Johnny is leasing a Ninety-eight Olds. It's dark green and serious. Saturday morning Loraine sits in the front seat, runs her hand over the upholstery, and thinks that she prefers the half-ton. It has a smell of oil and grain and she likes the way Johnny looks behind the wheel. This new car makes him look too earnest.

They're mostly quiet driving down the Number 52 through Steinbach, but when they turn onto the Number 12 and it begins to snow, tiny flakes melting on the windshield, Loraine talks about an aunt who lives in Grunthal. "She's got twelve kids," she says. "They live in a three-bedroom house and the husband's a mechanic."

Johnny doesn't answer. He's playing with the radio. "I love this," he says. "They're a family, I think. The Rankins. I saw them once on TV and they all look beautiful." He lights a cigarette and offers Loraine one. She shakes her head and Johnny looks at her, surprised.

"Anyway," Loraine says, "this aunt wanted all those children, just wanted them. Two died in a car accident. She still has ten. It's hard to imagine." Loraine knows Johnny is waiting for her to talk, to say what she has to say, but she's thinking now that something's wrong, that when she finally really talks he won't listen.

She says, "I gather eggs. Twice a day. I take six at a time. Three in each hand. It's strange these days to handle eggs. Not that they're fertilized in any way but still it's odd. I used to candle eggs at the hatchery. Watch them as they ran over a scanner, look for flaws, blood spots, bubbles of air. Sometimes I could see right into them, like I was looking into a perfect glass stone." She pauses, reaches out, and takes Johnny's right hand off the wheel and presses his palm against her stomach. "Here," she whispers.

Johnny's tongue is touching his top lip and his eyes wrinkle. He's taking her words and running them around in his head. Finally, he bangs a palm against the steering wheel. "Aw, no, Loraine, really?" A noise rises from his chest. Loraine cannot tell if this is joy or sorrow. But he turns and he smiles and "Yes," he says.

"You're happy then?" Loraine asks. "Really?"

And Johnny is, she can see that. Even later, after talking about it for a while, he hits at his leg. His excitement affects Loraine. Her fingers shake. She remembers this one time as a teenager, sitting on the rocks at Winnipeg Beach. She was wearing a bathing suit and talking to some boy she'd met two days earlier. She could sense the heat escaping from the boy's skin and her bum felt the roughness of the rock. Her buttocks feel now as if they've been scraped along rock.

Johnny's quiet for a bit and then near Sprague he says, "Jesus, Loraine, the thought of you is killing me." He looks at her on the other side of the car and clicks his tongue against his teeth. Loraine dips her chin and slides over and lays her head on Johnny's lap. He's wearing suit pants and they're cool on Loraine's cheek. She slides a hand deep into his cowboy boots and pulls at the hair on his calf. She wants to crawl inside him. "Hey, Johnny," she whispers.

"Hey," he says back. He pulls the car over onto a side road. He lifts Loraine's head and says, "Who'd have thought, you and me, huh?" And he takes her in his big hands and turns her small body, lays a nose on her flat stomach, gurgles and says, "Oh, my."

And as for Loraine, well, she'd let him do anything. She and Johnny have been lovers off and on for years now. He comes to her when he's lonely, or tired of his wife Charlene, and Loraine lets him because she likes his hardness, the way his jaw moves, his crooked mouth. Now, in the front seat of the Olds, she clings to him and won't let him go. "My little fucking monkey," he says. She chatters in his ear and sucks on his neck. "Yes," she says.

Johnny doesn't go to his appointment. Instead they cross into the States and drive the country roads, Loraine deep under Johnny's arm, and then they head back up to Steinbach for lunch.

Loraine watches Johnny eat. He likes to put things in his mouth; she is just one of those things. She says, "I'm worried about Chris. He's tough these days, doesn't talk."

Johnny's elation has worn off. He's stirring sugar into his coffee and staring out the large front window towards Main Street. "Chris's been hanging out with this Krahn girl," he says. "Melody's her name."

Loraine is surprised and hurt. It's unfair, Johnny knowing this. She wonders what this Melody looks like. She knows the parents but can't picture the daughter.

"Do you like Chris?" she asks.

"Sure," Johnny says. "Yeah." Then, "I was thinking. About us and what we're going to do. Leaving Charlene would kill her."

"Would it?"

Johnny is scratching at a match. It finally lights. He is looking over Loraine's head, at something only he can see. He refocuses, seeks out Loraine. "Yes, it would," he says.

Johnny pays for lunch and, out on the curb before climbing into the car, he pulls Loraine close and pushes his nose against her hair.

Loraine doesn't really like the town of Lesser. Most of the time she tries to stay away. She does her shopping at Super Valu in Winnipeg, except when she runs out of butter or milk and then she drives into Lesser and stops at the Solo store. Loraine finds she doesn't fit in the town. She's the wife of a dead farmer and it's still strange for women to run their own farms. She can't hobnob with the boys at Chuck's; she has no desire to. Lesser's an ugly little place with a sickness at its core; it's full of death and gossip and churches. This is what Loraine thinks. It's made a man like Johnny go all to pieces. He doesn't know any more who he is. He wants to be a Christian and a do-gooder but he keeps falling and people laugh at him; they want him to fail. And when he does fail he comes running to Loraine.

She remembers the day Johnny's father committed suicide. It was eight o'clock in the evening and she was in the refrigerator room, stacking flats. She'd seen Johnny earlier that day. He'd come by and they'd made love in the bedroom and the sunlight had fallen through the thin curtain onto his arms and stomach, and later, counting eggs, his scent was still in her nose.

Johnny had entered the refrigerator room and stood, leaning against the door, and told her about his father hanging from the tree and how he had no shoes, they must have been kicked off, and he told her about the dead dog and the bloody baseball bat. "Why on earth would he kill the dog?" Johnny asked.

Loraine didn't have too much to say. She kept stacking trays and glancing up at Johnny. She didn't want to touch him right then, either. "Sorry, Johnny," she said once, but he didn't seem to hear. She wasn't terribly sorry, she'd never really liked Mr. Fehr. He'd been stingy.

"How's Charlene managing all this?" Loraine asked. "Where is she?"

"At home. I miss you," Johnny said. "You."

Loraine shook her head. "No you don't, Johnny. You use me. I'm sorry about your father," she said, "but there's nothing I can do. You and me, we're apart. If you lay in my bed every night and I could hold you, not just have sex with you, then we could weep together, but what we have is nothing. We screw. That's all." Loraine was surprised at her own anger and at the word she'd just used. She hated it; so cold. She imagined that it was because her desire for Johnny had been spent that afternoon. Always, after the fact, she became rueful and disliked herself.

Johnny hung his head. Loraine picked up an egg and heaved it at him. It hit the plywood wall beside him. He looked up and grinned. Furious, she threw two more eggs. One hit the floor, the other he caught and cradled in his palm. "Hickety pickety, my black hen," he said. He put the captured egg in his jacket pocket and walked out. He left the door open. The chickens flapped and screamed in their cages. Loraine sat for the longest time, wishing Johnny would come back.

Loraine goes to parent-teacher interviews at Lesser Collegiate and she talks to Mr. Jameson, the Grade Nine Science teacher, and Ms. Holt, the English teacher. Science is okay, Chris could do better she is told, but he's all right. Outside the English class she waits for her interview and looks over Chris's writing folder and journal. She wonders if Chris knows his writing is available for her to see.

She reads, "Gonna write a cheap story about this woman who lives on a farm with her son. She's a wannabe and so is he." Loraine looks for the story but there is nothing else. Scribbled on the inside of the folder is this:

> *Sex is like math.*
> *Subtract the clothing*
> *divide the legs*
> *and multiply.*

Inside the pocket is a paper with Chris's sprawling handwriting:

> *Your father was a bastard,*
> *Your mother was a whore,*
> *This all wouldn't have happened*
> *If the rubber hadn't tore!*

Loraine blinks, reads it again, and then she slides the paper back into the pocket and closes the folder. Ms. Holt pokes her head out and smiles, her face round, her eyes oily. Chris claims she's a fossil and Loraine can see what he means. She knows that Ms. Holt taught Johnny. Taught him how to write a composition. She thinks she should ask about Johnny. Find out what kind of a student he had been, if back then already he was into sex. Of course.

They sit at a table and Loraine says, "It's so odd to be in a school. I keep waiting to be tested or something." She tries to laugh but it comes out too loud and she turns her head, stares at the wall.

But Ms. Holt is smiling and the two of them talk about living in this town, something Ms. Holt doesn't do. She commutes from Winnipeg. "Oh, no," she says, "it'd be claustrophobic."

Loraine nods. She leans forward and says, "The kids, when they write their compositions, do they have preoccupations? You know . . ."

"Oh, yes, at this age everything 'sucks', of course. Our themes are violence and sex but we're not allowed to write about either. When doing poetry, for example, we prefer the bucolic: pastoral scenes, rhyme, metre, odes." Her voice sings on until Loraine says, "Where does he sit? Chris. Which desk?"

Ms. Holt seems surprised, but she points to the back corner. "Some teachers," she says, "don't have desks. Just tables, and everything's a muddle. Hurly-burly. Me, I couldn't abide it."

Loraine goes and sits in Chris's desk. It's got a good angle on the room. Farthest from the teacher. By the wall. His name is carved into the top. So is Melody's. "Is he insolent?" Loraine asks. She doesn't really care any more. She hopes, in a small way, he is.

"Not at all. Not a peep from Chrissy."

An awful name, Loraine thinks. Not his at all. She wants to raise her hand and say, "Hello, Miss Holt. I'm a whore. A slut. I'm gonna have Johnny Fehr's baby. Remember Johnny? Picture's out in the centrum there, on the wall. Class of '75. Saw it when I walked in. Even back then he had that sneering smile, as if life couldn't beat him. Anyway, he's my main man."

But, instead, Loraine sighs and pushes herself from the desk. "Thank you," she says. "I've gotta run. Thank you."

Mr. Jake Wohlgemut, manager of the Lesser Credit Union, likes Loraine. She can tell. He sits in his chair, gaily swings his short legs, and stares at her neck, her mouth, her breasts, her shoulders. He fiddles with his tie and then says, "A new generator? No problem, Mrs. Wallace." Feet swing.

He is married to a tall big-boned woman with black hair. Gloria. Loraine tries to imagine them in bed together. All she can see is Jake working his way up and around Gloria's body like a mountain climber. They must have fun, she muses. Loraine often pictures couples having sex. She is not mean-spirited about it, just curious. She will talk to another woman and images will begin to flicker and jump; the rabbity hunch of the man's buttocks, nipples covered by big hands, the vein in the throat beating, the roll of stomachs.

Today, after getting her loan, she runs into Charlene by the Credit Union door. Charlene works here and is on her way out for lunch. "Do you want to come?" Charlene asks. They're walking out to the sidewalk together.

"I can't," Loraine says. "I've got chores." She's studying Charlene's face which still suffers from the scars of teenage acne. But her body's large and full, much bigger than Loraine's. Loraine wonders if Charlene is still holding Johnny at bay, as he claimed. How could you keep a man like Johnny away from a woman like Charlene? She wonders what Charlene's eyes and mouth do when Johnny is inside her.

Charlene's talking. Her hands are moving skyward and Johnny's name is on her lips. "We're seeing a counsellor," she says. "I told Johnny we'd have one more try. He's like a sheep. Do you want him?" She touches Loraine's arm, red nails. Loraine smiles at this tall woman. Her size is intimidating. Loraine lifts a hand quickly, says goodbye and walks to her half-ton. A little quip like that is so perfect, she thinks, like the light touch of God on a sinner's head. As if Charlene's known all along.

Loraine drives home slowly, down Main Street past Bill's Hardware, Herb's Electric, the centre, then the cemetery where Johnny's parents are buried. The mother died and the father couldn't take it, lonely perhaps.

There's an old woman standing in the graveyard. She's wearing a blue polka-dot dress and holding flowers. Loraine doesn't recognize her.

Beyond the cemetery lies OK Feeds where Johnny's big dark car sits in the lot. Then quickly the highway begins and Loraine picks up speed. In the distance there is this other graveyard, for buses and combines and tractors — Wayne Wiebe's Tractor Parts. Ugly. A sin, Loraine thinks, to allow one man to destroy the lay of the land. Past Wayne's and Lesser is lost behind her. The trees are bare, though there are still leaves blowing across the road. Smoke rises from a far-off field. She approaches the three-mile turn-off and coasts along the gravel road. Her barns become two white lines in the distance. She likes having her own place. She thinks about Charlene and how she's a woman who needs Johnny. Needs his money, his land, his house. But not Loraine, no. She doesn't need anything like that. Not today, anyway.

The following Saturday, eating supper, Chris says he's got a ride to town later — Brian's dad is going to a hockey game — so he's going to go hang out at the centre. "Okay?" he says.

Loraine nods and studies her son. He wears his hair long in back, not like the other skaters who walk around like skinheads. "I want you home by eleven," she says. She notices he has a second earring, something they haven't discussed. "You'll do the eggs with me tomorrow?" she asks.

"Yeah, whatever."

"It was our deal," Loraine says. She tries to keep her voice light. "You would help me on the weekends, Saturday and Sunday."

"Okay, okay. Johnny asked about you yesterday."

Loraine finds it strange to hear Chris talking about Johnny. She pauses and waits.

"He's weird, Mom. Not a bad guy, but weird."

"Yeah? Why?"

"I don't know. Kinda like he's in this time warp. You know, like you have those bell-bottoms in your closet but you wouldn't dream of wearing them. Well, Johnny'd wear his."

"Does he do religious stuff?" Loraine asks. She wants to keep Chris talking.

"Some. Not really. He's big into guilt. Says salvation is like doing drugs."

"You guys talk about drugs?"

"Some. Sometimes. He has this big speech. About how he used to get stoned and wasted but how now he's straight, and then he gets really excited and talks about angel dust and acid. Half the time we don't know what he's blabbing about."

"You like it there, at the centre?"

"No, not really. It's okay."

Loraine's mouth is hurting. She has a cold sore. She pores some salt into her palm, licks a finger and dips it. The salt, when eased between her gum and lip, inflates the pain. She hisses, licks her finger and studies her nails. "What's this Krahn girl like?" she asks. "Melody. Right?"

"Oh, all right. She's nice." That's all. No more is offered and Loraine won't push. Chris seems so childlike, so immature, she can't imagine any danger lurking. She wants to believe that. For Chris at this age, girls are dreams.

After her son has left, Loraine fills the tub and slides in. She touches her body, experimenting, believing in this, cupping her breasts and remembering Chris as an infant and milk dripping from her nipples. Johnny pulls her from the tub to the phone. She stands in the upstairs hall, dripping onto the carpet, a small towel covering her, and listens to him exclaim, "Loraine, I was just thinking, God, it's wonderful. Really. I closed my eyes and you were there, big-bellied, thick-legged. I wonder if your belly button will do that little trunk thingy the way my sister's did. I'd like to slip it in my nostril, I would. When do you feel the moving?"

"Not yet," she says. Loraine's pleased that Johnny's thrilled but there's too much excitement, as if he were playing house.

"What were you doing?" he asks.

Loraine considers. "Watching TV."

"Oh."

"You at the centre?" Loraine asks.

"Yeah."

"Is Chris there yet?"

"No, it's slow tonight. I haven't seen him."

"That's odd, he said he'd be there with Brian and Melody."

"Nothing," Johnny says. "He'll show. I've been thinking, Loraine. I'm gonna tell Charlene. Make some arrangements and then we can get together."

"Hold it, Johnny. I'm not sure about anything. You think I'm just going to lie down, don't you? I'm gonna say, 'Here I am, Johnny.'"

"I'm not pushing you," he says.

"Good. I like my life. I didn't do this to lure you into my nest."

"No?"

"I've got this boy who's fourteen. First I have to tell him I'm pregnant. Then you want me to say, 'Johnny's going to live with us.' The poor kid."

"You think Chris is pretty innocent, don't you?" Johnny says.

Loraine dislikes Johnny's tone, as if he were calling her names.

"Not at all," she says. "It's just, why dump all this shit on a kid whose main concern is his board?"

"Anyway," Johnny says, leaping away from Chris, "I keep thinking about you. I climb into my car and remember your bare ankle resting on the dash. That was fun."

"Of course," Loraine answers. She's cold standing on the landing, water rolling off her hair and down her back. Still, Johnny's remembering this makes Loraine want to rub up against something. She leans against the wall.

"Actually," Loraine says, "I'm naked. You got me out of the bath."

"Completely?" Johnny asks.

"Sure," Loraine lies.

"Thought so, I could hear the water dripping."

"Ah, fuck off."

"Okay."

"Bye, Johnny."

"Yeah, bye." These last two words are whispered and they produce a warmth at the base of Loraine's spine. She holds the phone a while and listens to the silence and then hangs up.

She climbs back into the tub and tries to forget Johnny but he keeps coming back; that mouth, the thickness in the stomach. And his smell. He's got body odour, not too bad, but it's there when he walks by or stoops to pick up a shoe; it flows from his shirt. The smell is strongest when he's dressed. Naked, there is only the slightest hint of sour sweat but it's not bad and anyway Loraine rather likes it, likes to push her nose and mouth into Johnny's armpit. Rest there. Like a dog.

The police bring Chris home at one in the morning. Loraine is frantic with worry and wants to hit her son when she finally sees him in the grasp of a cop. Constable Boucler. Loraine hears the name and then the officer says, "Your son stole a vehicle, Ma'am. He and a few other kids."

Loraine shivers. The wind is cold. Chris's face is dull, no emotion. He shakes himself loose and disappears. "Come in," Loraine says. "Coffee?" The man before her declines the offer. He's all uniform. The leather of his holster creaks when he shifts his weight. Loraine can see the black handle of his gun. "Whose car?" she asks.

"A half-ton," Boucler says. "Farmer from St. Pierre."

"St. Pierre?" Loraine says. "Way out there?"

"Yeah, the kids hit the ditch. The driver was shook up. Your boy trouble?"

"No, he isn't. Really, not." Loraine looks at the officer. He has a mole on his jaw and there are little black hairs growing out of it. She wonders why he doesn't shave it, if it's good luck or something. She wants to touch it. "Chris doesn't know how to steal cars," she says. "It would have been someone else's idea. He's a skateboarder, can't stand cars."

"He'll have to go to court."

"I see," Loraine says. They talk a bit more and then she watches the police car's tail-lights disappear down the driveway. She shuts the door.

Chris cries that night. Loraine sits at the edge of his bed and talks about prison. "It's a shit-hole," she says. "And you're going to end up there. In prison you just sit and stare at the wall or you worry about guys bigger than you, or you walk outside in the prison yard and there aren't any skateboards there, no music, no girls, nothing. A fine choice, son."

"I didn't do it. Roger Emery wanted to. He stole the car."

Loraine shakes her head. "Oh, Chris, it won't work. You were in the car. You're guilty."

That's when he cries. He lays his head on her lap and he weeps. She strokes his hair and after, when he's wiping at his face, he talks about how stupid the Emery boy is, and how Melody was there and how scared she was.

"I know," Loraine says. Pulling at Chris's hot ear she tells him she's going to have a baby, Johnny Fehr is the father, and, "Don't see me as bad," she says, "not bad at all, it's just something that happens."

Chris is confused, then excited. Later, he turns over to digest this news and he falls asleep. Loraine lies beside her son for a long time, listening to him breathe. There is a smell of alcohol emanating from his pores. Not too strong, but it's there. The world is a dangerous place.

Johnny doesn't come by for a week. He doesn't call either. Loraine begins to believe that she's all alone in the world and she'll live with it, when Johnny pulls up outside her barn on Friday afternoon. They sit in the usual spot, the kitchen, and drink Seven-Up and talk.

"I'm gonna be baptized," Johnny announces.

"Oh?" Loraine says. She's seen one baptism, at the Mennonite

Brethren Church, when they pushed a friend of hers under the water. The friend was wearing a choir gown over her brand-new dress. "What do you want me to say?" she asks.

Johnny folds his hands. "It's just I'm working things through," he says. "It's all about Charlene and me and you. Charlene wants to have one last go." He pauses. His top lip is dry. He wets it with his tongue and says, "She doesn't know about the baby."

"So," Loraine says, "baptism's going to make you love her?"

"I don't know. Phil Barkman thinks I need something to bring on the power of the Spirit. Maybe this."

Loraine wishes she weren't such a needy woman. She wishes she could slap Johnny's face, once, twice, and tell him to leave. But, when it comes down to her and Johnny sitting in the same room together, she is weak and can only imagine the rawness of his tongue after it has touched her, giving her back her own taste, and his mouth, all that space; she can fit her fist into that mouth. Has done it many times. Let him gnaw on her knuckles. She hates Johnny.

"I've been reading some," she says. "You know, that passage you told me about. The temptations. Well, they're not just temptations like throwing yourself from a high building, or eating bread when you're hungry. Jesus liked to talk in riddles."

Johnny is confused. "What?"

"Riddles. I mean, temptations have to do with everyday stuff: lying, stealing, cheating, hatred, revenge. I keep thinking of this math riddle I heard in high school. It's raining and you have to go from point A to point B in the rain. Will you get wetter if you run or walk?"

"I'd drive," Johnny says.

Loraine ignores him. "There is an answer but you're not sure what it is until you actually try it. And sex. Think about it. That was another temptation. I mean, was he ever tempted?"

Johnny's shaking his head. "That's good," he says. "You reading that. You're a smart girl, Loraine. You are."

Loraine reaches out and sandwiches one of Johnny's hands. Trips lightly over his fingernails. He must see her as simple, she thinks. As a farm girl who can't see beyond eggs and chickens and feed. She is a feeble and flickering light that he keeps running towards.

"Do you want me?" she asks.

"Of course," Johnny says. But, he doesn't move.

"You always will," Loraine says. "No matter where you are, or who you're with, you'll ache for me."

"I know."

Loraine says, "I'm going to get round and full. And one night, six months from now, you'll be lying beside Charlene and I'll be here by myself and I'll lay my hands on my big belly and feel the blow of an elbow or a knee and I'll be happy, Johnny. I'll be happy."

Johnny leans over the table and kisses Loraine. On the mouth. He's lost. His eyes are sad and sorry. He lets her go and she says, "I told Chris. Last weekend. And I told him who the father was."

"Aw," Johnny's big hand hits the table. "Why?"

"Well, what am I going to say? It was aliens?"

"There goes all my respect at the centre. The kids'll laugh. Chris'll spread the news."

"No, he won't. And anyway, what respect?"

"Who's getting nasty?" Johnny says. He's standing now over by the window, pulling on his jacket. His motions are jerky, he really doesn't want to storm out.

"Sorry," Loraine says.

"Baptism's next Sunday," Johnny says. He shrugs his shoulders, his face sheepish.

"You're not bad, Johnny," Loraine says. "You might think so, but you're not. You just do what you have to do and sometimes you end up hurting people."

"Really?" Johnny says. "God, you're wonderful, Loraine."

"No, I'm not," she says, and she means it.

Later, after Johnny has left, Loraine goes out to gather eggs. She rolls out the cart, stacks the trays, and wheels up and down the aisles. The chickens cheer. She works slowly. She is clumsy today and drops an egg. Another. Most eggs are cool, some are warm. When she's finished her chores, she steps outside and walks slowly back to the house. Gravel crunches beneath her rubber boots. The sky is clear and she feels like she is alone among the stars and planets and asteroids, all that stuff floating around in space. She thinks if she jumped high enough she could disappear.

AGAIN

Marijuana is making a comeback at Lesser Collegiate, so Mr. Isaacs, the high school principal, phones up Johnny Fehr and asks him if he won't do a few information sessions during Drug Awareness Week at the school.

"Maybe this is too bold," Mr. Isaacs says. "But I know you have a history and kids respect that."

Johnny doesn't really want to do it, mainly because he's not against grass. Still, he has an image to maintain, what with the drop-in centre, so he says he'll talk about drugs. His first session, on a Wednesday morning, is with a group of fourteen-year-olds. Johnny's wearing a dark green suit with a slight sheen to it, and cowboy boots, and he stands in front of the class, buries his hands in his pockets, and talks about how drugs and alcohol almost ruined his life.

"I was teetering," he says, holding up a palm parallel to the floor and moving it like a see-saw. His fingers are thick. All his life he's considered them long and fine-looking, but today he sees stubs. He's gaining weight, the skin around his ring is bulging.

He talks some more about hard drugs, about killing brain cells, and losing friends. "What happens," he says, "is people stop mattering. What

counts is getting high. I used to dance all by myself. I'd roll myself a
really large joint and lie in my room and imagine I was famous, or rich,
or dead. School didn't matter. Marks. What was cool was toking. I
hear that it's cool again. Am I right?" He waits for a response. A few
heads nod.

Johnny looks at the tender lives in front of him and he feels tremendous love for humanity. People are wonderful. What he's doing today is
wonderful. It's the right thing to do. He recognizes some of these kids.
Sees them at the centre on Friday and Saturday nights. There's Sherri
over there, Allison beside her. Johnny likes Allison; she helps him with
clean-up some nights and then he drives her home. She talks to him
about her parents, about her urge to run away. Johnny tells her not to and
Allison listens. One time she reached up and put her baseball cap on his
head. It didn't fit so Johnny gave it back.

Johnny can see Chris Wallace at the back of the class. Chris is looking
at Johnny, staring right at him. It's hard to know what he's thinking.

A kid in the front raises a hand and asks, "About grass, I was wondering, is it a crime? Like, can you be arrested?"

"Not for possession if you only have a little," Johnny says. "Just for
trafficking. So, for example, if I was smoking with a buddy and handed
him the joint, that's trafficking. What I have to do is lay the joint down
and then he can pick it up." Johnny rubs his hands together and a perverse glee fills him. He stifles it.

"Nobody sells grass here," someone else says. "There are no drugs in
Lesser Collegiate." The voice sounds disappointed.

"Are you sure?" Johnny asks. "Don't kid yourself. It's out there. One
last question?"

A girl with really short hair lifts a hand to her chin; her fingers curl as
if she were waving at someone. She says, "What happens if you don't
inhale? You know?"

"Nothing," Johnny says. "Nothing happens."

It's a Wednesday night and Johnny's sitting and thinking. There was a girl he loved at sixteen. Sue Klassen. They were baptized the same day. She went first, slid under the water, hair floated briefly, and then she reappeared and the gown clung to her body and he could see her shape as she slogged up the steps. Perhaps he loved her shape: wide hips, thick waist. Same look as Charlene, his wife, who is slamming her way around the kitchen.

Farmer's Almanac says no snow till December. They're always right. He's going to be baptized this Sunday. Again. Funny, wanting to do that, as if it can be perfected. He's not ready, not in his heart, but there's a desperation, a recklessness, and he's out of options. Sue married a doctor and moved to England. Three children and afternoon tea. Bum, spreading from age, pressed on a wooden chair. The tinkle of china.

Women. Amazing creatures. It has little to do with beauty or class or money. Some people like mountain climbing, cycling, or spelunking. Johnny likes women. They are intricately layered and it is his job to peel back those layers. Sometimes he passes by a woman in a car and catches a glimpse of just her head and for a brief moment he marvels, and imagines that woman picking up a tomato in the supermarket and smelling it, or studying herself in the mirror, rubbing her front teeth with her finger, mouth slightly open. Johnny bites at his tongue then and shudders, picturing the delicacy of that first layer, the thinness, the transparency, the anticipation of what lies underneath.

Of course if it doesn't snow, the farmers are going to cry. They bitch about everything. At Chuck's, over coffee, all you hear are complaints about the damn Americans. And quotas. They'll be gone soon. Loraine with all her layers seems the least worried. Johnny mentions this and Loraine shrugs her shoulders, and says, "So, what am I going to do? I'll keep gathering eggs, is what. And two years from now when the Americans ship up their cheap shit and poison us all, I'll say, 'I told you so.' Until then, I'll gather my quota and I'll sell it and I'll have this baby and I'll get by."

Johnny can hear Charlene from the living room where he sits looking out the big picture window at the yard. She opens the fridge door and digs for ice. It spills out onto the floor and countertop. One finally clinks into the glass, a splash of liquid. She's drinking too much lately; her face has been tight, her voice wobbling, like all her usual strength has been sucked from her. She's falling.

A car passes; a burst of light and then darkness. Charlene appears and stands in the doorway. She's holding her glass and sucking on an ice cube. She just stands and watches him so he watches back. Her size makes her homely tonight; her neck is slightly bent as if someone were pushing at the top of her head. Her mouth opens; she's about to speak.

"Was talking to the girls at the Credit Union," she says. Her voice slopes down, then rises quickly.

Johnny says, "Are you drunk?"

Charlene ignores him. She says, "They let slip some news that I think you probably already know."

There's a smell in this room that Johnny can't stand. Never could, even as a young boy growing up. It's a feathery, wet, mouse-dropping smell that appears only once in a while. But now it's back. Johnny shakes his head. He waits for Charlene to say more. He's not going to help her out here. Sometimes if you ignore her she just goes away.

But she keeps talking. "It was Karen. She said, quite by accident, that Loraine Wallace was going to have a baby and that the baby was yours."

Johnny looks right at her now. He wonders how it came to be that he married this woman, as if by some accident they met so long ago and he felt sorry for her or she for him and they ended up in the same house. She took his name back then so now she's a Fehr and it's odd, he thinks, giving up her name like that, he'd never do it, become her name. Rempel has the ring of disorder and loss.

He watches her. Her tongue touches her lower lip, her eyes close and open. He would like to be good to her, to hold her now and say proper things, but he can't, because her suffering is so obvious, so needy. "That's right," he says. "It's mine."

She wants to throw her glass. Her fingers squeeze and whiten. Her brow is shining. Johnny knows what she would smell like if he were to slide his nose along her hair. Defeat. When she gets like this she stirs up his own desperation.

"Come here," he says, and surprisingly she comes. When he stands and holds her he can smell her hatred. He takes her hand and kisses the wrist. "It's Loraine's baby," he says.

Charlene bites his shoulder. She clamps down and Johnny wants to howl, but instead he grasps, through her top, the flesh at her waist and he digs with his nails, harder, until they both break each other's skin and their eyes water. They butt foreheads. Johnny mumbles, "We've done things wrong."

"Shut up," she says, and kisses him. And then, there in the middle of the front room, curtains open to the yard light and the few cars and trucks that flash by on the gravel road, she undresses him.

She removes her own clothes and squats to take him in her mouth. Johnny lets her; she does this only when he has bitterly disappointed her. Johnny thinks that both of them are like those simians in the zoo, reaching out through the bars, stroking an arm, a shoulder, begging for a touch. He watches the back of her neck. The vertebrae glide beneath her skin. Her shoulders hump up and down. He poses his hands on top of her head as if praying. She licks and pauses. Looks up at him.

There is a gap at the centre of his being. Of hers too. Johnny knows this, knows he has to keep plugging it up over and over again. This is what he's doing now. He takes Charlene by the face and pulls her up and kisses the taste of himself from her mouth and nose and tongue. Then he lays her down on the braided rug his mother made and cups Charlene with his hands. His hairy belly slaps down on her soft round tummy and "Oh," she says, again and again into his right ear.

Later, she pours herself another drink but doesn't offer Johnny one. She sits in a soft chair, crosses her legs, and pushes with a finger at her sore wet mouth. Johnny dresses. He goes into the kitchen and puts an antibiotic cream on the teeth marks. His shirt is unbuttoned, he's still breathing with effort. He closes his eyes. There is a wetness in his underwear. He shifts his hips and buttons his shirt. Puts on a jacket and cowboy boots. He steps outside and before the door swings shut he hears Charlene's voice. He ignores her, finds his truck beneath the yard light, climbs in, and after starting up, shudders in the glow of the dash.

Johnny goes to the centre. It's either here or Carol's and tonight he doesn't want to face Carol. There is a cot in the back room and a shaver and shampoo in a cupboard; he washes in the sink. That night he sits in a vinyl chair in the darkness of the centre and he smokes. He phones Loraine but Chris answers so he just hangs up. When he finally goes to bed it's three in the morning but, still, he can't sleep. He turns on the black-and-white TV he has beside the cot and there are these people, a man and a woman, talking about a frying pan.

"Nothing stuck," the woman says, "It's wonderful." Her eyes open wide and she smiles.

"What is this?" Johnny says. "You're on drugs." He's thinking about Charlene, her black hair spread out on the rug, her eyes closed, and the constriction of her throat, on, off, on, off, as he moved inside her. The body is an amazing thing; muscles and shit and blood and veins, and somewhere in there, behind those closed eyes, is a little trigger that tells Charlene if she is happy or sad or horny or hungry or thirsty; and that's what makes her throat go on and off. Or maybe it's Johnny. He doesn't like to think about it too much.

"That's incredible, Tanya," the man on the TV says. "Nothing stuck." Johnny rubs his jaw. Tanya and the man keep discussing the merits of the frying pan so Johnny switches to a rerun of "The Rockford Files." His toes are cold; he puts on socks. He eats a bar from the dispenser over by the pool table and, when the show's over, switches off the TV. The centre feels hollow; water is dripping in the bathroom. He wonders about this place sometimes, what he's trying to prove. People in town, they laugh at him. Still, he believes that kids are more interesting than adults; teenagers are honest and hopeful.

Johnny wonders why adults are so cynical. That used to be the wonderful thing about Charlene; she supported him, told him he was fine, not to worry about others. Not any more, Charlene's losing it. He knows it's the baby, the blunt fact that he went and did this thing with Loraine so he'll have this other body out there; his genes, cells, maybe even the same slant to the mouth. This is too much for Charlene.

"So what," Johnny says. He finishes his bar and falls asleep, chocolate still melting into his molars.

The following morning he has breakfast at Chuck's. He sits with Joe Emery who talks about the road — he's a trucker — and about Melissa and his kids. Johnny knows that Joe's boy, Roger, stole a car the other night. Chris and Melody were involved but Roger was the big push. He waits for Joe to mention it but he doesn't. Later, driving to work, Johnny thinks people need to talk more, get stuff out in the open. It's no good, this hiding. He's guilty too, he knows it. Feeling this, he drives past the feed mill and turns up the three-mile road and over to his farm. Smoke rises from the chimney, a lazy curl, and he thinks that Charlene must have lit a fire.

He finds her in the living room, lying in front of the wood stove. She's on her back, snoring, wearing a T-shirt and panties. The house is cold, the fire almost out. Johnny touches Charlene's foot. Ice. He scoops up his wife, stumbles, then carries her to the bedroom on the second floor. He runs the bath, then removes Charlene's clothes and bends to her again. She smells of vomit and gin. Her breasts slide to either side as he straightens and carries her to the tub. He lays her in. She groans and pushes at the water; her red fingernails sink. He holds her head above the water and leans his chest against the tub.

"Charlene," he says, "I'm going to wash you." And he does. He wipes her face, pokes at her ears. He soaps her back, her front, her crotch. He scrubs her. Her hair he leaves; it's too long. When he is finished she is awake but still limp and heavy.

"Stand up," he says.

She tries but fails. He lifts her from her armpits and she hangs on to the towel rack as he dries her. "I'm sorry," she manages at one point. Johnny puts her to bed and goes downstairs to make coffee and toast. Charlene is sleeping when he returns. He touches her forehead. He kneels beside the bed and watches her face. He loves her again. What had seemed so desperate last night appears brighter today. Johnny remembers when he married Charlene and she talked about how some day she wanted five children and a grand house and when she said this she smiled and pushed at Johnny's chest with the heel of her hand, as if Johnny were on the edge of something and she wanted to check if he would fall. It was only later that Johnny saw Charlene as the earth's moon, halved, light and dark. It's the mother, Johnny thinks. Spreading herself like thick butter on Charlene. The mother calls Charlene and Charlene whispers into the phone and then finally hangs up and heads straight for the bottle. Clink, clink. These days she pours the drink while she's on the phone, as if this were a small form of rebellion.

One time Johnny said, "Why do you talk to her? She's poison."

"She's my mother," Charlene said and she swung her head back and forth and her hair followed.

"She changes you, makes you ugly," Johnny said.

"Does she?" Charlene's voice was tougher, as if the bile she'd collected from her mother would fall onto Johnny's brow. He didn't mind. He'd rather Charlene fight back than sit and pout and get slapped around.

"Yes, she does, look at you," and he pointed at the half-full glass in her hand where the clear liquid waved.

"Maybe you do this to me," Charlene said, and Johnny ducked his head quickly as if avoiding something solid hurtling through the air.

"Don't blame me," he said, and he pulled Charlene onto his lap. A splash of her drink fell onto Johnny's chest and Charlene put her mouth there and licked. Johnny's stomach lurched, but he said nothing, holding her head instead, wondering how it was that there were so many other people in the world who lived happily. How did they do it?

Bending over the sleeping Charlene now, Johnny touches her cheek and her nose and her mouth. He pats her rump through the blanket and thinks that he loves her and if it weren't for Loraine they could be happy sometimes. Charlene is like a field that has lain empty for years and needs to be harrowed, ploughed, even seeded. In her best moments, like when they are out in Winnipeg for dinner, just the two of them, and she sits across from him and her shoulders are big and she consumes food and drink and cigarettes and she says how much she trusts him and she is proud of him the way he's taking care of the youth of Lesser, that's when Johnny loves her best and then he wants to keep her forever. He wants to lay the length of her out and tell her, first in one ear and then the other, how her simplicity excites him.

But this is not always so. And Johnny sometimes sees that he too may be at fault, as if he has through the years been erasing Charlene; he is a waterfall, just big enough, and Charlene is a rock upon which he falls and he is slowly wearing her down. Johnny takes his hand off her bum now. Smooths her hair. Bends to kiss her. Like a child, she is easiest to love when sleeping.

That afternoon Johnny does another drug talk. This time it's to fifteen- and sixteen-year-olds. The supervising teacher is Ms. Holt, who never really liked Johnny when he was her student. He remembers a line she often said: *No event occurs twice.* He shakes hands with her and makes small talk. Odd, how things equal out, how this woman no longer has any power over him.

The kids this time are sleepy and uninterested. He recognizes one girl, Melody Krahn; she's friends with Chris. He sees them together at the centre. Ms. Holt gives Johnny an overhead projector to use in case he has notes or something important to show the group. He looks down at the glass top and sees himself; small-headed, sharp-nosed, a loose neck, a mouth that's too big. He smiles and gets his image back. Takes a breath.

"At your age," he says, "I was known as a stoner. I thought it was cool. I'd walk down the hall of this school, pull out a blunt instrument, and light up. Needless to say I didn't last long in school. I think you could ask Miss Holt here how appreciated I was by the teachers." The kids laugh. He's got their attention now. Ms. Holt offers a slight lift of her mouth.

"Movies, music, they make drugs look sexy. But I'm not sure, personally, how much we should celebrate them." Johnny pauses and looks around the room. He's preaching and he hates that. His heart's not in it today.

He tries again. "I don't think we should glorify the heads in our schools. The guys, like I used to be, who think they have a corner on genius because they're walking around stupid and stoned. Uh-uh."

Melody Krahn is shaking her head. Johnny doesn't know if she's tired or disagreeing. When he's finally finished, his mouth is dry and he wants to sip at something strong. Melody comes to see him as he's putting on his coat. She's wearing a T-shirt that claims Gandhi was just another skinhead. She pushes at her hair and says, "You don't really believe all that, do you?"

Johnny shrugs. "Of course, why not?"

"I dunno." She laughs, her eyebrows go up and then down. Her voice is fine, as if her life were full of secrets. "This short-term memory stuff you were talking about. You lost yours?"

"I lost my long-term memory. Ha!" Johnny flutters his hands at his sides like a little bird. "Hey, you've been at the centre."

"A bit."

"Good, keep coming, we need you there."

Johnny figures maybe he should have been a teacher. He feels good driving away from school. He lights a cigarette and immediately stubs it out. Ms. Holt had a second part to that saying. It went something like, *No event occurs twice, precisely because it has occurred once already.*

"Yes, that's right," Johnny thinks. He says this out loud to himself. It still doesn't make much sense but that doesn't matter, he feels intelligent saying it.

He drives past his sister Carol's house and, on a whim, pulls into the driveway. He lets himself in and finds Carol breast-feeding her new baby in the living room. The TV's on and Erica is flipping channels. Johnny sits and watches the baby's head beat a slow rhythm against Carol's skin. He is amazed by the colour of his sister's breast. So white. Perhaps it is the contrast, the round black head against her flesh.

"How's Roy?" he asks.

"Fine. He's got a road trip next week. Out to Calgary." She pulls the baby away. It comes up sloppy and wet.

"Here, let me burp him." Johnny stands and takes the boy. He smells the baby's neck and ears. The baby burps, its head wobbles. Johnny thinks about the little pea tucked inside Loraine's body. He misses Loraine, wants to lift her sweater and poke at her stomach. Maybe she'll show up at his baptism; he doubts it.

While Carol mixes tuna salad, Johnny rocks the baby and flips through a mail-order catalogue for women. There are bras and panties, stockings and skirts. The models are young. Johnny doesn't really notice the clothes. He can't think of any women who look like this; certainly not Loraine, Charlene, or his sister Carol. And that's fine. He prefers women who are flawed in some way, women who need someone like Johnny to dig for their centre and rescue them. Carol comes into the room licking mayonnaise from a spoon. She pauses, looks at her brother, and shakes her head.

"What?" Johnny says.

"Charlene called last night. She wanted me to come over. I couldn't. Roy was out till late. She sounded drunk, said you were gone."

Johnny nods. "I saw her this morning. She's okay."

"She's going to lose her job," Carol says. "She doesn't need that."

"She's got my money."

Carol ignores her brother. "She always knew you were seeing Loraine."

Johnny swallows. This is not what he expected.

Carol continues, "She could live with it, but now with the baby, that's killing her."

His sister's shirt has a wet spot on one side. Her full breast is leaking. The baby bangs his head against Johnny's chest, gums a fist. "Is he hungry?" Johnny asks.

"I just fed him," Carol says. Her own mouth is like Johnny's, he can see that; coy, greedy. Johnny's been watching his own body lately, observing its quirks, its descent, and he's been imagining his own baby not as a baby at all, but grown up like him, and he's wondering, Will it be happy when it's thirty-six? That's what he wants for the child, happiness. It'll be a girl, he's almost sure about it. He wants a girl.

He says to his sister, "Is Roy needy? Does he pull at you? Block you in?"

Carol shrugs. "Sure," she says, "but he's a man."

"Charlene and me, we don't have sex any more," Johnny says. He lifts a hand, touches the baby's neck.

"That surprises you?" Carol asks.

"How 'bout you and Roy?"

"We're all right," Carol says. She gathers up the baby, who's fussing, and holds him like a football. She sways in the centre of the room. "Roy's not like you though."

Johnny watches his sister lull her child to sleep. What she has become, this mother, amazes him. He's proud of her. He says, "And, who am I?"

"Roy doesn't always think about sex. He can take it or leave it. That's how it is. So, we live like that. Besides, children drain you. I'm beaten up by bedtime."

Johnny nods his head. "I'm going to be baptized," he says. "In three days."

"Well," Carol says. "Again?"

"Yeah. On the advice of Phil Barkman. He compared the earlier one to an infant baptism; though I was sixteen I probably wasn't terribly conscious. Conscious. That's what he said."

"I guess Phil Barkman knows then," Carol says.

"I guess. It's this Sunday evening. At the MB Church. You're welcome to come."

"I was at your first one."

"You were baptized once," Johnny says. "Weren't you?"

"Of course, everyone was," Carol says. "I was twelve."

"Huh. Anyways."

"You should see Charlene," Carol says. "She's gonna kill herself out there alone. Walk outside drunk. Fall over and freeze or something."

"I will," Johnny says. "Right after supper."

But, he doesn't. Instead, he goes back to the centre. Allison is there, sweeping the floor. She has her own key and often lets herself in. She's playing music. It's too loud.

"Turn it down," Johnny shouts.

Allison doesn't hear him. She's holding the broom, her back to him, and her head's bowed and moving slowly. Johnny tramps over to the stereo and turns down the volume. Allison swivels and smiles. "Thought I'd clean up a bit," she says, pushing a hand out at the room.

Johnny lifts an eye. "Nothing better to do?"

"Not really."

Johnny goes to his back room and phones his house. Charlene surprises him and answers.

"I'm just wondering," Johnny says, "if you want me at home there? You decide, okay? I'll do what you want."

Charlene's voice is calm. "I'm strong enough," she says.

"You wouldn't do anything stupid?" Johnny asks. Charlene laughs and then stops. Johnny listens to her quick light breaths and then says, "You'll call me, if you need anything?"

"Sure."

After he hangs up he sits for a long time, his eyes closed, and listens to Allison's music. She shouldn't be here, he thinks. It doesn't look right. Not these days. He puts on his coat, tells Allison he's going out, and drives down to the river and over the bridge to Glenlea. He could stop by St. Adolphe for a drink but he doesn't want to, not really. He turns up the 75 and drives towards Morris. The inside of a car at night is a wonderful thing. There is a glow, a low hum; it's his own egg. Johnny goes fast. His car is big and new and creaks faintly on the small bumps. Later Johnny pulls over and watches the traffic pass by. He talks to himself. "I am not a good man," he says.

When he gets back to the centre, Allison has left. Johnny brushes his teeth and climbs into bed. He stares up at the ceiling and thinks how believing in God makes him feel special. It gives him another side. He is not just one more philandering unbeliever, a descendant of an ape who, after spilling out his lonely life, returns to dust. In the darkness Johnny presses his fingers to his forehead, squeezes his eyes shut, cries a little, and whispers a need for forgiveness.

On Sunday, before the baptism, Johnny calls up Phil Barkman and says, "I don't think this is right. My life is not exactly on solid ground these days. Charlene and I are not doing well. Loraine Wallace is going to have my baby. I drive down the highway and big trucks bear down on me and I think I'm not ready to die, to be baptized. You see?"

Phil doesn't seem shocked or upset by Johnny's revelations. Johnny can hear kids playing in the background. Phil says, "You think there'll be a better time? I mean, you have to be sure. I can't decide for you. This one's all yours; not your wife's, not Loraine's, nor should it have much to do with this sense of imminent death you seem to have. Of course you want to be sure things are right with everyone in your life. Have you made your peace? But most of all you want to listen to the Holy Spirit. What does the Spirit want you to do?"

Johnny hangs up, still confused. He tries to read the Bible but nods off.

He sleeps too long and wakes with a feeling of both panic and anticipation. There are three cars in the church parking lot when he arrives. Inside he finds Melissa Emery, Phil, and one other man whom Phil introduces as his brother-in-law, Brian.

"Are you ready?" Phil asks.

"Sure."

"Turnout's low tonight," Phil says. He shakes his head.

"No problem," Johnny says. He finds himself amused.

The main auditorium is vast and bright. Johnny changes downstairs; he wears underwear, purple briefs, beneath a white gown. He keeps on his socks. His hands shake; he is cold. Phil is already standing in the water when Johnny walks up to the edge of the baptistry tank. He steps down into the water, grateful for its warmth. Through the short panel of glass, against which the water laps, he can see Melissa's red lips and Brian's bald head. Then, Phil has him by the shoulders, clasps his hands, and speaks into Johnny's ear. Asks him all those things that are necessary, things about Jesus and sins and the Holy Spirit, and Johnny says yes to all of them. Finally, he's submerged and then he rises again, water dripping off his ears. Later, he and Phil change into dry clothes in a Sunday school room in the basement. They rub towels against goosepimply skin. Their shared nakedness keeps them silent and thoughtful. Johnny turns his body slightly so Phil can't see his privates; though he does manage to sneak a look at Phil's and what he sees is nothing to brag about. Johnny slips his bare feet into brown shoes. His hair is tousled, his back still wet. Phil, dressed now, asks if he feels okay.

"Yes," Johnny says, and Phil hugs him. While they are holding each other Johnny thinks about how Phil looks when he's naked. He shakes his head and tries to recall Melissa Emery's red mouth. He hopes she will still be up there in that large vestibule, waiting to shake hands and wish him well. Then he remembers the voice he heard just before he went under the water. It was a groan or a chant, and he still isn't sure if it was Melissa Emery babbling with delight or his own voice crying out at the high varnished rafters of the empty building.

THE MIND OF CHRIS

Loraine is losing her son. For some time now he's been chafing. But as fall slides away and the world is at the edge of winter, Chris decides to take his hatred for this meagre life and throw it back at his mother. It's like Loraine is standing at the edge of a river and Chris is walking out into the middle where the ice is thin and dangerous. She calls out to him but he ignores her. There's nothing Loraine can do but watch. Some mornings, at breakfast, she watches him drop his chin near a bowl and spoon up cereal, and she thinks that all is okay, that Chris is still her little boy, that whatever ugliness she saw in him yesterday was exceptional and is dead today. But then he opens his mouth and Loraine must brave a barrage, a storm. He wallops away at his mother, at himself.

Like this morning, he is buttering his toast and Loraine is by the kitchen window watching for the school bus. She turns to ask him if he has his bag, his lunch.

"Why don't you go puke," he says.

Loraine's hands grip the countertop, the small of her back presses its edge. There is a hardness in her throat. "I'm finished with morning sickness. The first three months are the worst."

"Oh, the worst. Now we're waiting for the best. I'm so excited." He flaps his hands, mocking her.

"Your bus is here." Loraine can see it standing at the edge of the driveway. It's like a big bright yellow box on a black background. A painting. She calls out goodbye but Chris doesn't respond. She watches him run, his laces loose, his jacket flapping. Then he's swallowed by the doors; a mouth of a bird.

Loraine washes the dishes, then puts on a heavy coat — it was her husband's — and goes out to the barn to gather eggs. She's in the refrigerator room when the phone rings. She picks it up and talks but there's no response. She says hello again and then there's a quiet giggle and a voice breathy and loose that says, "Bitch," and then a click. Loraine holds her breath. The baby's fluttering and giving her goose bumps.

This baby. She wonders why she wanted it. She knows who phoned and she feels sorry for the woman. Johnny sometimes talks about Charlene, not in a bad way, just little details, like her habits, and bodily things. Loraine will ask, point-blank, about Charlene: how often does she shave, does Johnny like hairy armpits, does Charlene have nice breasts, whose are nicer, what about weight, is Charlene heavy, and does Johnny like lots to hang on to. Johnny doesn't seem to mind answering these questions. Often they're in bed talking like this and Johnny will touch Loraine all over. "I like *you*," he'll say.

But Johnny hasn't been around lately. And Loraine thinks maybe he won't be. When he gets into this baptism and Bible stuff he becomes more faithful and stays close to Charlene. That's all right, good for Charlene but, still, Loraine misses Johnny. She tries to understand how Chris might perceive all this. That's what frightens Loraine. Obviously, she's in the wrong; she has stolen another woman's husband and, according to Chris, the man wasn't worth stealing. But, it's more than that; Chris is just discovering his own sexuality and it must be troubling for him to know his mother sleeps with Johnny.

She talks to him one night. "You know, what Johnny and I are doing isn't wrong. It's terrible that Charlene gets hurt but if I love Johnny and he loves me, it's not wrong for us to be having sex."

"Did I say it was?" Chris says. "I mean, just because you're a slut doesn't make it wrong. Right? Everybody says that, 'Your mom's a slut.'"

"They do not."

"They think it."

"No, Chris. *You* think it. Look at me. Am I a slut? A whore?"

"Yeah, whatever."

"No, not whatever. I was wrong, okay. I shouldn't be pregnant. But I am. What do you want? An abortion?"

No answer. Glum face and angry ears.

"You have no idea," Loraine says.

"You talk too much," Chris throws back. They are in his bedroom, Chris lying in bed, Loraine on a stool beside him. Her neck is hot and red; she stops talking. She gets up and walks out on him, softly shutting the door, wanting to slam it. She creeps back in later when he is sleeping and stands looking at him. Lingers over him, bends to listen to him breathe. His bare legs are outside the blanket. They are getting hairy. She touches him lightly: hair, eyes, elbow, knee, mouth, hand, thumb, lips. She kisses him and smells his cheek, a mixture of Vaseline and soap. He has tiny scrapes on his arms as if someone has poked at him with a sharp object. His nails are bitten, his hair long, eyelashes thick. He mumbles and stirs. Loraine backs from the room.

One morning Johnny calls and tells Loraine that Chris punched a hole into his tongue. Johnny does not mean to say this, it is not the purpose of the call, but it slips out.

"A hole? What do you mean?" Loraine asks.

"Pierced. He pierced his tongue. You know, kids are into noses, navels, and so on. Well, Chris did his tongue."

"Like a hole right through?"

"Yeah."

"You've seen it?"

"He was showing some other kid at the centre. And there it was, a stud, right through the middle."

Loraine laughs. She doesn't want to, but she does. "Unbelievable."

"Don't tell him I told you," Johnny says.

"Sure, no problem, you'll just stay out of my life. Why'd you tell me? Do you think I want to know these things?"

"Yes. In the end, you do."

Loraine has to sit down.

"Actually, I'm calling about his trial," Johnny says. "Are you going?"

"I guess."

"I'll take him if you like."

"He'd let you?"

"He said so."

Loraine can't believe this, how her son has latched on to Johnny, a man he doesn't really care for. All his hatred is aimed at her. "Well," she says, "if he'd rather go with you, fine."

"Hey, it was his idea. I'm not stealing him from you."

"No?" It's quiet, and then Loraine says, "Haven't seen you, Johnny."

Johnny is slow to respond. He coughs softly and says that Charlene needs him. He's torn, but he's got to make some decisions. "It's a moral thing," he says.

"A what?"

"Moral. You know, duty."

"Oh, I see. I get it."

That evening, at supper, Loraine watches Chris eat. She looks for flashes from his mouth but there's no sign of gold. He eats quietly. Loraine attempts to engage him. "You going into town tonight?"

"Uh huh," he says.

"How?"

"With Walker."

"Seeing someone?"

"Some kids."

"You still see Melody?"

"Yup."

"Does she hang out at the centre?"

"Some."

"Johnny called. He asked about your court appearance. The thing is, do you want me to go or Johnny?"

"Johnny."

Loraine's poking at some cauliflower on her plate. It crumbles and falls away. She can see that Chris is embarrassed. He doesn't want his mother to see him in court. She accepts this and says, "Is Melody going the same day?"

"Yeah."

"And Roger?"

"A different time."

"Do you still see Roger?"

"Not much. He's a jerk. What is this?" Chris pushes back from the table.

Loraine watches the tendons move on his hands. She remembers when he was two, she'd circle his wrist with her fingers and feel his narrow bone there and marvel at how frail he was. She hates the sound of her voice now, whiny, wheedling, as she says, "Before you leave you've got eggs to gather."

Chris turns and looks at his mother, distaste for this life forcing his mouth open and revealing his tongue, almost oversized, Loraine thinks, and she sees for an instant the tiny red spot at the centre of that fleshy organ, and then the mouth shuts and Chris is gone.

The day of the court appearance, Johnny picks up Chris at nine in the morning and Loraine manages to kiss her son on the cheek before he leaves. Johnny stands in the doorway, his head bent a little, hands sticking into the pockets of his jacket. Chris is already in the car. Loraine keeps her distance and lays her hands across her belly. "Thanks," she says.

"For what?" Johnny says.

"For doing this."

"Achhh." He waves his hand and dismisses her.

"He's so angry," Loraine says. Her body's twitching being so close to Johnny. This happens when he's around, excitement rises from her stomach up to her throat and then trickles around in her back. She lifts her nose. When he's gone, raising a hand, obviously wanting to kiss her but knowing she won't let him, Loraine folds laundry and thinks that she's lonely. She has no one she could call a friend. Except maybe Helen but Helen hangs out with the book club group and it's a collection of women Loraine doesn't feel comfortable with. They're sassy, she thinks. They all live in town; they either work at good jobs or don't have to work. Charlene wouldn't have to work at her job. Johnny's got lots of money. All those women read too and Loraine doesn't have time to read. She takes care of chickens. That's what she does. Sometimes she dreams she's at the bottom of a large tube and chicken feathers are floating down the tube and landing on her. At first it's soft and cozy but the tube is high and the feathers keep coming and finally the load becomes unbearable and Loraine wakes up gasping for air.

She'd like to move. Sell the farm and go to Winnipeg, get a job there, but she doesn't know what she'd do. She never finished university; Jim plucked her out of school and moved her onto this farm and then died and she was left with an eight-year-old and twenty thousand birds.

Loraine finds herself in Chris's room, on his bed. She clutches his folded socks and thinks about how good it would be to take her son by his cheeks and hold him, face him, and talk, talk, talk. She wants to crack open his head, lick the ugliness out of the cracks and crevices of his brain. She wants him to be excited for this baby, to come with her and select a crib, to help name the baby.

Smother, smother.

Then she lies back on his bed and does something dark; opens his drawing book and pages through it. Inside are sketches and caricatures and little bits of writing. There's a note to someone, Melody maybe, that never got finished, but it begins: *Dear M, Huh-Huh Cool, was hoping to do some with you, ruby lips that kicked ass. It ruled. It ruled.* Beneath this is the word *Nirvana* in scrolled handwriting. Loraine sits up and puts a tape in Chris's player. She listens and dawdles. She tries to dance to one song but can't feel the beat.

She turns off the music and picks up the book again. She feels nervous and excited, like having Johnny on a Sunday afternoon, expecting Chris to bang through the door at any moment. Chris has drawn a picture of her. She recognizes her own arms and legs. She's standing in the garden, leaning on a hoe, and she's looking off somewhere as if something important were taking place far far away. For some reason Loraine is pleased looking at this drawing. It is flattering, even though it was done last summer, before Chris became angry and ridiculous.

On the last page there is a letter to Melody. *Dear Melody, Hey was thinking be nice to unzip you, or you me, and we could put our fingers where we shouldn't. Maybe fuck, too. Sure, fuck. I like the way your tongue feels, cool little bumps that match my bumps. You can do what you want. You want?* There is more and Loraine reads the whole thing and wishes she hadn't. Then she reads it again. Loraine finds herself turning red because the language is both childish and daring. The only thing that relieves Loraine is the sense she has that the letter was never meant to be sent. Or read. She is amused at one point, though. It's a quote from a TV show. She reads it.

Come to Butt-head,
Come a little closer.
I just want to feel every part

of me, touching every part of
you. Especially the thingys.

She laughs.

Loraine cooks pasta and salad for supper and she makes fresh bread, planning to invite Johnny to stay. When Johnny and Chris return, around four-thirty, Loraine is walking from the house to the barn. Chris looks so small beyond the windshield; the glass warps him, he's out of proportion, not her son at all. The car stops and Chris flies towards the house, not acknowledging his mother. Loraine leans into the car, rests her arms on the door and says, "So?"

Johnny lights a cigarette and lifts his shoulders. "Okay. Forty hours of community service. Here in Lesser."

"That's all?"

"What did you want, prison?"

"In a way, yes. I'm happy, really. But he'll never learn."

"I asked the judge if I could use him at the centre. No problem."

"Ah, Johnny. He'll never do it. He'll shirk."

"He'll do it. We have to report back. It's good, I've got this bathroom I want redone. He can do the bull work." Johnny reaches up and touches Loraine's face. "Your skin is perfect, tighter."

Loraine doesn't move, just lets him touch. "Do you want some supper? It's made."

"No. Chris is sick of me. I shouldn't." He kisses her then, on the cheek, as if she were his daughter and not the mother of his baby. Loraine is toying with this vision of domestic bliss, of Johnny joining the family and them all sitting down to an evening meal and Johnny reaching out to cup Loraine's belly. She wants him, reaches down and puts a hand at his crotch. She's wearing gloves so the effect is comically surgical. Johnny doesn't seem to notice.

His voice low, he asks, "How's the baby?"

"Good," Loraine says. She stoops and lays her mouth on Johnny's neck. "I've stopped puking and she's moving."

"I think about you," Johnny says.

"Good." And then Loraine, imagining Chris watching from the house, pulls out of the car. Her waist is cold where her parka lifted. "How 'bout Melody?"

"Ten hours."

"And Roger?"

"His was moved back. Next month. That boy's clearly bad. Chris should stay away from him."

"He will."

After, when Johnny is driving away, Loraine watches his car and thinks how considerate he is these days, unusually kind and fair, as if his life were brimming with hope and happiness and he was doling out the excess to people surrounding him. When Johnny's like this Loraine doesn't mind as much him going back to Charlene. She just has to wait. It's a nasty fact, but Loraine knows that when it comes to Johnny choosing, he'll pick her over Charlene. He will.

On Friday night Loraine drives Chris and Melody to Winnipeg and drops them off at DJ'S Roller City. Melody sits in front with Loraine and Chris is in back. Melody wears braces and when she talks her s's slide around. It's dark in the car and Loraine can smell the girl beside her, it's as if she's sprinkled baby powder on her shoulders. Loraine carries the conversation, asking about the Christmas concert, the school teams, the teachers. Melody likes to talk, Chris is silent. At one point he leans into the front, his head close to Loraine's shoulder, and he runs a hand along the back of Melody's hair. Loraine pretends not to notice and turns on the radio. She only has AM so must do with country or classic rock.

"That's lousy," Chris says.

Loraine turns the radio off. She says, turning to Melody, "Did Chris tell you I'm pregnant?"

"Aw, Mom, give it a break," Chris's voice complains out of the darkness.

Loraine continues, ignoring her son, "I don't know about you but I think it's better to talk than to pretend or go 'round with your eyes closed. I'm pregnant. It's a fact. Maybe it's not a great situation, but there it is."

"Hey, I think it's neat, Mrs. Wallace. When are you due?" Melody's voice cajoles, slippery, full of saliva. An undertow there. Things are deeper than they seem.

"In five months," Loraine answers. "The baby's about this big." And she holds up a thumb and forefinger showing the size of the fetus. "Like a good-sized frog."

Melody laughs. Chris groans.

"Tell her what your mom said, Melody," Chris says.

"Chris. Don't." Melody turns in her seat and glares.

"Oh, it's okay," Loraine says. "People talk. But I don't worry. It's my baby." She pats her stomach instinctively and looks across at Melody who has her boots off and is resting her feet on the dash. Melody smiles; a flash of metal. Loraine feels affection for her.

She leaves Chris and Melody at the door to DJ'S and drives to The Bay and shops till nine o'clock. Then she eats something at a nearby restaurant. She risks a glass of wine. It's been so long since she's pampered herself. The dining room is almost empty but Loraine doesn't mind. She sits and looks out the window onto Portage Avenue. It's a busy intersection so there's lots of foot and vehicle traffic. After the farm it's like a movie. People are just so fine here, everything in place, slick. Loraine feels frumpy.

Back at DJ'S it's fairly dark inside, only a big glass ball turning in the middle of the rink, so her frumpiness doesn't really matter. She stands at the edge of the rink and stares out into the centre looking for Chris and Melody. They're at the far end, coming around slowly, holding hands. Chris is talking. Melody smiles and punches at him, her thin arms flashing out and then back. Loraine sees that the girl is both exciting and dangerous; she's not that innocent. Her body is a piano wire being stretched. Loraine knows the feeling. She doesn't know though if her son can handle all this. She thinks that Chris is about to get hurt.

There are a lot of native girls skating. They all seem to be wearing red pants and white T-shirts and their hair is black and wavy as if they'd all gotten perms at the same place. Most are thin but there's a chubby one who can't quite keep up. Chris and Melody drift by again, this time Chris is skating backwards and his tongue hangs out. Loraine can see a flash of gold, then his mouth claps shut. Finally, Melody spots Loraine and pulls Chris over. Melody jabbers while Chris lingers behind her.

"Wanna skate, Mrs. Wallace? It's easy."

"No, thanks."

Up close like this, leaning into Melody, Loraine is aware that the girl is stoned. Her eyes, even in this dim light, are swimming. She's too happy; holds on to Loraine's hands. Chris, Loraine supposes, is in the same state. Not knowing if she wants to deal with this, she lets them keep skating and seats herself at a small table and drinks coffee. She thinks about a girl like Melody, her father the pastor of a Mennonite church, and how likely she is, how necessary her actions seem. Johnny, more familiar with the underbelly of a stringent religion, has told Loraine that pastors' kids inevitably go wild. They are programmed to either kill themselves or do heavy damage. Johnny speaks from personal experience; though his father wasn't a pastor, he was a strict, fanatical man, eventually driving Johnny to his own extremes.

At one point Loraine sees this couple holding each other for the longest time by the far wall. Later, when they part, she recognizes Chris and Melody. In fact, driving home later, they sit in the back seat while Loraine plays the chauffeur. They whisper and push at each other. It's harmless, Loraine wants to believe. Then, remembering that letter, she almost asks Melody if she has protection; Loraine doesn't want the girl hurt, she likes her spunk. She remembers what it's like to be faced with the prospect of sex at this age, all excitement and clumsiness and mishap. Like sticking your nose into a gopher hole and being bitten.

She plays some music softly and, pulling into Lesser, thinks the two children in back must be sleeping, it's so quiet. She sneaks a look in the rear-view mirror and in the light of a street lamp sees her son entangled in Melody's arms, his head pressed against her chest. Lights flash from a passing car and Melody's face flares and disappears. For a moment Loraine sees how perfectly happy she is and this, for some reason, makes Loraine sad.

In the morning Chris has a low-grade fever.

"My tongue hurts," he says. He touches his mouth. His speech is thicker today as if he were fighting words past a rag.

Loraine feels his forehead and offers him juice and toast. She goes out to work in the barn and when she returns to the house at noon Chris's fever has gone up. His lips are dry, his tongue fatter.

Loraine says, "Your tongue's infected."

The boy just stares, he doesn't speak.

"You put that in yourself? That hole?"

Chris nods.

"Was the needle, or punch, or whatever, clean?"

"Yeah. I think so. Melody used it but I washed it."

"Boiled it?"

"No, washed it. It was just Melody, it's not like it was this bum."

"Well, there you go. Just curious. What did she pierce?"

"Her nipple." Chris says this and winces. His tongue is growing. The fever has made him yielding and honest. He's telling Loraine stuff he normally wouldn't. Loraine shakes her head and wonders if she should call Mrs. Krahn and have her check out Melody's breasts, just to show her what's happening — the woman's naive.

In the afternoon Loraine drives Chris to Emergency in Steinbach. They sit side by side surrounded by a worried mother holding a hot baby, a middle-aged man reading the paper, and a Holdemann couple with six

children. Four girls, two boys. The girls are wearing these polka-dot ker-
chiefs. Loraine stares and watches the eldest daughter, who is close to
Chris's age, tend her baby brother. She's a big patient girl with thick calves.
The little boy toddles past Loraine, grabs a magazine, and gurgles. The
Holdemann girl hovers, hands ready. Loraine, so close, sights the pale skin
at her nape. Unblemished. She wonders if Chris has noticed this girl. How
pleasing. Loraine wants to touch the hem of her dress. She thinks that if
she were to be given another life she would choose to be this girl. Walk a
path where doubt does not exist, where the rituals consist of dressing and
eating and praying and having babies and standing in a large kitchen with
several other women, bending before a yeasty dun-coloured bowl, laughing
at some tidy joke, flour on the cheek. Nothing dirty there. No fear.

The little one cries. The girl scoops him up. Her dress sticks between
her legs and she pulls it free. Loraine turns to her son, whose head lolls.
Later the doctor shakes her head, prescribes penicillin, and says to
Loraine, "Watch him. Something like this shouldn't be ignored. You
especially have to monitor his breathing, swollen tongue and all."

That night Loraine dreams she is swallowing an eel and choking on it.
She wakes, her fists clenched, and goes to check on Chris. His breathing
is light and fast. His forehead is hot, his lips dry. Loraine sits by his side
and when he stirs, offers him water. He drinks quickly, still groggy.
Before he lies down again he kisses Loraine on the cheek. His eyes are on
fire; he is mad. Loraine kisses him back quickly, feeling as if she is taking advantage of her boy.

Chris's mouth moves. He garbles a sentence and says, "Oops!" Then he
says, clearly, in whispers as if confessing a private sin, "Melody doesn't
believe." He slides back onto the pillow and sleeps.

Loraine watches him; the hall light falls across his face. She would like
to trade places with her son. She could so easily take his pain, his confusion and say, "There, you are healed. Go now."

She strokes his cheek. His mouth is big, like Jim's was; stretched now, pulled by the weight of sleep, it is grotesque. Beautifully so. Ugly is beautiful sometimes. Loraine knows that and this is what attracts her to Johnny. He can be so ugly. Inside too, but there's also a purity there; he's raw and furious, and this makes him less elusive, more honest. She would like to hold him now. Just that. She lies down beside her hot son and holds him instead.

Though the fever subsides a little by the evening of the next day, Chris remains dull and listless and his forehead and chest are blotchy. He is weak, too weak to eat properly. He drinks ice water and lets the cubes rest on his tongue. In this state he forgets who Loraine is and allows her entrance to his body. She helps him walk to the washroom, his legs wobbly and unfamiliar, and she holds his hips from behind as he stands and pees into the bowl.

"I'm not looking," she says. She runs a bath for him and helps him undress, guides him into the tub. He makes a half-hearted attempt to cover himself but once prone in the water simply sighs and closes his eyes. Loraine splashes water across his chest and watches his penis float. It's shaped like Jim's; remembering Jim like this loosens a shard into her throat and the quick pain makes her eyes water, as if that innocuous little muscle were a tunnel to her past, to a time before Johnny. Johnny's penis, when limp, is long and thin and when Loraine talks to it she mocks it. Then she puts her mouth on Johnny's chest and says, "You're teeny, teeny." He doesn't like that.

"You can go now," Chris says. His eyes are open and he's watching Loraine stare at him. He draws a cloth over his crotch.

Loraine reddens. "Okay, if you need help, call me."

Later, they watch TV together and though Chris's eyes are still grey and wet and weak, he seems revived. He eats some soup that Loraine makes — and he talks.

"You know this stuff Johnny talks about? About being saved?"

"Yeah?"

"Well, I'm thinking it makes sense, somehow. You know, like we're all lost in a way."

"You think so?"

"Yeah, sometimes."

"I see." Loraine pauses, then says, "Johnny's a little hysterical at times."

"What do you mean?"

"He goes overboard."

"'You think you're better than him?" Chris asks. Loraine can sense that the testiness and resentment still exist in the dark corners of his mouth. But she doesn't answer, knowing he's frail and unable to damage her.

His eyes close and he sleeps. She stays, is tickled by the thought of him needing her. He is not himself. Soon, maybe tomorrow, he will lash out again, his voice resentful, his thin shoulders sharp with anger. However, at this moment, he is frail.

He chants and rambles, drifts into sleep and then reports back to her. Loraine cannot be sure but she thinks he speaks of beauty and kisses, of the sweet tongue of Melody, of a pierced nipple which resembles a ring through the snout of a pig, of the first inkling of death, and of a baby roaring at its mother, mouth open.

At one point he startles and says, "I like Melody, she's funny."

"Funny?"

"Yeah, like she doesn't care. Nothing's important." A pause. "That's her line."

Loraine nods and Chris slides back into a silent reverie. His mind is a weightless insect, a butterfly rising and tumbling, brushing up against a stone wall here, a tree there. The slightest commotion makes it jerk and falter. For the moment Loraine wants to capture that dizziness, cup it in her palms, and keep it safe.

WINTER

THIS DARKNESS

Though she plans on going to work Friday morning, Charlene doesn't even manage to get dressed. She sits naked on the toilet and groans into her hands. The room is cold. The furnace must have cut out during the night or the wood stove needed stoking. Her dress and stockings are laid out on the bed. She put them there last night, before opening the bottle and dipping into the heat that slid down her throat so easily. She stands, turns, and throws up into the bowl. Not much there.

"God," she says, wiping her mouth with a towel. On all fours now she studies the green growth at the base of the toilet. "Clean it," she says. She bends her neck and confronts her breasts which hang and swing. She can see her crotch way down there, an intricate forest at the end of a passage. Lying down on the throw rug she pulls a bath towel on top of herself. She squeezes herself tightly. A memory comes to her of when she was young and sick and her mother served her lunch in bed, soup and crackers and ginger ale, but she threw it up. She had been afraid that she would choke on her own vomit. Her mother held her head and washed her face. Then together they lay in bed and both fell asleep. That was a happy moment. Rare.

At ten o'clock Charlene manages to dial the Credit Union. The receptionist, Judy Penner, is curt and prissy. "Mr. Wohlgemut's been asking about you," she says. "Here, I'll put you through."

Charlene's head aches. Her mouth puckers and then she slides back into her boss's life, bowing to him, telling him that her life has not been pretty lately.

The man is terse, yet cloyingly patient, as if informing her that she has erred but will now be forgiven. Charlene wants to hang up but instead she says, "My husband's been seeing this other woman, you might know her, Loraine Wallace, and until I get this sorted out in my brain I'll have to stay away from work."

"Oh," Mr. Wohlgemut says. "Yes. Mrs. Wallace. I just loaned her money for a new generator. I'm sorry."

Charlene thinks about how when she is called into this man's office, or she meets him by the vault, she pictures holding him like a child, and he lays his head on her breast and smiles up into her face.

Charlene says, "Loraine's going to have a baby."

"Oh."

"I'm sorry, Mr. Wohlgemut. Forgive me. Will you take me back Monday morning?"

Charlene can hear the man's pencil tapping on the desk. She knows what he's thinking. There's all this sexual stuff twisted into her story and in some way he's excited and wants to take care of her. "Yes, shh, listen," he says. "Could one of the girls from here help you out? It's slow today and Luisa could come."

"I'm fine. Thanks. That's awfully sweet."

"Don't hesitate to call."

"Yes."

After Charlene hangs up she stares at the ceiling and then gets up and takes three Tylenols. There is a half-full bottle of rye on her bedside table. She studies the bottle for a long time. Her teeth are chattering. Her whole jaw shakes. She hasn't eaten for days. Johnny tried to serve her toast and coffee the other morning, Thursday it was, but Charlene just pushed it away.

Finally, she sleeps.

In the afternoon she wakes sweaty and confused and lies with her eyes closed until she has grasped who and where she is. There is a fly banging against the windowpane. Odd, she thinks, this time of year. It is windy; she can hear the trees creaking, the eaves whistling. She calls Loraine, listens to the hum of the phone and imagines Loraine walking, reaching out for the receiver; there is that second, just before the conversation, which cradles the unknown.

Loraine's voice is careful, almost unsure. Charlene doesn't say anything. Just listens to Loraine's breath, little sharp noises.

Loraine again. Voice rising. Louder now.

Charlene wants to giggle.

"Who is this?" Loraine asks. "Hello?"

Charlene can hear chickens in the background so Loraine must be in the refrigerator room off the barn. Did they do it in there? she wonders. Did he lay her out on a flat of white eggs? Charlene does giggle now; a noise from the back of her throat.

"Hello," Loraine says again.

"Bitch," Charlene says, and hangs up. She sits and watches the phone, as if it will ring, or leap up and strangle her. Her hands are shaking again.

She finishes the bottle of rye that afternoon. She manages to read at the same time. It's something she's supposed to finish for her book club which is meeting Saturday night. That's tomorrow. She wants to go but isn't sure if she'll make it.

The book is a thin collection of poetry written by a woman who's obviously in love with her father. It's not like they're having sex but this girl's definitely got problems, Charlene thinks. Talking about her father's cock; sick, in a way. Charlene reads that particular poem three times. It was Avi Heath who suggested this poet. Mona, who's part of the club, announced that Avi was pronounced "Eh-vee"; she smirked when she said this. Anyways, Avi is new at the club and doesn't realize poetry is not well accepted by the other women. Still, no one wanted to hurt Avi's feelings, so they agreed. Charlene wonders if Avi has problems with her own father. She doesn't understand why writers need to do this, cut open and spread themselves out, battered and bloody, between the pages. Everybody craps, so what? There is another good one though, where the writer's having sex with her husband or lover or whomever, and reading it, Charlene thinks, That's me. The poet is remembering the night before and marvelling at what she actually did: all fours and her rump in the air like a flower. That's nice, Charlene thinks, a flower.

She eats crackers and drinks apple juice around five in the afternoon. A square of sun is falling onto the counter. It's so silent out here, in this house, planted on this yard, at the edge of a quarter section. Sometimes she hates it; today it's pretty. You look out the window and there's a wind-break of trees and beyond that the flat earth which eventually disappears. Perhaps it's the liquor but at the moment she's proud of where she lives. She feels hopeful and calls Agnes at Lesser Beauty Salon; makes an appointment for late Saturday afternoon. A trim. And her nails too. By eight o'clock she's thirsty again. She looks for more liquor but there is none. She sniffs at the bottle she finished in the afternoon, licks the neck, sticks her tongue inside. "Fine," she says, stashing the empty bottle under the counter. "Better that way."

Saturday afternoon her Mustang won't start. She grinds the battery down to a click and takes Johnny's half-ton. At the salon she says to Agnes, "Make me beautiful."

Agnes washes Charlene's hair. Touching has not been a big part of Charlene's life lately and it's wonderful, the fingers rubbing her scalp and neck. She closes her eyes. Later, cutting at Charlene's bangs, Agnes says, "I've got this new conditioner you should try. Does a great job on the ends."

"That bad?"

"Not too."

"I'm hungry," Charlene says. "Hasn't been a good week for food."

She senses that she must reek of alcohol and wonders if she should explain herself.

Agnes pauses, holds the scissors up in the air, and closes her mouth. She's awfully pretty, Charlene thinks. She married a Ski-Doo dealer, right out of high school. Charlene thinks that Agnes maybe didn't even finish school. There was a baby, a girl who's now sixteen. Agnes says, "I've got a cinnamon bun in the kitchen, I could get it for you."

"No, it's okay, I'm just blabbin'."

"How's Johnny?" Agnes is working on the back now, Charlene can hear her breathing.

"Oh. Well? Johnny's Johnny. You've probably heard."

"A bit," Agnes says, as if waiting for more.

Charlene's quiet for a while, and then says, "I think something happened to him the day his father died. Like a tiny brittle piece snapped inside him, you know. Since then he's been all over the map, not that he wasn't like that before, it's just now he's worse, like a runaway train." Charlene shuts up. She doesn't know why she's saying this. Agnes isn't really her friend.

"Men are full of fits at this age," Agnes says. She laughs, her breath is sweet. Her scissors keep going and her breasts touch Charlene's back. "Rick, well, I sometimes think he's going to disappear. One day I'll wake up and he'll be gone. Of course, he thinks I'd miss him, hah!"

Charlene laughs. Her head feels lighter and she stops worrying about betraying Johnny. "It's just strange," she says to Agnes, "knowing there's another woman who's going to have Johnny's baby. The town's too small for that."

"Personally, if you want my opinion, I'd kill someone, I really would," Agnes says. Her mouth is this taut line and Charlene figures she isn't joking. Agnes finishes cutting and switches on the blow dryer. It's too loud for Charlene to talk, so she closes her eyes and imagines herself not killing anybody, but happily pregnant, her belly a mound that Johnny straddles.

Later, she drives down Main Street and looks for Johnny's car. It's not at the centre, nor at Chuck's. OK Feeds is closed, but Johnny could be out on a trip. It seems she's always looking out for Johnny. Even when they're in the house together she listens for him, every little creak tells her what he's doing. His toothbrush tapping the sink, or him banging through his sock drawer. She misses him, wonders if his ears ever listen for her, if his eyes roam and flit, checking for little signs of her presence. She knows the answer.

She heads up the 312 towards her turn-off but when she arrives she doesn't slow down, she just keeps driving to the 59, and left up to Lagimodiere and then east, stopping at Deacon's for gas. On the road again, driving into the falling darkness, she picks up speed. The half-ton has a shimmy, the windshield moulding rattles in the wind. Charlene holds tightly to the wheel, her knuckles yellow in the dim light of the cab. Trucks float by across the divide, their overhead lights signalling safety. Beyond Richer, into the trees of the Canadian Shield, she passes a moose by the side of the road who looks like he's mounted, he's so frozen by the light. A bit further on she has to pee and pulls to the side of the road. Flipping through the glove compartment, looking for toilet paper, she finds only a small plastic bag of grass and papers. "Johnny, you little sinner," she says. She steps outside and pees in the ditch. She pulls up her jeans and drips into her panties. Back in the truck she rubs her hands together over the heater. It's a cold night, no snow yet, and this makes it even worse. She leans back against the passenger door and rolls a joint. Her foot taps the steering wheel as she smokes and stares out into the night. There is something wrong here, she thinks. She's running, in a way, but nobody knows that she's gone. The girls at the book club will wonder, but they won't fret or worry. Johnny's not even home so he won't notice. Life will go on.

Charlene's finding it hard to breathe. Perhaps it's the grass, too strong for her. It's like someone has a towel over her face and is just barely letting her come up for air. She pulls at her jaw, opens the window, rasps out into the frosty night. Then she drives, too fast, and her lungs find new air, but still there is a lump inside her that reminds her of something swallowed too quickly, like a large cube of ice aching in her gullet. She sings a tune for comfort and the pain subsides.

The moon comes out and for a while she does what Johnny likes to do with a full moon: drive without the lights. On divided highway it's safe, everything's just shadows, and there is a sense of gliding through space in a tree-walled tunnel; the only thing that really tells Charlene where she is is the shudder of the road in her hands and the engine vibrating her feet. But, eventually, the lights come back on. The dark scares her, and cops.

For Charlene, the best thing about a hotel room is the sameness, the knowledge that she could be anywhere in the world: Sri Lanka, Chicago, Vancouver. But not in Lesser. Lesser has no hotels, certainly not an inn like this one in Kenora, which stands at the edge of the Lake of the Woods. Charlene lies in bed in her panties and bra. The TV is on. She stands and rummages through the mini-bar, pulls out a little bottle of whisky, cracks the cap, takes a shot, and breathes out through her nostrils. That night she works at the stash of petite and expensive bottles layered in the mini-bar. In between there somewhere, her head swimming, her voice descending, warped and hard from the ceiling, she orders room service: sweet-and-sour chicken, rice, fried mushrooms, and a salad. She drinks ice water and coffee, then finishes the alcohol. She sleeps, dreaming of swollen stomachs, deformed babies, and fathers with big heads. She wakes at noon and phones for a late check-out, her need to languish, to lie back and forget, overruling her frugality.

It is her headache that brings her home, back to her long driveway and the bare rowed trees lining the road, and the green and white house with the old kitchen lino. The lights are on; Johnny is home. Charlene finds him in the kitchen, reading the Bible. His hair is neatly combed, he's wearing a suit, his face glows. He does not ask where she's been, his focus is elsewhere.

"It was great," he says. His fingers splay on the table. The tips of his thumbs are bitten and ragged.

"What?" Charlene says. She has no idea what he's talking about. He looks as if he's about to jump across the table and devour her. His eyes swim. He may cry, she thinks.

"I'm sorry, Charlene," he says.

"What, what is it?"

"I love you," he says. "You're beautiful." Charlene stands and holds the back of a chair.

"I was baptized tonight," Johnny says. "Remember?"

Charlene senses that she may never rise above the man across from her. He's eating, pushing bread and cheese and jam into his mouth. His eyes shine. Charlene thinks she should sit on his face, erase the glow of God from his countenance. She circles the table, wraps her arms around his neck, and talks into his collar. "You smell like water," she says.

Johnny doesn't answer, he keeps eating.

"Who was there?" Charlene asks.

"Phil, a brother-in-law of his, Melissa Emery."

"That's it?"

"Yeah."

"Did Melissa speak in tongues? She does that, doesn't she?" Charlene kisses Johnny's ear. She's surprising herself, her bum itches and she wants Johnny to touch her, drag those mangled thumbs along her skin. She does not care about him, she wants only the knowledge of her own body.

"I don't know," Johnny says. "I thought she was speaking in tongues but I couldn't be sure. My head was underwater."

Charlene laughs. He takes her questions so seriously.

"Actually," Johnny says, "she's amazing. No other person in this town can ascend to delirium at the push of a button like Melissa Emery." Johnny shakes his head, reaches up to take Charlene's hand.

"Maybe she's unhappy," Charlene says. Then, she says quietly, past Johnny's ear, "I was thinking about the other night. Remember? On the rug, desperate, like we were two animals and that's all. I figure I don't want to be just an animal, Johnny. I'd like to think there was more to me than just the odour and look of an animal." She takes the heel of her hand and pushes it against Johnny's mouth. "Bite," she says.

He doesn't. He holds her wrist and manoeuvres it gently, hangs on to it as if it were delicate and easily breakable. Then he settles Charlene onto his lap and pulls her head to his chest as if she were a small child.

"You were gone," he says.

"Hmmm," she responds.

"Where?" he asks.

"Just gone."

And in bed later they are both naked, and she lets him hold her because she needs to feel something. But he is chaste, still elevated by this goodness he sees in himself. His hands, his voice, his whole body is tender and full of love and for a moment Charlene believes that Christianity is the best thing for Johnny. When he's mucking about with redemption, he exudes compassion, not love necessarily, but pity and mercy. And she'll take it.

Just before they sleep, Johnny says, his voice full of singsong, "Phil Barkman's got this tiny penis, hooded and blue. I saw it."

"Did you?" Charlene asks. Her eyes are closed. She reaches behind her and finds Johnny's rear, his legs; she slides her hand between and grabs hold. "Hooded and blue," she says. She's holding Johnny, not moving and he's curled into her, already sleeping. "That's nice," she says.

It could work. Monday morning Johnny and Charlene are rosy and giggly, poking at each other in the bathroom. Johnny farts and blames it on Charlene. She slaps at him as he shaves, and later she sees the mark on his back, the outline of her hand, and she laughs, bends to kiss it and says, "Sorry."

Charlene sings as she dresses. She's nervous but excited about returning to work. She eats Cheerios while Johnny reads the Bible to her.

Ephesians. "Listen," he says. "'So then do not be foolish . . . And do not get drunk with wine, for that is dissipation, but be filled with the Spirit.'" Johnny pauses, looks up at Charlene, and wets his lips. "Isn't that great? It just speaks to me. *Be filled with the Spirit.* Have you ever wanted that, Charlene?"

Charlene laughs. She lifts her arms to the air.

"It's possible," Johnny says. "I could talk to Phil, he'd pray over you."

"Wonderful," Charlene says. "As if we need another one in the house."

Johnny's face crinkles. He bends back to the Bible as Charlene eats; milk dribbles down her chin and she wipes at it with the back of her hand. "'Husbands, love your wives,'" he reads aloud. He looks up. His eyes will spill real tears, Charlene thinks. And then, at the end of chapter six, he reads slowly while Charlene putters with her lunch. "'For our struggle is not against flesh and blood, but against the rulers, against the powers, against the world forces of this darkness, against the spiritual *forces* of wickedness in the heavenly *places.*' Wow," Johnny says.

"So, what does that mean?" Charlene asks.

"It's a big battle," Johnny answers.

"I already know that, so how does that help me?"

Johnny holds up his palms. "It's funny. I always struggle with my tiny earthly body, the things of the flesh, you know. But, I'm thinking that I'm setting my sights too low. This is big stuff. There is real darkness out there, up there, not just in here . . ." Johnny thumps at this chest. "I don't know," he says. "I could be wrong."

Charlene rolls out some wax paper. She's humming to herself but she's remembering herself stretched out drunk on the kitchen floor just a few days ago and she marvels at how high one can climb, how quickly one falls, and she accepts that today she is happy and tomorrow may be different.

"Maybe it's the mind," she says, pointing at Johnny's Bible. "The mind is like a heavenly place, and then there's all those possibilities for wickedness there." Like her on the phone, whispering obscenities in Loraine's ear. She's repentant now.

Johnny's still chasing this problem. "I heard Harry Kroeker say once it was politicians. They were in high places and wicked."

"He's probably right." Charlene says this, but her mind's back on work, on how the women will treat her. Before leaving she asks Johnny if he wouldn't mind looking at her Mustang. "It's dead," she says. "All I get are clicks or maybe a tired groan."

"Sure," Johnny mumbles, still brooding at the table.

The week has a flow to it, in fact the buoyancy is frightening, as if only goodness and mercy were available in this world. Charlene, knowing this to be impossible, keeps waiting for the fall. Johnny cooks supper Monday: a chicken dish and rice. He makes instant pudding for dessert and opens a bottle of wine. Charlene drinks too much and talks really fast. She's closing up the spaces, disliking the sound of Johnny chewing, the clink of silverware. Johnny is slow, a little dazed, as if he'd spent the afternoon sleeping or smoking drugs. Noting this, Charlene says, "I found your little stash in the glove box."

"Oh?"

"Some leftovers, really old. Hard to roll."

"Must have got left there in summer."

"We haven't smoked together in a long time," Charlene says. There is something lovely here, tempting Johnny in this way.

He holds up his hands. "I'm squeaky," he says. "I really am."

"I was wondering," Charlene says, "if we'd ever do anything at Christmas. You know. Fly south, Mexico maybe, lie on the beach."

Johnny points a finger at his chest. "I burn. And I don't speak Spanish." Then he says, being more careful, "But really. You want that?"

Charlene worries she is sounding greedy but she thinks it would be so safe down there, away from here. She waves a hand, splashes the last of the wine into her glass. "It's a notion I had, a silly one."

"Not so silly," Johnny says. An attempt at kindness.

Tuesday is level, Wednesday fine. Thursday, Mona calls about the book club and wants to know if Charlene will be coming the following week. "We never really got to the book of poetry," she says. "Conversation wandered, recipes and things. And Avi asked if she could bring this new professor friend, who's just moved into town. Bought some land out by Cleary's."

"A guy?"

"Yeah, so we debated. Nancy didn't want it, said it would break up the intimacy. Deb asked if this guy was single. He is. Although I wonder if he and Avi aren't friends, you know? The guy's a physicist or into religion, I forget which."

"Maybe he's lonely," Charlene says. "So, what did you decide?"

"We didn't. We're going to vote next time. You should come."

"I don't know what to vote."

"Well, whatever you want. Did you read that poet?"

"Yes. What would you say about that book with a man present. I mean, strange stuff."

"It's poetry," Mona says.

"I liked some pieces though," Charlene says. She's on the verge of a defence of sorts and wonders why. "I'll see," she says. "I'll probably come."

"You okay now?"

"Yes, better. Much."

Once again Charlene begins to fit into the flow of life in Lesser. The women at work feed her gossip, things like Melissa Emery's son, Roger, needing to go to court. Supposedly Melody Krahn and Chris Wallace were involved too. "They all stole a half-ton," Judy Penner says. "Out near St. Pierre."

And the pastor of the United Church is having an affair with Mrs. Cornies. She's the grain elevator manager's wife. Charlene doesn't know her except to recognize her red hair. Mr. Cornies comes in to pay bills sometimes; he's always dusty and coughing. Serving him makes Charlene sneeze. She's not happy to hear about someone else's affair; it saddens her, makes her cynical and scared.

Her mother calls from the city. Though they don't see much of each other they talk once a week by phone. Sometimes her parents come out to the country for a visit but they don't really like it. Her mother's face, especially, becomes this oval of disappointment: with the town, the house, Johnny.

"What about Christmas?" her mother asks. "We're trying to make plans."

"Johnny and I were talking about Mexico," Charlene says.

"Really? That doesn't sound like him."

Charlene ignores this. "We thought two weeks right over Christmas. There's this cheap package I saw."

"Well, you decide and let us know. Is Johnny still doing that youth thing?"

"You mean the centre?"

"I suppose."

"Yes, Friday and Saturday nights."

"What does he do all that time, just hang out?"

"He talks to the kids, gives them a place to be. He's good with teen-agers."

"I should hope so, he's lousy with adults."

Charlene draws a slow breath and makes little rabbit movements with her nose. She hates to argue with her mother. It's tasteless, boring, and always slides in the same direction. Still, she says, "I don't know why you pick on Johnny. You hardly see him, you don't know where he's going, where his mind's at."

"I look at you, dear. I'm still waiting for you to blossom. I'm sorry, but he grinds you down, I can see it."

Charlene doesn't respond. Finally, her mother says, "Are you okay?"

"Yes, sure, why not?"

"Well, last time we talked you and Johnny were going to see a counsellor."

"It's better," Charlene says. "We've decided we don't need to spend money on a counsellor. Johnny's at home, we're talking, he's making meals. We're happy."

It is only later, after hanging up, that Charlene thinks about happiness. She lied; Johnny's happy, she's not. She knows she will never experience the pure joy Johnny drains out of life. There is not enough of that joy to go around.

She dreams. She is lost, standing beside a deserted road, and a young girl with blonde hair picks her up, stops beside the road and beckons her into the car which smells of orchids. When she gets into the car, the girl at the wheel is dead. She dreams about Loraine Wallace. Loraine is naked and at full term. She is having the baby and Charlene can see the head crowning. Then Johnny is there and he's trying to push the baby back in.

At first Charlene doesn't tell anyone about these dreams, even though they scare her. Then, in late November, on a Saturday, she decides to go to the book club. It's the night of the vote, the decision regarding Avi's friend. Deb says that before she votes she'd like to see a picture of the guy. Everyone laughs and Mona says she had a dream about him. He was splitting atoms, the way someone would split firewood. "Little explosions were coming off the axe," she says.

Then Charlene jumps in and talks about her dreams, the one about being lost and the one about Loraine. When she's finished, nobody speaks. It's as if she's stepped over that fine line of decorum — she's embarrassed the group.

Avi, the new woman, says, "It's normal. Completely. Dreams allow us to be violent, to murder, to pull heads off, to lust, fornicate. I would say your wish in that one dream, Charlene, is to disappear Loraine's baby. And not only that, but to have Johnny do it for you."

"It's not that I hate Loraine," Charlene says. She twists her fingers until the knuckles turn white. "I don't even know her. I guess I'm jealous."

"Well, of course, you're jealous," Avi roars.

"Oh, not only because Johnny slept with her, sleeps with her, see, I'm not even sure about that, though I do know he's been faithful for at least one month. But, you know, it's the fact that she's going to have his baby. That was supposed to be my job."

"You want to kill the baby," Avi says.

Charlene nods. "I guess so," she says, and these three words chill the group for a moment, especially Nancy and Mona, the ones with children, and then Helen titters. She's sort of friends with Loraine, but still she titters.

"I had a dream too," Helen says. "I was eating cream cheese cake. Eating and eating and I couldn't stop so I just kept expanding. Oh, right, and I was eating in bed and I rolled over at one point and smothered Jimmy. He died." Helen laughs and slips an olive onto a cracker.

Charlene loves Helen, who is a big woman and makes no apologies for it; when she laughs her body rolls and her eyes squeeze and shut and then open again.

Finally Mona says that they have to decide about Avi's friend Michael. "Personally, I think it would destroy the intimacy of the group. It's not like we just talk books. Look at us, we delve into personal matters, and with this man around we'd lose that closeness."

"I agree," Nancy says. "I've always seen this as a kind of coven, a place where magic is possible. A woman's magic."

"Hey," Avi says, "I don't want to push it. Michael's new in town and I thought it would be a good entry point. But that's okay."

"Why doesn't he try Phil Barkman's group? Is he religious?" Helen asks.

The women laugh.

"In a way, I suppose," Avi says.

"Really?" says Mona. "I thought he was a physicist."

"Well," says Helen, making little impatient shooing movements with her hands, "it seems we've got nays all around. I guess it makes sense. I personally couldn't imagine talking about this poet with Jimmy in the group." Helen plucks at an elbow and says, dangling the book by two fingers, "What is this?"

"You're mocking me," Avi says. She is hurt.

"No, no, love. Jimmy would mock you."

And so they go around in a circle and talk about the poems. Mona likes the one called "The Pope's Penis." "I love it," she chortles, "and I'm not even Catholic."

"That's exactly why you love it," Avi says.

Deb says she doesn't like any of them. They're crude and not really poems anyway.

"Why not?" Charlene asks.

"Because they're like stories, and not very good ones, and there's no rhythm or rhyme. I'd like to do an Amy Tan novel."

Nancy says she had a lot of favourites. "It's all so explicit," she says. "I mean, 'A Woman in Heat Wiping Herself.' Yuck! Still, I read it twice. My favourite though was 'It.' The description of the sex, of being folded over like paper, of being stunned. It was all so honest and strangely familiar."

"Yes, I liked that too, that one." This is Charlene talking. Her face is flushed and she's opening her book to that poem. "Except I didn't get the last part where she talks about the river and these boatloads of children. Why talk about dead children in the middle of a poem about sex?"

"The river means death," Avi says. "Kind of like the river Styx."

"But these children never died, did they?"

"It seems not, but I think we always expect them to die or we don't expect children at all."

"Hey, well, that's me," Charlene says. She's smiling but she's got a pain in her side.

Helen says, "I remember a river we crossed when I was young. In Saskatchewan, on a ferry."

There is a pause and then Charlene says, "My favourite was 'Looking at my Father.' May I read part of it?"

Heads nod. Deb looks sleepy.

"Go ahead," Avi says.

Charlene folds open the book. "This is the last of it," she says.

> *I know he is not perfect but my*
> *body thinks his body is perfect, the*
> *fine stretched coarse pink*
> *skin, the big size of him, the*
> *sour-ball mass, darkness, hair,*
> *sex, legs even longer than mine,*
> *lovely feet. What I know I know, what my*
> *body knows it knows, it likes to*
> *slip the leash of my mind and go and*
> *look at him, like an animal*
> *looking at water, then going to it and*
> *drinking until it has had its fill and can*
> *lie down and sleep.*

When Charlene's finished she says, "I think I know why I like it. I like it because it reminds me of Johnny."

That night Charlene lies in bed waiting for Johnny to come home. Around midnight she hears the car door slam, then the sound of footsteps up the porch stairs and Johnny's in the kitchen, pouring himself Cornflakes, and then the rhythmic click of the spoon on the glass bowl. Charlene watches the ceiling above her and predicts Johnny's moves. Rinse the bowl, blow his nose, run a glass of water, up the stairs, brush his teeth, pee, drop his pants across the laundry hamper, socks in a ball, sigh.

Through all this Charlene is aware, at a deeper level, of having in some way betrayed Johnny. By baring herself earlier that evening, by holding Johnny up as a picture of parts, old and used, she feels she has dismissed him as a joke. The other women seemed to have missed the longing, the adoration, in the words that she read. What they saw was a sickness, and this is not what she intended. Because, above all, she loves Johnny.

His shape approaches, and now beside her he reaches out and touches her hip, waist, elbow. He warms his feet on her calves.

"Yaiee," she says, pulling away.

"You're not sleeping?"

"Not yet. How was it tonight?"

"Good," he says. "Great turnout."

Charlene rolls and throws a leg over Johnny's hip.

"You're naked," he says.

"Hmmm." Charlene puts her nose on Johnny's neck and breathes in smoke and outside air and sweat and the perfume of the centre where Johnny likes to burn incense. His hands are cold on her head and face. They kiss and Charlene tastes Cornflakes and Crest. "Can we?" she says and pushes herself up so she's sitting on top of Johnny. She lifts herself slightly and pulls down his shorts. He is not yet hard so she takes him in her hands and coaxes him. When he is ready she slides him inside her and puts her hands on his shoulders. Johnny is quick, and after, when they are lying beside each other, only hands touching, he asks, "Aren't you going to go to the bathroom?"

Charlene squeezes his hand and says, "No." Later, when Johnny is sleeping, Charlene tightens her bum and holds her breath, as if by some physical exertion she could wish the movement up inside her. She has an image in her head of frantic babies in white suits trying to break through a rubbery wall and finally one succeeds and then the wall closes again.

Four more times that week Charlene initiates sex. Each time Johnny is surprised, and perhaps it is this surprise that produces a tenderness in him. He is careful with Charlene, lets her have her way. He asks, "Is this okay?" "Does that hurt?" He licks her ears and kisses her eyes. He must know, but if he does, he does not let on. He slides up from beneath her like a child, face glowing, contented, fists full of candy.

On Thursday, they lie in the darkness of their room and Charlene, the wetness dribbling between her legs, asks about Loraine.

"Have you seen her?" she says.

"Not for a while." It seems Johnny is both embarrassed and proud.

"How many months is she now?" Charlene asks.

"I dunno. Four?" Johnny is tired. He falls asleep quickly, his bare shoulders breaching the blanket. Outside the moon is full, the night cold. The room seems brightly washed, as if daylight were catching Johnny and Charlene still in bed.

Charlene senses tonight that her plan has failed. She has miscalculated. Her stomach is slightly bloated as if preparing for evacuation. She folds her hands and closes her eyes and when she finally sleeps she dreams. And in the dream Johnny and Loraine are practicing their breathing. Loraine is on her back and Johnny kneels beside her, chanting in her ear. Loraine is beautifully huge. Then Johnny stoops to Loraine's crotch and when he reappears he holds the tiny head of a baby between his teeth.

Charlene wakes up and pushes herself into a sitting position. She is breathing hard. She moans, shoves at Johnny and says, "I had a nightmare."

Johnny grunts and turns away.

"It was awful," Charlene says. "Frightening."

Johnny's sleeping again and Charlene's still afraid. She goes to the bathroom and sits for a long time. When she wipes herself she feels sticky. She checks the toilet paper and finds traces of blood mixed with semen. Failure tugs at her somewhere; she is not sure, perhaps at her stomach, between her shoulders, and down her spine. In the hard light of the bathroom she lays a liner across her panties, washes herself, and slides in a tampon. In the next room, Johnny sleeps and sleeps.

And then on Friday afternoon, around five, Loraine Wallace drops by. Charlene is making herself a small meal, Johnny is at the centre, and she hears a knock but thinks it is an icicle dropping off the eaves or the wind blowing. But the sound comes again and when Charlene opens the door there is Loraine, her face hooded by her parka, her feet moving on the squeaky snow of the step.

"Hi, Charlene," she says.

Charlene doesn't respond, just stands there and lets the wind whip at her hair and she thinks how cold her neck feels.

"May I come in?"

Charlene nods and Loraine enters and then the coat is off and Charlene's offering supper, but Loraine says no, she's eaten. So Charlene serves tea and stands with her bum against the kitchen counter and watches Loraine handle the sugar and milk.

They are not friends. They rarely talk. Charlene lights a cigarette and moves her hand to her throat. Her teeth ache.

Loraine says, "This is really abrupt and maybe uncalled for, but . . ."

"You're going to have a baby," Charlene says. It's amazing, Loraine is showing. As she sat, Charlene saw the curve of her belly beneath her blouse. Loraine is small, compact, her stomach a slightly inflated balloon. Charlene finds that the roof of her mouth is gritty, she's short of breath.

"Yes," Loraine says. "I guess that's why I came. Sort of." Physically Loraine appears so healthy; face rounding out, cheeks pink. Her whole body screaming *Yes*.

"To taunt me," Charlene says. She can't help it. She is both angry and brimming with admiration. She wants to fall on her knees before this woman.

"No. No." Loraine stands quickly, hands fumbling for her coat. "I'm sorry, I'll go."

"Don't." Charlene stands, pulls at Loraine's arm. Her fingers clutch and pinch. She lets go; Loraine's skin is cool and smooth. Johnny must love that, he has an eye for details.

Loraine sits down again and says, "I was hoping we could talk. Last night I was sitting by myself thinking about this baby and I wondered if you were sitting by yourself too."

"Johnny and I are doing really well these days."

"Oh, well. I assumed so. I haven't seen him," Loraine says. "Where is he tonight?"

"At the centre." Charlene knows that Loraine knows this, otherwise she wouldn't have come. She watches Loraine's lips approach the teacup. Charlene says, "I was thinking, when the baby's born, we should cut it in half. Part for you, part for me. You've read that story, haven't you?"

"Johnny never told me you had a sense of humour. You want to touch?"

Charlene surprises herself. She swallows and, "Yes," she whispers. Loraine comes around the table and lifts up her blouse. Charlene puts both hands on Loraine's stomach, one above the belly button, one below.

"You can't feel anything right now. When I lie down and keep still, it moves. At first it was like a gas bubble, but now it's like a small animal in a gunny sack."

Charlene thinks she should pull her hands away. Suddenly she is self-conscious, touching the same body Johnny touches. If she slid her hands a little lower, she could scrape the edges of Loraine's pubic hair. His hands here and here. Here. Little Johnny inside there.

Charlene looks up. Loraine is looking down at her. She takes one of Charlene's hands and holds it. "Sometimes," Loraine says, "I imagine taking revenge. As you must do? Do you?"

Charlene nods. She feels inadequate. Inferior. It's not just the baby. It's Loraine's confidence; coming over here, showing off her stomach. Charlene thinks Loraine's laughing at her. Even now, she's talking, saying she doesn't want to hurt anyone, especially not her son Chris, Charlene neither, and Charlene thinks how Johnny must gloat, shuttling back and forth between his lover and wife. This is all about greed, but it's not Johnny's greed, it's the women's. Charlene knows how when she lays her weight down on Johnny she could crush him, her need is so great.

She says now, "Forget the baby. Let's cut up Johnny. I'll take the head, you can have the body. I like to pull at his eyebrows with my teeth, roll my tongue on his eyes. His mouth is best, I like to sit on that sneer."

Loraine is giggling, holding herself as if she may pee. "Oh, that's bad." Then, she says, "He's got body odour, you ever notice?"

"Of course," Charlene says. She feels as if she's been drinking. She's talking like a fool.

Still, Loraine's playing along, her belly protruding, her hands splayed near her crotch now, mouth smiling. Charlene feels sudden revulsion for everything as Loraine says, "And always worried about his size. He says it's because of his father, a death-sex thing."

"He said that?" Charlene is hurt. Her eyes burn.

Loraine understands her slip, and says, "He's not smart."

"No, he's not," Charlene agrees. "Phil Barkman's smaller, that's what Johnny said."

"Really?"

"Yeah, he saw him at the baptism. Funny, coming home from your baptism and talking about the size of the preacher's prick."

"Huh."

"I got my period last night," Charlene says. Loraine takes this in, her mouth moving; the house is talking as the wind blows. Charlene watches Loraine's mouth and thinks how things go round in circles. Johnny on Loraine's mouth, then on Charlene's, back to Loraine's, mouths on bodies, the transmission of germs and saliva and body fluids. Charlene's never really thought about it till now but she assumes Loraine is healthy. It's Johnny they have to worry about. "I don't know why I said that," Charlene says.

"It's okay," Loraine says. She lifts her small shoulders as if shifting an uncomfortable load. She pulls her coat up over her back. It is chilly in the house; there is nothing left to say.

Charlene offers more tea but Loraine declines. Their parting is pleasant, they even hug carefully, as if they were hesitant lovers. Charlene tells Loraine to come again and Loraine says she will. After Loraine is outside, Charlene stands and watches for her car but it's blowing snow so she sees only a flash of a red light and then nothing. It feels like a blizzard. She stays by the kitchen sink for a long time, facing the window, looking past the lace curtains she sewed; looking out into the darkness.

At one point she realizes she is crying but doesn't know why, she is not sad, not angry. The clock shows 8:00 p.m., still early. In the fridge she discovers some wine, and drinks that; holds a glass by the stem and takes large gulps. The chill of the wine hurts her teeth. Her throat aches. Later, she scours the house for more liquor but the bottles are all empty. She sits at the table and smokes, then remembers the little bottle of cognac, Hennessy, that she took from the hotel room in Kenora. She drinks that quickly, not bothering to pour it into her glass. She sits for what seems a long time and enjoys the warmth inside her, wishing for more.

She remembers Johnny pointing out a place in Île des Chênes that sells liquor. An old man and his daughter who make a living at this. She pulls on her coat, goes outside and starts the half-ton. The snow is hard and thick and swirls around the truck. At the gravel road Charlene turns right towards the 312. She shouldn't be out in this mess. She wonders if Johnny will make it home tonight. The store is closing as Charlene pulls up at the centre of Île des Chênes. She scrambles up the step and bangs at the door. An old man in a camouflage jacket lets her in. Charlene knocks snow from her jacket and says, "Thank you." She asks for two bottles.

"That's fine," the old man says. "That's fine." He wants to talk but Charlene ignores him. She pays and wades her way back to the truck. She drives slowly, hugging the shoulder. At one point, a semi blows by and Charlene moans, lost for a moment. Back on the 312 she feels safer, and actually takes a second to wonder why she is so desperate, as if there were a cliff edge somewhere up ahead and she were running pell-mell for it.

She can't see anything on the gravel road. The world beyond the windshield is a dark blanket. The headlights are useless, they pick up driving snow. The half-ton crawls. A few times Charlene stops, gets out and walks out onto the road to feel with her feet where the ditch begins. She's wearing little cotton gloves and her hands are numb. Finally, like a lighthouse warning boats from rocks, she spies the timid and cloudy yard-light of her farm. At least, she thinks it's her yard.

The truck slides into the ditch as Charlene attempts to find the driveway. As if it had been invited, it settles carefully into the snow at a slight angle. The engine sputters and dies. Charlene gathers her bottles and purse and strikes out for the house. People die doing this, she thinks; they just crawl up to the door and die. She finds the house and shoulders her way into the front room. Though the wind still howls at the windows and knocks at the roof, the silence of the house is shocking.

It's cold. Charlene brushes off her clothes, turns up the heat and stokes the wood stove. When her hands have warmed, she takes a glass and pours herself a drink. She swallows, her throat burns, her stomach jumps, and she wonders what inspired her to risk a trip like that. Then she remembers Loraine standing in the kitchen. Like a young girl she was really, flagrantly peeling up her blouse, or did Charlene do that? But, still, Charlene's not angry, just disappointed, and that's why she's bowing before this golden liquid.

Charlene thinks about her own life. She refuses to be beaten down. Even now, with this turmoil in her life, she's risen above the people of Lesser. Still, they see her as a joke; she's the fool. Everyone looks at her when they do their banking. The men smirk as if she's easy now, a fine target. They think that if Johnny's doing it, she should want to even things out. Just last week Mr. Hamm asked her if she believed in equal rights. Charlene smiled and pretended not to hear. "Will that be all, Mr. Hamm?" she asked. He looked at her breasts then and Charlene reddened, her neck hot. She didn't mind Mr. Hamm, she talked to him sometimes, but he had no right to stare at her breasts.

Charlene hates her breasts. Thinks they're too large. She lifts a hand now and cups one through her sweater. Too heavy and full. By fifty she'll be sagging to her navel like her mother. She finishes her glass and pours some more; a little spills onto her lap. Half the bottle's gone. It's eleven o'clock.

That's the thing about Loraine. She's so small. All over. But her breasts especially. Perky little things. Nipples not too big. Johnny must love them in his mouth. Nausea hits her. Charlene folds herself at her stomach. She swallows. The phone rings, a sharp clanging that circles around the room and lands on Charlene's head. She tries to remember where the phone is. She stands, wobbles, and laughs. The kitchen. The damn thing is so loud. She's wanted to get a pulse phone, but Johnny likes the noise; his hearing's going on him.

"Twelve, thirteen, fourteen." Charlene isn't sure if she's counting her steps or the number of rings. My, that bottle had some strong stuff. She'll have to be careful. She winces, draws a breath and lifts the receiver.

"Charlene, it's Johnny."

"Hi, Johnny." She's concentrating, inching out her words, working at the syllables.

"Where were you? I've been trying to phone. You had me worried." He doesn't wait for an answer, just ploughs ahead. "I'm staying at the centre tonight. We're locked in because of the blizzard. A few kids are here too. We're going to wait it out."

Charlene pulls back from the phone and looks around the room.

"Charlene?"

The phone goes back. "Yeah?"

"You all right?"

"Fine, just fine." She has this sense of always talking on the phone with Johnny and him asking if she's okay. "Are *you* okay?" she says.

"Yes. You drinking, Charlene?"

"No. Loraine came by tonight."

"She did? Why?"

"Oh, didn't you know? We're friends." Charlene waits, listening to Johnny breathe. "I don't know," she says finally. "I don't know." Then quickly, she adds, "Johnny, do you like my breasts?"

"Of course."

"I wish you were here, Johnny, you could do me right now."

"Charlene, you are drunk."

"So?"

"Listen, Charlene," and here Johnny lowers his voice, "I'd love to be with you right now, I really would, but you have to put the bottle away. Okay?"

"Sure."

"And don't go outside. Turn up the heat. Crawl into bed and I'll be there in the morning."

"I got my period, Johnny. Last night."

Johnny's lost. Charlene can almost hear his mind grappling with this comment. "Is it bad?" he asks. "Different?"

"No, the same." Charlene pours herself another drink. She hopes Johnny can hear the splash though she knows he won't. She's being spiteful. She says, "You see, I wanted to have a baby."

"You did?" Johnny says.

Charlene laughs. He's so stupid. "Yeah, except my timing was off. I should have aimed for the week before."

"Listen, Charlene, I've got to phone other people. Parents. But, we'll talk about this. We can have a baby."

"Really, Johnny?"

Charlene pulls away and pours another glass, but when she tilts her head back to the phone and listens for Johnny it's too late, he's gone. She makes it back to her chair, opens the stove door and leaves it ajar. She moves in closer to the heat, throws in two more logs, lights a cigarette and closes her eyes. Perhaps she should have asked Loraine to stay the night. They could have slept together in the big bed upstairs. Would be lovely to have that swollen body close to hers. Loraine's not a bad woman. Good to see and touch her. Nice to touch people. Very. Loraine must feel the same because she didn't seem to mind being stroked. Johnny's a lucky man.

Charlene wonders what it must be like to be a man and make love to a woman. She cuddles her drink and thinks about Loraine's body, about her knotty shoulders, the fine-balled tightness of her stomach. Full of baby. Charlene remembers playing with this neighbour boy, Ronald, when she was young. Charlene was the man, Ronald was the woman, and he put a pillow under his T-shirt for a baby and Charlene would put her hands up inside and pull the pillow out and spank it and hand it back and say, "It's a boy." One time she undressed Ronald and he undressed her and he tried to stick himself inside her but he was too young for an erection. Charlene liked the secrecy; whispering with Ronald behind the garage in the damp coolness of the fort they had built. A dirt floor, a rickety shelf holding seashells and a chipped ceramic tea set. A reed mat laid out. Ronald on his knees, Charlene on her back. Ronald's chest pale in the light. His eyes dim. And later Charlene telling him that she was going to have many children. "I want to be a mother," she said.

It's cold. Too cold. She stands, catching herself on the arm of the chair. She couldn't find her slippers. The place is a mess. She's been meaning to clean it up, not vacuum or anything, just tidy, but time is short and she keeps finding other and better things to do. Loraine must have thought Charlene was a slob: dishes everywhere in the kitchen, Johnny's boots and shoes scattered, a fried egg abandoned on the stove. Loraine is neat and tidy. Her house must be like that too. Her farm, her barn. And sex. Is that tidy too? Johnny likes it messy, Charlene knows that. She can't imagine Loraine going down on Johnny. That pretty mouth, the lipstick just so, those hands that Johnny loves, so perfect; do those hands go everywhere? But then, the most unlikely people are wild in bed. Like Nancy Stone from the book club. She used to drop hints about her sex life. Made a reference to anal sex once and everybody was grossed out. Charlene wonders about Johnny. He'd like that. If Charlene did it for him, maybe he'd stay.

She's surprised to find herself on her knees. She's facing the shelf which holds knick-knacks and family photos and the few books she and Johnny own. There's Johnny's Bible. It's got a leather front with gold lettering. She pulls at it. Opens it. *This Bible belongs to Johnny Fehr,* she reads. "Belongs?" Charlene says. She shakes her head. Fans the hundreds of pages. When she was a teenager she tried to read the Bible all the way through. She got stuck in Leviticus. Ridiculous. Whoever thought all those men's names were important? She leaped to the Gospels then. She remembers reading and waiting for a light or a voice, something that would let her know who she was, or who she should be. Her mother had been so proud of her. "My daughter Charlene is reading the Bible from beginning to end," she would tell her friends.

Charlene puts her nose inside the pages and smells. She breathes again. There are some things she likes in here. What Jesus says is good. Especially those words about faith and hope and love. Did Jesus say that? Charlene thinks those are probably the most important words in the Bible. She once told Johnny this and he nodded seriously and agreed. There's more though. Stuff about a *noisy gong* and *tongues ceasing*. She should tell Johnny this too. No sense chasing after *tongues*. All that fades in the end. Everything fades. Even Loraine will eventually fade. When Johnny tires of her and the baby. The baby will interfere with their time and Johnny will be impatient and then he'll come back to Charlene and Charlene won't say, "I told you so," she'll just take him back and think how predictable he is, like the little boy she never had. She wonders if Loraine and Johnny talk about her, or if Johnny compares the sex and tells Loraine about it. Do they talk about God? About Johnny leaving Charlene? Charlene wants to ask Johnny these questions. She could phone now. No, Johnny said he was busy. Leave him be. Tomorrow.

Charlene reaches out and touches the stove. Burns herself. She sucks on her fingers. Takes the bottle of whisky and drinks. She has a thought. She giggles and takes Johnny's Bible and carefully rips Leviticus from its centre. She throws it into the stove. Johnny won't notice. Like Phil Barkman and Melissa Emery and the Bartel brothers and all the others, Johnny gets by on a New Testament diet. That's what's important. Except for the Creation story; Johnny likes that one. God snapping his fingers. Magic.

The stove needs wood. Birch. Birch burns the best. "Cadillac of firewood," Johnny calls it. Charlene fumbles with the wood, it tears at her hands. Stoke. Stoke. One log bangs the edge of the door, flames slide across it and the log drops to the floor. Oh my. Birch bark burns so quickly. So sweetly. Crackles, like bacon frying. Can write letters on it too. Letters to Johnny. Love letters. She remembers writing Johnny little notes, just after they were married, and leaving them lying around for him. In his boots, his jeans' pocket. Once she wrote something lusty on the toilet-paper roll. Johnny liked that. He called her from where he was sitting and then he stood and held her, his pants at his knees, and laughed and said, "You're a horny, silly girl."

"Am I?" she asked, looking up at his chin, her hands fisted at the small of his back.

Charlene, on her knees, reaches out and pushes at the sparking log. It skitters across Johnny's mother's rug and halts at the edge of the couch; can't quite reach it. The flames die, she thinks. This braided rug. Charlene recalls being here with Johnny, seems so long ago. He laid her out, ass against the braids, fingers kneading her breasts, and she cried out some foolishness. Johnny with his leaping tongue. Stubby Johnny. Light in his eyes, darkness at the edges, like if you didn't stay close enough to the heat, you'd get lost.

Where's the bottle? On hands and knees she moves across the floor. Bottle's tipped over, little bit of rye that's left soaking the rug. Beautiful colours. "The rug is on fire," she says. "Too bad." She stands and stomps with her stockinged feet. She laughs. "Fuck," she says, "this is not good." She stands there, looking for a blanket, a jacket. "Should smother it," she says. She can't see anything. The phone. She must find the phone but she can't remember where it is. She wonders if her mother will call. She usually does on a Friday night. Though it's late, isn't it? Her mother will be sleeping. That's better, anyway. Hate to have to fake being sober.

"A bucket," she says. "There's a hole . . ." And then she's on her stomach and the walls are brightening and there's a grey creature creeping across the rug. On hands and knees she moves towards the kitchen, manages to stand and grab the phone. She dials the centre but it's busy. She tries her mother's number. A man answers. Up from the depths of sleep. Wrong number. She tries again, directory assistance. She tells the woman, "My house is burning," and then she hangs up.

Outside. She should go there. Out there. But her coat's missing and she'd freeze and a clarity comes to her through the haze of smoke and alcohol and she sees two choices and they are freezing or burning and though the machine shed is a haven across the yard she'd never make it in her condition.

She wets a rag and holds it across her mouth. She's not too drunk to reason, she thinks. Johnny would be proud of her. "Get down," she tells herself. She does this. Lies on the kitchen floor, curled up against the far cabinets. She faces the beige wall. Finds herself staring at the grease and dirt that has collected over the years. A bit of a crayon drawing. Old. Probably Johnny's creation from way back. A brief sentence too. Charlene's face is wet. She is crying. Everything's come loose now. This is a dream, she thinks. That's good. Yes. A dream. She licks her tears and realizes they taste real. She cries harder. Johnny as a young boy. Right here. Touching the purple letters with her fingers. She's never seen this before. Wishes she'd known about it. Like finding his childhood gum under the old table; she takes it as a message or something. He must have been learning to print. Excited by it. Wanting to try it out everywhere. Johnny gets so excited about things. It's easier to breathe now. Maybe the fire's dying out. Nothing to feed it. She wishes she had Johnny's enthusiasm. A while back he tried to get her to pray with him. "Fine," she said, and she even kneeled beside him but the hollowness made her giggle, like they were playing a game and Johnny wasn't even aware how silly he sounded. Perhaps she should pray now. Beg forgiveness. She calls out, alternately, "God, Mother, God, Mother," but there is no answer, only a growing heat at her back. She wishes she weren't so drunk. Then she could save herself. She decides suddenly that she should confront the danger. Easier that way. She turns onto her other side, her back to the wall now, and lies there, knees up at her chest, rag at her mouth, sobbing, "Oh Jesus, save me." And then, in the background, faintly beyond the roar, she can hear the telephone ring, and she believes, heart fluttering with relief, that she has been saved.

THEORY OF EVERYTHING

For a month after Charlene's death, Johnny is stupid with grief. His doctor prescribes something strong but he doesn't use it, he needs to suffer. So, his nights are spent keening, his days driving the country roads from customer to customer, stopping in small, unlikely towns, where he sits in the coffee shops and dully watches the pattering of the locals. He makes his rounds: Île des Chênes, St. Agathe, Landmark, St. Malo, Grunthal. He finds that he likes to watch the waitresses. They bring to their work a lilt that somehow lifts Johnny from the hell he is living.

He begins to find his regulars; like Holly, in Morris, a single mother of three, who is vicious with her gum and sits with Johnny at her breaks and sometimes touches his hands. He tells Holly about Charlene and Loraine and the baby. He does not want to sleep with Holly, though he finds her toughness attractive. It is his grief that has made him sexually immobile. He, of course, blames himself for Charlene's death and he is also aware of those in and around Lesser who whisper that he or Loraine were involved in that awful fire.

He dreams of fire. It burns at the edges of his sleep and even awake he imagines Charlene's clothes catching fire, her body a log that roasts slowly from the outside in, though he knows, having spoken with the fire inspector, that a house-fire is not hot enough to destroy a body. Charlene's body was found, charred and unrecognizable, yes, but the shape was there; that is how the inspector put it. Johnny had pushed, wanting to know, and after some hesitation, the man, pink eyelids squeezed over pale eyes, said that a person who dies in a fire, their body remains intact; bones, inner organs, and such. Johnny winced. Swallowed. He recalled Charlene's tic above her left eye, and again, with compassion this time, the movement of her throat as they made love. These days, at night, he goes to sleep in fear, knowing he will discover Charlene's eyes following him, narrowing, opening, narrowing again.

It is stunning to remember her, especially the smell of her hair after a day at the bank, the scent of money-dust, similar to twine and bales. He liked Charlene's smell. Every woman gives off a particular scent and Johnny knows which ones he likes. He shies from the hint of tin, is attracted to women who radiate a faint moisture, that of water sprinkled onto dust. And that is all he has left of Charlene. Perhaps that is where the pain comes from. Her death might not be so final if he had something left of her: pictures, shoes, make-up. Something to touch, to smell and remember, something to sort through and pack up, put away: Charlene in boxes, ready for the thrift shop. Johnny feels the absence of something to heave out the window. His grief, of course, is mostly for himself, for what he is now missing. He recalls wanting her dead sometimes, a sort of adolescent wish for a new life. But now, Johnny rues those old dreams. He finds solace nowhere.

And then, two days before Christmas, he visits Loraine. Loraine was not at the funeral, in fact, Johnny, who hasn't worked much in the past month, has not seen her for six weeks. When he arrives on a Sunday morning, she is in her housecoat and slippers. She is bigger now, when she walks she seems to lean backwards. Johnny is amazed at her fleshiness. They hold each other just inside the door. They do not speak, just fold into each other's bodies, and Johnny thinks that he needn't ever say another word again; nor move, nor eat, nor drink.

Loraine's size reminds him, eerily, of Charlene, especially her width. Loraine still has the light touch he remembers, her fingers press his back, skitter across the hairiness of his forearms. She is crying. Her body shakes. Johnny will not cry. He cried one night in his sister's basement, early in the evening when he heard Carol and Roy talking upstairs. Actually, they were arguing intensely in whispers and this made Johnny cry.

He pats Loraine's back and stares past her head out the window towards the road and the snow-covered fields and he sees that life out here is desolate, empty. God, floating above this land, must laugh at a house like this, flanked by two barns; three grey spots stubbed into the snow. The world could go on and on and then suddenly end.

There is nothing else, just Johnny and Loraine, and the mixing spoons sticking out of the jar, and the worn covers on the kitchen chairs, speckled green, and Chris moving upstairs, his footsteps heavy and restless, and the tap dripping and Loraine's belly, the wet spot on his shirt, and the lust seeping to his crotch and the discomfort there. Nothing else. No one else.

Just this.

The Christmas tree is up. Loraine holds Johnny's hand and guides him to the living room. She leaves him and circles the tree, her hand reaching out to brush baubles, angels. "It's a blue spruce," she says. "This new guy in town, Michael Barry, brought it by. He was with Avi Heath. She was friends with Charlene. They brought it last Saturday. I didn't know what to say. I felt they were taunting me but they weren't."

Loraine pronounces the silent *e* in that last word, *were-ent*; it's like that man who used to work at the Solo store in Lesser and counted out the change: *sixtee-en*, *seventee-en*. Johnny finds it endearing, as if Loraine were blending into this town.

He watches her slide around the tree. He wants to pull her close and yank the belt on her housecoat, see what's underneath. Her arms are lifting and dropping, her fingers doodle the air. Weakness and passion enfold him. He gapes.

"Actually," Loraine continues, still dealing with Michael and Avi, "it was nice to see someone. I'm lost out here. I get nothing except the little tidbits from Chris and he offers so little. He's ugly again these days." She stops and picks at some tangled tinsel. Her hair is pulled back and dirty. She's still full of sleep. "You all right?" she asks.

Johnny pauses, fumbles for a cigarette, then thinks better of it. "It's like I'm guilty. I can feel it. Everybody thinks I wanted Charlene dead. But, I didn't."

"I know you didn't," Loraine says. She appears distracted, stooping to pluck a few dry needles from the rug, standing again and running her hands over her housecoat. "Do you want coffee?" she asks.

"Sure."

They sit and find they have little to say. The movements of Chris reach them from upstairs and both of them take comfort in this.

"How is he?" Johnny asks.

"You see him, don't you? He says he works at the centre."

"Yeah, but how are you two doing?"

"We talk about the baby sometimes and then he gets a little excited. Mostly he's raging."

"You gonna have anybody with you, like at the birth?"

"My sister, maybe. But, she's out on the other side of Winnipeg and it'd be tough to get to the Victoria on time. I labour fast. Chris was three hours."

"How 'bout me?" Johnny says this and his tongue touches his lower lip.

"You're serious." Loraine may laugh. "You'd never do it."

"Would so."

"You don't know anything about labour, birth, breathing."

"I could learn."

"But what would people think? Isn't that why you haven't been around? Appearances? Johnny, the rebel, gone careful. Funny. People'd think for sure then we killed Charlene. Torched her house so we could be together."

Johnny is drawing a line across the table with a wet teaspoon. Loraine is lovely like this. She is the little round chestnut he used to hold in his hand as a boy. The kind of nut that squirted from between the jaws of the cracker. Split it though and it was great to taste. Meaty, a little dry. He wants to crack her now.

"Maybe you did," he says. "Burn the house down."

Loraine stares. Her knuckles are white.

"You were there that night," Johnny whispers.

"Aw, screw you, Johnny. Right. I took gasoline, dumped it all over the house, and lit it. Poof. Wonderful to see Charlene burn."

Johnny's grinning. He can see that Loraine wants to hit him. The tendons in her forearms are jumping.

"You didn't deserve her," she says finally. "You don't deserve me." Her voice slows and then her anger drops away. "You talked to her? That night? Jesus, Johnny, I'm sorry."

Chris comes into the kitchen then, says hi to Johnny, and pokes his head in the fridge. From the back, Johnny thinks he could pass for Loraine before she was pregnant. His shoulders angle like his mother's, his neck, when exposed, appears frail and ropy. The boy grunts something at no one and walks out of the room, cheese and bread in hand. Loraine is looking at her nails, nibbling a little finger. She's calmer now, understanding Johnny's need for provocation. Johnny, though, figures that he and Loraine are sinners, they have skidded into the slough together, and if what he says now is bad, the fact is Charlene in some way needs to be redeemed.

"Well, of course, you didn't *do it*, Loraine," he says. "It just probably crossed your mind. I mean, her death is such an easy way out. And then you being there, and me calling and hearing her drunk, fully drunk, all of it adds up to a good-sized push."

"Oh, stop it, Johnny, stop trying to sound so intelligent."

"The police came to see me," Johnny says. "A Constable Boucler.

You've met him. Him and this woman. Rose. That was it, Constable Rose. They sat in my office and talked."

Loraine is alert now, her eyes wider. "Why?" she asks.

"A formality. Wanted to know where I was that night. Did Charlene drink. Was she depressed. Suicidal. I told them that only my father was suicidal. They didn't find that humorous."

"You answered them?"

"Why not? Charlene was dead. You see, everything I do these days is for her. I figure if it'll help lift her up, then fine. They never asked about you. Don't even know you were there."

"So what. Go ahead, tell them."

Johnny thinks that Charlene's death was a devious last attempt to separate him and Loraine. It could work. They could lean into each other and slap away until there was nothing left. Johnny doesn't want that. He says, "What's going to happen to us? We gonna fight? Make love?"

Loraine's eyes are red from too much sleep. She rubs them and says, "You think this is funny."

"I don't think it's funny. I'm hurting. Everything's crazy. Sometimes I'm driving down the highway, and it wouldn't matter if I rolled the car or not."

"Well, I'm not going to lay you back down in my bed just like that," Loraine says. "Throw you a feast. Life's too easy for you."

Johnny lights a cigarette now. Loraine slides him an ashtray. He catches her fingers before she can pull away, holds on tight. "I was thinking about the baby, about how it's mine too."

"Oh?"

"Yes." Johnny sucks on his cigarette and pinches it between thumb and forefinger. He isn't sure what he's getting at, if he wants to scare Loraine or warn her, or just say he needs her. "You read about all these fights to abort babies, or give 'em up for adoption. One wants to, one doesn't."

"I'm doing neither," Loraine says.

"Yes, I know."

"So, what is it you want?"

"You," Johnny says. "The baby. I want a life in a house, with someone I love. I want to wake up beside you, feel your heat, then get up and bring you the baby and listen to the baby feed. In a way, I loved Charlene. I see that now. I've done some bad things. I don't want to do them any more. I want to love you."

"And eventually kill me?"

Johnny can see that Loraine doesn't plan to say this, because her chin quivers and she gropes at and strokes his wrists, fiercely, as if they were smudged and dirty and she were cleaning them. He knows, with a bone-deep knowledge, that he has one more chance, and Loraine Wallace is that chance. It's like he's been underwater this past month and now, see-ing Loraine, he has finally surfaced and he's taking big gulps of air.

"I'm having a Christmas dinner," she says. "On Boxing Day. Chris and Melody, Avi and Michael. You. If you want."

"Avi and Michael again? What, you rubbing shoulders with smart people all of a sudden? Weren't they Charlene's friends?"

"Avi's in the book club, but I didn't think they were great friends. It's true, Michael seemed more willing. 'Love to come,' he said. Avi just nod-ded, but she didn't say no."

"I don't know," Johnny says. "He's a professor of something and she's a psychologist of something and what are they doing hanging around Lesser? They'll just stare at me and call me names."

"They're too sophisticated," Loraine says. She stands and leans across the table and kisses Johnny on the jaw. Her stomach touches the table-top and Johnny can smell her breath; coffee. Her gown slips open and he can see her breasts, not the nipple and everything but the tops, the smooth slant to the edge of the nipple. Everything's a little bigger. Rounder. Full of promise. He wants to leap at Loraine but instead watches her settle back, pull her belt tighter and smirk at him. A tingling warmth creeps across his shoulders.

"A gift," he says. "You're a gift."

And then he says, his mind flapping, his eyes centred on the oval of

Loraine's face, "I remember the day Charlene died, and it was strange and frightening, but good too. For some reason I thought of those little blonde hairs you have on the tops of your big toes. Fine and fair. You know what they do to me. Well, anyways, I thought of them and I wanted to fuck you, Loraine. Fuck you."

The morning after the blizzard when all the kids who'd spent the night at the centre were safely picked up or delivered home, Johnny drove his Ninety-eight Olds down the 312 and followed the grader, driven by Hank Birton, along the three-mile road out to his farm. Hank's job was to clear the mile roads around Lesser, and Johnny convinced him to do his road first. Johnny had tried to phone Charlene that morning but the line was dead. It had happened all over Southern Manitoba. People were locked in, power and telephone lines were down, snowmobiles whined down Main Street.

Out on the three-mile road, Hank kept a steady pace. Johnny followed and marvelled at the blank page all around. Without Hank chugging before him Johnny could have imagined a new world, a form of rapture even, where everyone else was taken and he was left. Johnny wondered about the rapture sometimes, when it would happen, and where he'd be. It would be best, he thought, if he were dressed for work, or at home, reading the Bible. He didn't want to be caught napping, or worst of all, lying naked with Loraine Wallace. He knew Loraine wasn't a Christian, not in the right sense, and it confused him sometimes to think about him being taken and her left. It didn't seem fair, somehow, because really Loraine was a pretty good person. Charlene too. She'd be left. She had nothing but scorn for God. Johnny's God, anyway.

Hank stopped the grader, dismounted, walked over to the car and climbed in. Together, Hank and Johnny smoked cigarettes, shared coffee from Hank's thermos, and talked about the storm.

"I was in Winnipeg," Hank said. "At a hockey game. Barely made it home and all hell broke loose. Lost my dog. Pearl. Couldn't find her last night and she didn't come in this morning." He pointed at a rabbit flashing across the snow. "Saw a deer this morning. She was outside the door to my garage. I considered getting my gun, then thought better of it. In a flash, she lifted her head and was gone. White rear bouncing." His hand waves across the cab and back to his thermos.

"Deer are everywhere," Johnny said. "I've got one that feeds by the wooden granary. Like a drive-thru. Sometimes he brings his friends."

"This new guy," Hank said. "Michael Barry. Word has it he hunts. Fishes too."

"Really?" Johnny said. "I thought he was a religion professor."

"Physics. Anyway, you're religious and you hunt."

"Don't like it much though, and it's just that people into books and things, I mean, I didn't imagine him ripping bullets into animal flesh."

"All types," Hank said. He belched softly and screwed the cap on his thermos. "A witch's cunt out there," he said, and heaved himself from the car.

Johnny watched him settle back into the cab, relieved to be moving again. He was worried about Charlene, what state he'd find her in. She'd sounded too careful on the phone, for sure drunk, and beneath that false calm she was hazy and blubbering.

In the distance the wind-break of poplars lining Johnny's yard appeared. Hank was picking up speed now, settling into a rhythm. The house couldn't be seen from here, you had to turn onto the driveway.

Passing the driveway the grader's blade caught something, faltered, and then continued, pulling from the drifts the rear end of Johnny's half-ton. The grader chugged and groaned, ripping the box off the truck before Hank understood what was happening. Johnny climbed out of the car and walked over to his half-ton.

He was thinking about his truck but he was also trying to make sense of this. He looked over at the house and saw the big elm, which stood behind the house. This is the wrong yard, the wrong farm, Johnny thought. We've gone too far.

Then he said, "Where's my house?" His eyes caught sight of the black-ened skeleton of his home emerging from the snow and he said, "Charlene." He said her name softly but insistently, as if calling her to come see something important. Shocked, he floundered to the house.

Hank, following, had to pull Johnny, hands blackened, his face ugly with confusion, from the mess.

"Where is she?" Johnny said. He pushed at Hank. He pushed again so that the man almost fell. Johnny moved away, circled the house, and waded to the machine shed. Called out to Charlene. Then the granaries. Nothing. No one.

He ran back to the remains of the house and pulled up some half-burned planks. "She's dead," he said as he scraped at the corner where the kitchen had been. "Look," he cried, "a spoon," and he held it up for Hank to see. He put it in his pocket and rummaged about some more. Hank was standing behind him, calling his name, kicking at the timbers, pleading with him to stop.

"Get away from there," Hank finally said, pulling at his arm, and it was that sharp tug that forced Johnny to stop. He stumbled back, realiz-ing at that moment that he didn't really want to find anything, certainly not pieces of Charlene. Turning, he looked up at the sky and then back at the ground.

Hank kept holding his arm and they slogged back through the drifts, their breath steaming and the bright winter sun making the snow shine. They climbed into Johnny's car, left the grader idling. And while Hank drove Johnny back to town, Johnny laid his head back and closed his eyes and listened to someone moan in a greedy and helpless voice.

Johnny when he prays, gets down on his knees. He does this because he needs to appear abject and also his knees begin to hurt after a bit and this too he considers necessary, as if suffering a little is a sort of balm for his soul. That night, at his sister's house, after everyone was sleeping, Johnny knelt on the cement floor of the basement and tried to pray. For an hour he struggled with short phrases of grief and supplication but his efforts seemed small and selfish. He climbed into bed, rubbed his cold knees, and thought about Charlene's teeth gleaming past gold as she tipped her glass and her throat moved and the alcohol sank and her eyes lit up.

He recalled just three hours before, calling Charlene's mother. She howled into the phone. The father had to wrestle the receiver from her and say, voice shaking, that they would come by in the morning. "For what?" Johnny had the audacity to ask.

There was no response. The old man hung up the phone.

Johnny lay there that night, his mind numb; but not completely numb. Pieces of it were excited too, as if he were setting out on a new journey, like starting his life all over again, and guiltily he thrilled at the prospect. When he finally slept, Charlene came to him in a dream and offered him her mouth and eyes and ears and arms and legs and he woke up panicky, fighting off his dead wife and thinking about Loraine, that forbidden fruit, and he realized that he could finally have her. Forever and ever.

Phil Barkman spoke at Charlene's funeral. Watching him and listening to him, Johnny was sorry he'd asked the man to participate. Phil was too excited, too happy to have three hundred people staring up at him. He talked about heaven and hell. He spoke of Charlene's goodness, her inner beauty. He mentioned grace and salvation and the mind of God. He spoke of all these things with an authority he didn't really have. Still, he sounded convincing.

He told a story about two men, one rich, one poor, and how the rich man went to hell and the poor man went to heaven and the man in hell wanted a drop of water to cool his lips. "Charlene will need no water," he said. He raised his fist then, and shook it, calling out, "Because she is where the streams are cool and the water is fresh."

Johnny thought of fishing and standing in hip waders and drops of water hitting his cheeks as he let his line fly, and he was happy to be alive.

Later, there was a gathering in the church basement. They ate buns and butter and pickles and cheese. No jam, no dessert. Older women served coffee and people brushed past Johnny and bent low to whisper in his ear. He nodded and murmured thanks.

Many people got up to say something about Charlene. They spoke of her sense of humour, her poise, her tenacity. One woman said, "I think of Charlene and those things she wanted and those she didn't get," and she looked right at Johnny. Johnny bowed his head and thought he heard Charlene's mom say yes.

The women from the book club got up as a group and each read a poem or some prose they remembered Charlene liking. Johnny, listening, was surprised at the amount of love spilling out all around him. He had this sense of being misunderstood, of himself misunderstanding; he even thought at one point that of course these folks could be generous with Charlene: they never had to live with her.

Johnny was sitting beside Charlene's parents. Mr. and Mrs. Rempel. Mrs. Rempel cried softly throughout the service and the small meal. Mr. Rempel held her hand. He had arthritis and his little fingers were bent like bows. His knuckles were chafed, their sharpness reminded him of Charlene's. This moved Johnny.

The following day he drove to their home in Winnipeg and shared with them how he'd found Charlene. He explained about the night before her death; he did not say she was drunk. He sensed from Mrs. Rempel an animosity, hatred even. Her eyes were fawn-like and drooping in grief and she focused on his face and wouldn't let him go. He would try to stare her down, but found himself clearing his throat and turning away.

Mrs. Rempel wanted to know about this other woman. Her eyes enlarged. Disdain appeared and then evaporated. She said, "You had another woman, didn't you?"

Johnny did not respond at first. Finally, he said, "It doesn't matter."

"Of course it does. You were having sex with that other woman."

These particular words, erupting from Mrs. Rempel's mouth, had a certain power. She punched out the syllables and it was obvious to Johnny she was not free with herself; just like Charlene, who could leap from bawdiness to modesty but was never really at ease with the fact of sex.

"Yes," Johnny said. "I was seeing another woman."

"Charlene told me, you see. Last year, already."

"Ahhh." Johnny wanted the conversation to stop. The baby would be next.

It was.

"And there was going to be a child?"

"Yes." Johnny's voice was small. He wanted to run. This woman was merciless.

"She probably killed herself."

"No."

"Oh, I don't mean she deliberately set fire to that house. Charlene never had the capacity for that kind of thing. She didn't have a particularly strong backbone. Bit of a jellyfish, wasn't she, Peter? If she'd had any kind of self-awareness, she would have walked out on you. She was too beautiful."

Johnny wanted to disagree. She wasn't beautiful. Instead, he said, "It wasn't all me. She had her own brain. Her own problems, that had little to do with me. And besides, you raised her."

"Stop it." Mr. Rempel, in the background, leaned forward in his chair and almost tipped.

Mrs. Rempel's eyes were deep and stark as if she'd seen a vision. She turned to her husband and said, "This Johnny Fehr, he is a sick man. A very sick man."

But Johnny had his own vision: one of Charlene's head nodding up and down, her teeth deep in his own flesh. He cleared his throat and said, "No, he's not, Mrs. Rempel, he's not."

After he's left the Rempels', Johnny goes to a drive-thru and orders a hamburger and a Coke. He parks, idles the car, and sits in the warmth watching the traffic on Henderson Highway. It's a cold day and the exhaust billows and hangs. Pedestrians scuttle, huddling under their coats. Johnny wonders where Charlene is, if she's looking down on him. "Charlene," he says, and the sound of his voice startles him.

The day before, at the internment, the weather had been so harsh that people had to stand, backs to the wind, and stomp their feet. The snow squeaked, Harvey Bergmann sang a song, his mouth a perfect black hole. Charlene's coffin hung above the grave on black straps which were connected to a pulley system. It was an oak casket, lined with white satin.

"What's the point?" Johnny had asked the undertaker, a few days earlier. "Her body's a mess."

The undertaker, a short, soft-voiced man with a black mustache, had said, "People like the idea of a casket, it lends a solidity to the mourning. I'd suggest standing a photograph of Charlene on it. Do you have one?"

Mrs. Rempel had a picture of Charlene. It was taken just before her marriage to Johnny. She was standing in front of the summer cottage; her dress was knee-length and flowery. A breeze or a toss of her head had messed her hair slightly; she was smiling and looking away from the camera, off towards the lake or perhaps a person standing out of the picture. She looked expectant, happy. At the funeral, people said how lovely Charlene was in the photograph, and even Johnny found himself going back to sneak looks, as if he couldn't quite believe that this was the same woman he had married.

The mounds of earth at the graveside were covered with a green outdoor carpet. It reminded Johnny of a cheaply finished patio deck or a mini golf course. Johnny had the urge to point at it and laugh, but he didn't. He kicked at a loose clump of dirt. The diggers would have had to heat the ground, he knew that. They probably set up gas heaters and scraped the defrosted earth away with a backhoe. Frozen earth was like rock.

After Harvey Bergmann had closed his mouth and his words were whipped away by the wind, Phil said the final prayer. Johnny heard Phil's voice but the words made little sense, something about the dead in Christ rising incorruptible. Johnny's toes were cold in his thin black boots. His lungs ached. He lifted his head at one point and saw in the bright sky a sparrow flit by and disappear. Johnny realized he was standing all alone. The rest of the people gathered by Charlene's grave were holding each other, either out of grief or because of the chill. No one was holding him.

The tips of his boots just touched the green rug. The hard powder of snow sifted onto the shoulders of his black coat, covered his arms, his hair, fell in behind his collar. After the prayer and a short song the mourners left. Johnny stayed on, watching the casket sway slightly in the wind. Then he turned and walked back to the hearse and climbed in beside Phil Barkman who was waiting for him.

For Christmas dinner Johnny dresses in a black suit. No tie though. He's wearing Roy's clothes because his own were destroyed in the fire. The jacket's a little tight, the pant legs short; the image is of a man not finished growing. He brings gifts, a cassette for Chris, perfume for Loraine, and he carries a bottle of white wine.

He has not spent much time with other people since Charlene's death and so is uncertain about his behaviour. The few times he entered Chuck's for coffee he felt an obligation to exhibit grief, and usually he failed. Even in the earliest days, when his sorrow was immense and carved up his insides, he seemed not to deliver what was expected. He laughed when in fact he shouldn't have laughed at all. He talked about hockey and curling, inconsequential events. He drank coffee with other men and saw what they saw: Johnny Fehr, a hollow, flawed man. A sinner thick with desire. The unfortunate instrument of his wife's death. But, a fortunate man too, and how, to be led so easily into another woman's bed.

And Johnny too, standing at Loraine's door the day after Christmas, tapping lightly on the knocker, sees he is a lucky man. There is the knowledge that he has in some way been snatched from a downward spiral.

Melody answers the door, her braces gleaming, saying, "Hi, Johnny," and in turn, Johnny leans down and kisses her on the cheek, this girl he barely knows, brushes past her lips actually and he breathes in peanuts and sage; her cheek is downy, the eyes long and narrow in the light. She accepts his kiss, doesn't flinch.

"Merry Christmas," he says.

"You too, Johnny," she says, careful with him, as if he were precious. She stretches out a hand and takes the wine. He sheds his coat and boots and follows Melody. She's wearing jeans with holes in her bum; he can see paisley boxers. Her top is a sleeveless knit, her arms are white and thin. Johnny's brief contact just now with Melody has made her more accessible, worth studying, and he wonders for a moment how brave Chris is with her.

Loraine is in the kitchen fiddling with the dressing. She looks up and smiles. Her face is reddened from hovering over a turkey all day. She licks a finger and says, "I hate this part, too hectic."

Johnny kisses her on the cheek. She is heavier, even though he saw her two days earlier. The damp brow, the belly pushing against her light top, her lips blowing out exhaustion, all this makes her sloppy and maternal. Johnny wants to stagger and fall, he is so happy. Loraine, however, does not have time to dwell on the state of his mind and her body. She shoos him off to the living room where he finds Avi and Michael buried in a couch, sipping wine and muttering in each other's ears.

The TV is on, a football game, but no one's watching. Michael stands and shakes Johnny's hand and then they make small talk and nobody says anything important, though they seem to want to. Avi gets more wine from the server and Johnny watches her. She's tall and sort of awkward as if she were a large baby bird learning to fly. Johnny thinks she may have had too much to drink but realizes quickly enough that this is her walk. She's wearing dark blue culottes and dark stockings. Her calves are thick down to the ankle. Her hair is short, offering a lot of neck, and her eyes are big and steady. When Johnny focuses on her face she looks right back at him and says, finally, "I knew Charlene, we were in the book club together. I'm sorry."

Johnny can't get away from her eyes. He nods. That's all; he's learned not to attempt more.

"How are you doing?" Avi asks.

Johnny draws a knee up and plays with a hole in his sock. "Fine," he says. "Now. For a while there I was angry and full of revenge and guilt."

Avi lifts her chin. "I see," she says.

Johnny can see that this woman doesn't like him. Her face and body are hostile. This does not surprise him. He can tell she has a modern touch; university-bred, hawkish, predator, out to devour men like him. Still, he finds her greedy mouth, her sharp nose, exhilarating. Behind every woman like this, Johnny thinks, is a needy woman who wants to be coaxed. She is a challenge. *Bed me,* her body says.

Johnny slides deeper into the chair he has chosen. "I'm still low," he says. "Some days I feel I may slither around in muck for the rest of my life. But," he brightens, "these are the necessary stages, aren't they. I have to leap from rock to rock across the pond of grief."

Johnny wonders where this line came from, he is not usually poetic. His phrase seems to have surprised Avi as well. She half-lifts her glass and says, "I liked Charlene."

Johnny smiles and says, "So did I."

Michael, saving his woman, interrupts at this moment and asks Johnny if he likes to hunt.

"For what?" Johnny asks, wary of this new man from the city who should ideally be worrying about forests, not killing animals. He is a burly, hairy man. Big jawed. Thick chested. He could crack Johnny.

"Small game, birds, geese, ducks. Or big. Bear, deer, moose."

Johnny slides even lower. "I do a little," he says. "Every fall I do the goose thing. I've never hunted bear." He does not admit that he dislikes hunting. He goes for the drinking, the time out with the men.

"I'll take you sometime," Michael says. He is leaning forward, his teeth shine. Johnny wants to rub his finger along them.

Avi's head appears at Michael's shoulder. Her nostrils go in and out. She says, "Michael's one vice is hunting. His house is full of pelts and stuffed animals. It's eerie, especially the little birds. Of course, I'm against hunting."

What are you for? Johnny wants to say, but he doesn't. He's watching Avi's tongue appear and then disappear as she savours her wine. Her mouth is close to Michael's ear, she's leaning into him and Johnny understands at that moment that these two are lovers — not that he doubted it before. But now it's so obvious, the quickness of breath, even the scent of them together. Johnny wonders if Avi likes to lie naked on one of those hoary bears, if she cradles that fanged mouth as Michael climbs her.

His thoughts, both perverse and creative, are interrupted by the appearance of Loraine. She's removed her apron and she's pushing back her hair. Her arms are bare, the undersides white. She is exhausted and content. Johnny rises and offers her his hand and then the chair, but she refuses both.

"We're ready," she says, and bends slightly towards Michael and Avi, the strange guests Johnny finds he does not like, one for her impertinence, the other for his love of dead animals, something Johnny, the country boy, is expected to share. But he doesn't. The thump of a big bird hitting the ground has always managed to sicken him.

Melody, picking up a slice of white meat, wants to know what a physicist does. The word, hissing through her braces, makes the occupation sound tired and deflated. However, Michael seems not to notice her difficulty and, armed with an answer, wants to illuminate the group. His fork points at the ceiling, his eyes lift in thought. Johnny wonders what Avi sees in a man like this, though he does consider that they deserve each other.

"We look for ways to explain the world," Michael says.

Johnny looks over at Loraine but she is intent on watching Michael whose whole physical self has changed. The snarly aggressive hunter is replaced by a glowing fanatic. His head is lit up in a way that suggests photons travelling at the speed of light, his eyes are bright with weightlessness, as if drifting through space.

"Illumination," he says. "Everyone lives for that moment, for those three minutes or three days, where we break through the mundane and experience bliss."

Loraine says, "Sounds religious," and she looks at Johnny, who, with that last statement, is scratching his head. This does sound like a spiritual event, something that Johnny can understand.

Michael confirms this. He says, "It is religious in a way. Rather like Paul on the road to Damascus being blinded by a light. A form of salvation."

Melody interrupts. This confuses her. "But," she says, "you don't believe in God, do you?"

Michael laughs. Avi is quiet. She doesn't like Michael controlling the conversation. "It may seem odd," Michael continues, "for a scientist to believe in God. Some physicists do. There is a particle physicist, John Polkinghorne, who took up the priesthood."

Johnny is impatient. He wants to make jokes, to laugh at this man who is tarnishing Johnny's domain. He is making light of religion, of faith. The man is all brain, a sort of walking grey matter, who obviously has no sense of pleasure other than killing animals. Johnny holds up his hand as if in school and says, "So, when you look for this God of yours, you and your colleagues, you ignore happiness and fear, joy and pain. Your God is a mathematician and that's that?"

Michael doesn't get to answer. Avi shakes her head and says, "This isn't fair to Loraine. She's worked hard at the meal and surely doesn't want to suffer through descriptions of muons and superstrings." She pronounces these words carefully, with familiar distaste.

"But it's fine," Loraine says. "Really." And then she pours Michael more water and says that if she weren't raising chickens she would study math because playing with numbers has always struck her as a way into another life. "All those theories," she says, and rubs her hands together. Johnny is amused by her girlish excitement. She appears quite taken with this professor. She tucks her fists under her chin, rests her elbows on the table, and says, "Because that's what it is, isn't it? Theories."

"Sure," Michael says. "But theories give us our truth, as close as we can come to it anyway."

"You have something you follow then?" Loraine says.

"Theory of Everything," Avi breaks in.

Michael looks at her, clears his throat, and says, "Yes, but I can't adhere to it completely."

Johnny wants to laugh. Melody, bored now, whispers something to Chris and they disappear.

"Oh," Loraine says, and before she can continue, Michael says, "If we believe the cosmos is rational then we should be able to assign a graspable logic to our world, that is, we should be capable of taking the forces and particles of physics, as well as the structure of time and space, and blend them into a single mathematical plan."

Johnny isn't really listening. Everything is nonsense, gobbledegook, even this "Theory of Everything." It strikes him as contrived and desperate, as if Michael the physicist were an elevated form of Johnny Fehr the feed salesman, both of them striving for illumination — one through molecules and mind, the other by praying and running his nose along the base of a woman's spine — yet, for all their trying, they are both worming around in a primal soup, somehow failing, eyes staring up into a blackness that is like pitch. Johnny wants to tell Michael Barry one thing he has learned: look for everything and you'll end up with nothing.

After dinner Loraine apologizes and says she has to gather eggs. Johnny wants to help her but Avi jumps in and says the men can do dishes while the women work in the barn; she seems excited by the prospect, so Johnny lets her go. He is standing at the sink, hands deep in water, as Loraine and Avi walk out across the yard. Avi is wearing a green parka that is too short in the sleeves, and big white boots. Johnny watches her throw her wide forehead up at the sky and shout something. Loraine turns and smiles and Johnny thinks how it is impossible to really know someone, even if you live with that person, sleep beside her, and enter her body now and then.

It's his fault that Charlene died. He lacked the imagination to find the other Charlenes hidden somewhere beneath her dull skin. He has sinned. He admires these young people from other countries who are thrown into arranged marriages and learn to love their partners. He thinks that that is wonderful and he hates the craving in his own life, in the lives of the people he sees around him.

He turns to Michael now and asks, "You and Avi. You live in the same house?"

Michael looks surprised, but not unwilling to answer. "Yes," he says, "we do."

Johnny says, "I like living with a woman. Though I'm not terribly good at it." He laughs and then stops, because he's close to crying. "Living by myself now, most of the time at the centre, I'm lonely and I start thinking that I'm full of boring chaos, like a dripping tap." Johnny doesn't know why he's telling Michael this. He doesn't really like the man, though at this moment Michael seems gracious and willing to listen.

Michael has nothing to say so Johnny keeps going. "What I find amazing," he says, "and you understand that I'm not laughing, is how people like you spend your lives looking for order, even arranging it, but you wouldn't have shit to say to someone who's grieving. I'm a Christian, you see, born again many times, and *I'm* at a loss. Sometimes I think God has really screwed up. Not that that stops me from believing. No point in that. I like the feeling. Do you believe?"

Michael has a way of pointing at the air as he speaks. It makes him look silly, as if he were stabbing at dust motes or invisible rings. He says, "You're right. I have nothing to say to you. About Charlene. A priest would do better."

"I'm not Catholic," Johnny says.

Michael is thinking. "Maybe those who accept mysticism to explain the unexplainable are deluding themselves. And maybe the more comprehensible we make the world the more pointless it all becomes. Maybe."

Johnny thinks the man is full of crap. Still he likes him a little bit now. He's not jumping all over everybody; perhaps because Avi's not around.

Later, when Avi is back in the kitchen, talking and laughing about all the eggs she broke, Johnny passes by her and a shiver skips across his back. She's a mixture of cold air, ammonia, perfume, and the tiniest trace of sexual heat, as if she were hungry for Michael, or someone else. She crosses her legs and says, "It's odd, to be stealing eggs. I feel so guilty."

Loraine looks at Johnny and closes her eyes. She is tired; Avi has worn her out. Michael senses this too and suggests they go. Loraine doesn't argue. She asks if they could drop off Melody at home. "Chris needs a ride too," she says. "He's sleeping at a friend's in town."

When everyone has parted and the house is quiet, Loraine stands in the middle of the living room and tells Johnny he can stay the night if he likes. He'll have to sleep on the couch though. The blankets are in the hall closet.

"I'm tired," Loraine says. "I'm gonna shower, scrub off the turkey, and then go to bed." She walks over to Johnny, leans down to him, and kisses the top of his head. "Thanks," she says and strokes his face.

He keeps his hands at his sides. Her knee touches his, one of her hands rests on his head.

"You okay?" she asks.

He nods.

"Good night, then."

He lies on the couch and listens to her bathe and then the house is silent, and Johnny is by himself, thinking about Loraine, who will still be damp and fresh smelling, her bum warm from the bath, a red line marking her skin where the hot water lay against her body.

In the morning, before the winter light creeps in through the windows, Loraine wakes him as she climbs under his covers. She wraps her legs around his hips. Her body is fierce but her voice is tender as she says, "Love me, Johnny."

It is nice to be surprised. To have it swoop down and claw at you. Johnny, holding Loraine, is surprised. He feels as if he has been offered an unexpected present, and gently, gently, he unwraps it. Loraine is urgent, but Johnny takes his time. He lays his head on her stomach. He bows down before her, kneels on the rug beside the couch, his legs bare and chilly outside the blanket, but he doesn't notice. He talks and prays to this woman. "You are good," he says. "Good."

Loraine reaches down and pulls him up so they can share mouths, and eyes, and noses, and tongues, and Johnny would swallow Loraine whole if he could. There is nothing else he wants. He has everything.

BLISS

In early February Loraine phones Mrs. Krahn and asks about Melody. "Has she been any different lately?" she says.

"No, not really," is the answer. "She knows we don't approve of her crowd, but, well, we are limited, you see."

"Yes, we all are," Loraine says, and then adds that Melody and Chris are having sex.

It's quiet for a long time and finally Mrs. Krahn says, "Oh. Oh, my. Are you sure?"

"Yes," Loraine says, "I'm sure." She does not explain that she was shopping in Winnipeg on a Thursday afternoon and returned to find Chris and Melody in her son's bed. They were both naked, on top of the covers. Loraine hadn't known they were there when she opened the bedroom door and discovered the rounded whiteness of Melody's bum and Chris's foot, an innocent and vulnerable limb. Loraine slipped downstairs and made a big to-do about her next entry, banging the back door, shouting out Chris's name.

Later, when her son appeared, Melody at his side, the two of them were pulled together, but seemed somehow puzzled, as if they were descending from a mountaintop and were sobered by the common sight of Loraine unpacking groceries.

That night, Loraine asked Chris if he and Melody were having sex.

He looked up from his math homework, surprised. "What if we are?" he asked. "You gonna stop us?"

He was like a rat, Loraine thought. She disliked what she was doing. She poked at some plants, talked into the dirt. "It's supposed to be fun," she said. "I mean, if you are having sex, and I'm not saying you are, age has something to do with how comfortable you feel. Like, will she get pregnant?"

"We're not stupid," Chris said. "Not like you."

Loraine expected this; she was quick with her response. "It's never occurred to you that I wanted this baby, has it? I'm thirty-six. How old are you?"

Chris snarled and thumped upstairs. Loraine sat at the kitchen table, cleaned the dirt from her nails, and felt washed over by helplessness.

Funny thing, on the phone now, Mrs. Krahn wants to know Chris's age too. "How old is he?" she asks.

"Fourteen," Loraine says.

"Melody's sixteen."

Loraine waits, expecting some logic. Then Mrs. Krahn says, "She just got her driver's, last week."

"Yes, she told me." It sounds, though Loraine can't be sure, as if Mrs. Krahn is crying. There's a whistle in her voice, a quick intake before she speaks, and then a shakiness.

"I said to Leonard, just last night, that Melody was scaring me. He agreed. So we've stopped her using the car. She just can't have it. This made her angry of course. She hates us."

This sounds like a pathetic confession, something Loraine might say. Mrs. Krahn is surprising Loraine. She anticipated anger and outrage, not submission and helplessness. The kindness in her voice is perhaps the veneer of a pastor's wife: the woman must take care, be generous and forgiving.

Loraine becomes careless. "I suppose you could blame Chris," she says. "He's a little out of control lately."

"I don't know," Mrs. Krahn says. She doesn't sound convinced.

"Is she using any protection?" Loraine asks.

"Sorry?"

"I was thinking. We can't forbid them to see each other, short of chaining them in their rooms, so I wonder if Melody's on the pill or something. I know I'm gonna give Chris condoms. Even so, Melody's the girl. She's got to look out."

"See," Mrs. Krahn says, as if aiming a finger over the phone, "Leonard wouldn't have it. You know. It'd be like condoning it."

"How 'bout you?" Loraine asks. She's getting a feel for this small woman. She's only seen her once, in the aisles of the hardware store, and there she seemed cowed and timid, not at all the mother of colourful Melody.

"Of course," she answers, but she stops, as if what she desires and needs is far from the core of her real existence and in the end, denied. She breathes quickly, a slight rattle in her throat. Loraine listens, thinks of dry seeds, and Mrs. Krahn says, "You're expecting."

"Yes."

"Hnnnh. When?"

"Late April."

"Melody told me. She said you were happy."

"I am."

"It will be a change, won't it?"

"Of course, but we'll manage."

"The father will help?"

"You mean Johnny?"

"I suppose. Is he?"

"He is."

Mrs. Krahn doesn't say much else, though it seems she wants to. Loraine thinks, just before hanging up, that if she could look into the other woman's eyes, she would discover there the cold ashes of a fire long dead.

And then one day, upon Loraine's suggestion, Johnny packs up his few
belongings, says goodbye to his sister's basement, and moves into the room
connected to the barns at Loraine's farm. It's a place Jim built before he
died; for the hired help who never materialized. It's small but there is space
for a single bed, a hotplate, a dresser, and a shelf. The shower and toilet
are accessible via the refrigerator room so Johnny's got all he needs.

When Loraine makes her offer she also says, "I would even consider
letting you live with me if it weren't for Chris."

"Well, what's he gonna think, I'm a boarder in this little shack?"

"He's naive enough."

"Marry me," Johnny says. On this particular day they're painting the
little room bright yellow and when Johnny says this Loraine's paintbrush
stops moving. She waits for Johnny to speak. He has specks of yellow on his
nose and forehead from painting the ceiling. He says again, "Marry me."

"No."

"So, some day then?"

"Sure, some day."

Johnny eats his meals with Loraine and Chris. He uses the washer and
dryer. He gathers eggs in the morning and cleans out the barn on sched-
ule. He is like the hired hand. Chris accepts his presence grudgingly,
Loraine loves knowing he's near. Sometimes, late in the evening, she
stands by the kitchen window and looks across at Johnny's window and
she gurgles and smiles, holds her belly and sighs.

Lately, she feels the baby pressing her pelvic floor. Her crotch itches,
her vagina squirms. She scratches wildly at herself but this brings little
relief. She thinks maybe it's the hair of the baby's head making her itchy.
She believes, too, that she's carrying a boy because her testosterone level
is up: she's horny. She felt this way when she was carrying Chris. There
is nothing romantic about her feelings. Some days she feels she could rip
a chicken from its cage and stick its head up inside her. She both loves
and despises this lust. She asks Johnny if this is how he feels all the time
and he smiles, shakes his head, and says, "Not all the time."

She goes to him. Late at night, after she is sure Chris is sleeping, she

creeps from the bed, her body throbbing, and she scrambles into clothes
— one time she throws a coat over her naked body — and flies through
the winter into Johnny's shed. She wakes him and wordlessly rides him,
clutching at his shoulders, her head thrown back, a silent howl floating
upwards. The little electric heater clicks. The room is musty and close.

Once, Loraine finds herself kneeling on the floor, her head resting on
the linoleum, her belly nestled in her thighs, her bare bum in the air, and
she says, "Come, Johnny. Do it."

Johnny crawls up her back and blows in her ear. The linoleum is cold on
her knees. Their bodies slap. When they are done she trudges back over the
hard snow and she feels spent and a little embarrassed, though not sorry.

Loraine likes to sit by the kitchen window. Sometimes she remembers
Charlene and how it was before Charlene died and Loraine allows herself the prick of pleasure in feeling guilty for being here, for holding this
chipped mug and staring out across the fields.

Johnny no longer speaks of his dead wife. Once, he mentioned the life
insurance, a fairly large sum, and said, "I really don't need to work."

He talked about selling his land, about leaving Lesser. Moving to the
southern states, Florida.

"No," Loraine said, "I couldn't."

"You love your chickens," he said, and again he broached the subject
of marriage, said it didn't have to be a white wedding, in fact Phil
Barkman could marry them in the barn.

"Really?" The idea, for a moment, appealed to Loraine. Then, she
grew serious. "I don't trust you Johnny. I like you. I love to have you
close, but there's something about us I don't trust."

"I can understand that," Johnny said, too easily. Loraine took his hand
and kissed it, saying, "My sister wants to have this party for me. A weird
one. Some Indian custom thing. Navaho. That's just like Claire. We'll all
sit around and eat millet."

"Am I such a bad man?" Johnny asked.

"Sometimes. Sometimes."

All her life Loraine thinks she's been looking for something. It's as if there is a slot inside her, like a keyhole, and ice and wind and dread and pain blow through that hole, and then Johnny comes along and he slides himself like a key into her and he opens her up, climbs in, curls his warm body up inside her, into that hole the size of Johnny.

This is why, these days, Loraine can sit at the kitchen table on a cold winter's day in February, spin a mug in her hands, and wait. She's planted geranium seeds in tiny humus trays and the little green shoots are appearing. She talks to them, pours water at their feet. The cat rubs against her legs. The baby knocks at the wall of the uterus. Last night she risked staying with Johnny till morning. At one point he held his head against her belly, exclaiming at each blow, each rubbery extension of the stomach wall. "Great," he said, waking her in the morning blackness, dressing her under the blanket, first sliding on her panties, then sweater, then pants and socks. He slid his rough palms under her T-shirt and shaped her breasts. She took his head and tangled his hair in her hands and yanked fiercely, pulling his head to her mouth

"I could weep," she said.

He stood her up and wrapped her parka around her. "Go," he said, "back to your nest."

Now, as she sits in the kitchen, talking to her plants, she remembers the smell of Johnny's hair, the texture of it, like coarse string. Then he is there, stepping out of the barn, knocking a boot against the door, popping in the latch. He crosses the yard, smoking a cigarette, looking up at the sky and then down at his feet. He sees her in the window and smiles; doesn't wave, just smiles and looks as he keeps coming. His exhaled breath rises and disappears above his head. Loraine thinks that if she were to fall, she'd want Johnny to catch her.

Loraine's sister, Claire, has chased the kids out with their father for the afternoon and there's a circle of women sitting on the floor, Loraine in the middle. Incense is burning, Loraine is holding a cup of scalding tea between her palms, and there's a round-faced woman called Prue brushing Loraine's hair. Prue brushes and hums a soft tune, over and over again. At one point she leans forward and whispers past Loraine's ear, loud enough for all to hear, "You will have a beautiful baby."

This is like a spiritual gathering, Loraine thinks. A meeting of witches. She loves the feel of the bristles in her hair, the pressure of Prue's fingers on her shoulder. Meryl, a good friend of Claire's, reads a poem and then plays a song on a recorder. While she plays the women look at their hands or their feet. A few watch Meryl's wet lips on the mouthpiece. When the recorder is silent, the women do not speak. Finally, Claire says, "I have this for you," and she hands Loraine a copper bowl, the size of her cupped palms.

"You made this?" Loraine asks.

"Yes."

Loraine leans over and kisses Claire on the mouth. Claire is her younger sister. She has lived a happy life — three children, a husband who did not die; her life is organized, pulled together, easy. Her mouth is full and generous, like her life. She is more beautiful than Loraine. Tall like a tree, Loraine thinks. She smells something green and leafy. It is the incense.

These women who surround Loraine are practically strangers. Still, they are kind strangers. They do not care where Loraine comes from, who the father is, or why she is having this baby. They know nothing about Johnny or the fire or Charlene and the guilt that flows and ebbs, flows and ebbs. Even Claire has only a vague notion of Loraine and who she is. These women are present because Loraine is about to give birth. They are celebrating.

All afternoon people touch Loraine. She has her feet massaged. Kaye, a midwife with round oily eyes, asks if she can touch the stomach. She lifts Loraine's shirt and places warm hands on Loraine's skin. The baby's head is found, a foot, an elbow. Kaye lays her ear on the bulge and rises, eyes shining. "You're so tight," she says to Loraine. "Like it's your first."

"It's been fourteen years."

Loraine closes her eyes, imagines herself a queen bee surrounded by drones. Kaye's eyelashes are tiny wings brushing her navel. Like Charlene's fingers; her kneeling before Loraine on that kitchen floor. Loraine shudders and starts.

"Easy," Kaye says, pushing her backwards, one hand resting under her neck.

There is a difference, Loraine thinks, between a man and a woman. With Johnny a lot is external, as if when she finally gets close to him she needs to scrape her skin against his. With a woman like Kaye it's as if they are together in a warm field that goes on forever and ever, no edge, and so there is never any fear of falling. Loraine opens her eyes. Kaye is eating date cake, there are crumbs on her lips. Claire is talking about having a baby at home.

"No doctors, no nurses, no intrusions," she says. The women nod.

Loraine sits up, adjusts her top, and says, "I couldn't do it. I'd be thinking about my chickens."

Kaye laughs. "Arrange all that beforehand."

Meryl says, "I was tortured in the hospital. They pinned me down and tore the baby out. I swore, never again."

Loraine doesn't remember it being so awful with Chris. Just fast. She says this. "With my boy it wasn't bad. He was quick but the doctor was great. And I like hospital food and they keep your baby for you at night. What can I say?"

The women smile. Claire takes her hand and squeezes it. "I'm going to be with Loraine. We'll be fine."

Loraine feels as if she's erred in some way, said something wrong. The women are still warm but it's as if messages are being passed to and fro and Loraine is missing them. She holds Claire's hand and takes a piece of cake. She is disappointed. Not terribly, but still there's a small twinge in her throat. At least with Johnny the pain is massive and she knows what's happening. Not here. She doesn't get it.

The day ends well though, with Kaye promising to drive out and see her on the farm. They all kiss and Loraine generously accepts these intimacies. Gifts are also given: canned apples, home-baked buns, the copper bowl, and two books, *Natural Ways of Childbirth* and *The Prophet*.

Claire says she will attend the refresher course with Loraine. Her children have returned and she's standing in the foyer hipping her two-year-old. Looking at Claire, Loraine feels huge, like a holstein.

"You look great, Claire," she says. She kisses her nephew, who ducks and bobs. "So thin."

"*You* look great. I love a pregnant woman."

"So does Johnny. He's living on the farm now. Not in the house, I was worried about Chris, but in that little room Jim built next to the barn." Loraine says this quickly, wanting to give Claire some glimpse into her life. She never visits. Rarely asks about Chris.

"You like him then?" Claire sounds surprised. She's met Johnny once, by accident, when Loraine and Johnny were having dinner together in the city and Claire was in the same restaurant. That was four years ago, back when Loraine and Johnny were tenuous, still gaping at each other from a distance.

"Yes," Loraine says. "We're going to marry."

"No." This is a squeal, a bark of amazement and disbelief. "Well." Claire shifts the baby to the other hip, pushes back her hair. Her elbows are dry. The winter air has done her some damage. This is comforting to Loraine. Elbows and knees, they're hard to keep looking young.

"Well, we're not gonna marry right away," Loraine says. "Johnny was devastated, you know, by Charlene's death. It sounds kind of screwy, I know, but we're good together." Loraine wants to leave now. She's sounding all wrong and the impression is one of desperation. She is not desperate. She doesn't know why she talked about marrying Johnny, although now that the words have rolled around in her mouth she almost likes their taste and feel. She grins. Leans once again into Claire and kisses her jaw, just below the ear. "Bye, thanks," she says.

Johnny is amused by the two books. "Oh, my," he says, "Gibran. We had a high school teacher who liked to read this to us. Put us all to sleep. And, what's this?" He picks up the birth book and cracks it open. "Pretty graphic," he says. He flips pages and Loraine watches him. He is impish tonight; his ears are red and he has a looseness to his body as if he were a puppet or rag doll. Loraine comes up behind him, leans over his shoulder, and lays her cheek on his.

"You smell good," she says.

"Really?"

She touches his hair. "You showered?"

"Just finished in the barn."

Loraine breathes deeply. "See that," she says, pointing, "In a tub. France. It figures."

Johnny says, "These women are pretty easygoing with their bodies."

"European," Loraine says. "It's not supposed to be a turn-on."

Surprisingly, Johnny is embarrassed. "I know that," he says. "It's curious. That's all."

Loraine punches him. Sucks on his earlobe. "My feet are swollen tonight. I gotta sit down."

"Here." Johnny pats his lap and pulls Loraine around and plunks her down. "Elephant," he says. He slips his hand inside her top and plays with her belly.

"Claire was talking about this massage I should do," Loraine says. "The perineum. She gave me a bottle of vitamin A liquid and said to try it."

"Perineum?"

"Hmm, like at the base of the vagina. Claire says if you massage, you won't need an episiotomy."

"I could do it for you," Johnny says.

"Sure you could. But I think I'll handle that. Did you see Chris today?" she asks.

"He was around and then Melody came by with her dad's car. Picked him up."

"That's odd. Mrs. Krahn said she was grounded."

"She probably begged and lied," Johnny says. "Kids are good at that. Especially lying."

"They're having sex, you know."

"I figured," Johnny says.

"Oh, you figured. What makes you so clever?"

"I work with kids," Johnny says. "I know when they're sleeping around. Or think they'd like to. Sometimes it's the most unlikely ones. Like us, huh." He laughs. Loraine doesn't.

"They're too young," she says. "I think there should be a law that you can't have sex until you're ready to look after kids."

Johnny draws a finger along the inside of Loraine's arm. "So soft here. Like your thighs."

"I told Claire we were gonna get married," Loraine says. She stares past Johnny's chin and listens to him breathe. In. Out. In. Out.

He says, "So, you were fooling around, making a point."

"Sort of."

"But there was a part of you that said yes."

"I guess."

"How big?"

"Like this?" Loraine holds up a little finger and touches Johnny's nose. His voice is slow. "That's big." He pulls Loraine's head down and puts one of his earlobes against her eye. Rubs it around.

"I drove by your old place today. On the way home," Loraine whispers.

Johnny takes Loraine's ear now and traces it.

"I hadn't driven by there yet," Loraine continues. "I always go around. But today, I did. Everything's gone. The house, the tree."

"I hired Hank Birton to raze the place."

"So, clean slate," Loraine says. "Pretty easy."

"Not really," Johnny says. His hand goes up and scratches his jaw. "I'm gonna sell."

Loraine feels Johnny's heat, the hardness of his chest, the sharpness of a hip. She gets off his lap and takes a chair across the table from him. She waddles these days. Like a goose. Her hips are spreading, they move as if almost detached and she feels she could pull them from their sockets. She misses her pre-pregnancy body. Johnny's smoking. Loraine looks at him. "Will anyone buy?" she asks.

"Doesn't matter."

Loraine knows now why Johnny seems so young and springy tonight. He doesn't care. Chris is like this a lot. Hands twitch and play. Eyes roam all over, never resting on one thing. Loraine begins to feel that Johnny could run tonight. She'd just have to say the word and he'd walk out that door, hop in his car and go. She wonders if she should let him, if she really wants to spend the next years of her life looking around corners for Johnny Fehr.

Of course, she'd just have to say, "Come here, Johnny," and he'd do that. He'd never say no. And there's something disgusting in that too, makes her feel lousy and cheap. Loraine doesn't know what it is, perhaps the time with Claire, looking at her sister's life and the easy flow of it, but at the moment she dislikes Johnny. He's eating bread and peanut butter now. The cigarette's smouldering in the ash tray. He gets whatever he wants.

She wonders who Johnny really is. If he could be violent. Hit her. "Did you ever hit Charlene?" she asks.

Johnny looks surprised. "What a stupid question," he says finally.

"Just curious."

"You think I did?"

"I didn't say that. It's just men are strange. I know a woman whose husband took her to bars. He made her wear a trench coat with no clothes underneath."

First Johnny says, "And she did it." Then, he says, "That's sick. I'm not sick."

"You're right. Not like that."

"How then?"

"It's more subtle. Like maybe you think you're better than me."

"Do I?"

"Maybe you are."

"Well, maybe." Johnny's trying to be funny but it's not working.

"Like, your religion," Loraine says. "You've got me beat there."

Johnny doesn't answer. He slides out another cigarette and says, "It's like any discovery. When you see it you can't believe how you lived without it all your life."

"Why can't you show me?"

"You'd just make fun of me." He's still moving weird. He puts a foot on a chair; his socks are dirty. "You've got nicer teeth than me," he says.

"Ahhh." Loraine looks at Johnny and imagines him talking about her, about her tits and so on. It happens. Some men do that. She remembers how it first was with him. Like jumping. As if she'd be high up somewhere, and she'd jump and he'd catch her. Jump. Catch. Especially the sex made her feel this way. She wanted to steal him, was fascinated by every little bit; the gaps between his toes, the hair of his knuckles, his odour. She would clamber all over him, sniffing like a furry animal and it was everything: funny, sad, desperate, pleasing. But it was the sadness that made it so rich. Like maybe this would be the last time.

Loraine focuses back on Johnny across from her. He's talking, about money and bonds and his land. Then he's telling her about Phil Barkman and the healing power of his hands. He holds his own hands up as he speaks, spreads his fingers, and Loraine can see the flesh bulging around his ring and she feels old. She wants to go back to how it was before; she wishes it were possible to stop the movement of the clock. She wants to tell Johnny this but she isn't sure he'd understand.

She opens her mouth. "Come here," she says.

SPRING

METHODS OF TORTURE

Living with her.

Loraine at the kitchen table, buttering toast. Her knuckles white where bent around the knife. Her tongue curling out, touching her top lip. It is spring, and warm; she is wearing a tank top, purple, and she hasn't shaved for a while. The sight of those bristles as she stretches the knife across the table makes Chris stoop to his shoelace and from this position he looks up at the armpit of his mother: concave, the beginning of her breast like dough rising, the light blue vein along the inside of her arm.

He has forgiven her. All those grievances of the past, those hateful words, his own disgust for her — this is gone. It is as if he has had a grey film peeled back from his eyes and he now sees clearly. These days she seems so easy. She has pulled the rocker into the kitchen and, when she is not eating at the kitchen table, she rocks herself into a trance, her legs up, her gaze focusing on some small spot on the ceiling. Or, she pages through these books she picked up in Winnipeg, at the public library. Books on childbirth. There are pictures of women: big, naked, standing in profile or facing the camera, mess of bush, breasts sloping and then turning up at the tips, hands usually clasped under the belly, supporting the load. There is one of a Danish woman. Her long hair covers one breast, her eyes are dark and mournful, her hips are narrow, her shoulders thin; it seems to Chris, who has only really seen Melody naked and even that has been hasty and unstudied, that this is a girl, much younger than his own mother, and that she has been surprised by the growth of her belly, as if the fetus were an unwanted limb. Her thighs do not touch; Chris can see right through the gap.

Chris likes these pictures. They make him want to be near his own mother, to sneak looks at her belly, her legs, her breasts, her neck and ears, the top of her head. She has become, since about the fifth month, a boat sitting lower and lower in the water. He would like to stow away on her, enter a deep and inner hold, and lay himself down and ride her with the swell. Sometimes, when she has discovered the spot on the ceiling, he approaches her from behind, leans in until they are almost touching, and breathes deeply.

On Sunday mornings he brings her breakfast in bed. He makes toast and juice and climbs the stairs to her room and lays the tray on her lap, his hands brushing lightly at her thighs.

"You're so sweet," Loraine says. "Thank you." Her voice is a whisper, as if she were leaning forward and telling him a secret.

Chris's neck tightens. He is embarrassed, though he cannot help himself. He sits at the edge of the bed and watches her chew. Her cheeks are rounder now, her chin double. The backs of her arms shake when she laughs, though she doesn't laugh much. One of these mornings, weeks before the baby is due, he says, "You should laugh more."

Loraine is wary, one eye half-closed, her brain still groggy, "Oh, I should? Give me a reason."

"The baby."

"Ah, yes. Do you want to feel?" She pushes aside the tray, lifts her T-shirt, and takes Chris's hand and lays it on her tummy. "Sometimes it kicks, really hard. There. Feel that?"

"Yes." Her skin is hot. His hand burns.

"Here, lower," and she guides his fingers lower. She is smiling. "That's its head. It's dropped. A few weeks before the birth it engages and gets ready."

Chris looks at his hand. At hers. She is sitting up now and a shoulder brushes his ear. He looks up at her face and she asks, "Are you scared?"

"No, are you?"

"Kind of. I forget what it was like with you. Except the speed."

Chris wants to touch his mother's lips. He thinks what it is like to kiss Melody. Melody is hard and thoughtless; greedy. This woman here, this big full-of-baby woman, is the best: like a tub of warm milk.

"Do you want some more toast?" he asks.

She looks at him, frightened by his kindness. "Are you sick?" she asks.

Sometimes, he is burdened by shame. He does not want it to be this way, in fact, he is unsure when this compulsion began. There is a clear memory of an early morning, back in February, when he stumbled to the bathroom and lifted the toilet lid. His mother had not flushed, which was not unusual these days; she was absentminded. Chris stooped to the bowl. Her shit was long and thick and lay perfectly coiled like a snake as if Loraine had laid it down with her own hands. All one piece. Chris was repulsed. He was aroused. It was like coming upon his mother naked in the bath. It had the same effect. He had discovered the wonderful torture of desire.

Back in February, when Johnny moved into the little shed across the yard, Chris knew what his mother did at night. He heard her creep downstairs and from his bedroom window saw her run across the snow to Johnny's beacon of light. She disappeared and Chris waited. Occasionally he saw shadows beyond the curtains of that tiny window and he imagined they were talking and drinking tea.

One night after Loraine had left the house and flown across the yard, her feet flicking behind her, Chris went to his mother's bedroom and lay down on her bed. He curled up in the still-warm recess she had left. He smelled her smell. He climbed out of bed and rummaged through her drawers and put on a pair of her panties. Pink. Cotton. He picked up another pair and held them to his nose. Her. He heard a noise and crawled back into her bed. He blushed and stripped.

He fell asleep and vaguely remembered his mother sliding under the covers later, her knees cold, her hands on his neck as if he were the headboard or a pillow. She didn't move him. In fact, she held his head for a while as if it were a precious and delicate bowl. In the morning he awoke to discover the twisted blanket, thrown aside by his mother, and her bare speckled shoulders. He lay still for the longest time and watched her body rise and fall. She had a different smell this morning, a mixture of the barn and something wet and old. Johnny. The little room. Chris shuddered. His experience with Melody so far had been less than grand and it was by this he judged all sex. Why then, he wondered, would his mother run headlong through the dark and the snow, to a man who was chubby and weak, and who smelled of sweat? He reached out a finger, brushed his mother's spine and understood that she didn't know he was there; in the darkness of the room last night she had not noticed him.

Johnny was moving around in the kitchen now. Chris didn't worry about him coming up. He never did. He only worried about Loraine waking. And yet, he did want her to open her eyes, to discover him beside her. He climbed from the bed. Loraine moved slightly and adjusted a leg so her foot peeked from beneath the cover. Chris went to his bedroom and lay there, full of regret. He must have slept briefly, because he became aware of Loraine and Johnny talking downstairs, their voices muffled and distant as if the house were underwater.

What Chris felt was dirty and lovely. It was full of possibilities and surprises and weakness and doom. On subsequent nights, he watched his mother cross the yard to Johnny's place and always she fairly flew, her elbows moving out and sideways, her long heavy coat, hiding her pregnancy, swaying back and forth as she aimed her mounded body at the glowing yellow rectangle. Chris watched her go and then he studied the window and the shadows and he imagined Johnny filling his greedy hands. He fell back onto his bed.

He returned to his mother's bed a few times, even dug again amongst her underwear. One other night he fell asleep, his face on his mother's pillow, and she reappeared to discover and wake him, calling him "sweetheart" and kissing him, guiding him from her bed and back to his own. That night she smelled of saltwater and melon. Her body was like a sheet waiting to be folded. She laid him down, pulled his blanket up, and said, "Good night."

His disappointment was bitter.

With the coming of spring and the nearing of the birth, Loraine's journeys out to the shed become fewer and fewer. Chris keeps track. One week she goes twice. The next, not at all. The following week, once, skittering around the large puddles which now occupy the yard. Chris wonders if perhaps he is sleeping through these meetings. He forces himself to lie awake and listen, but no, she is not leaving the house.

Her presence becomes bigger and bigger. Some days Chris feels she may split the house apart. She is solid, nothing moves her: not his anger, not his desire, not his fear. She is unaware.

Johnny has Chris doing some work at the centre; Chris is still filling in the hours for community service. Together, they go to Bill's Hardware and pick up some studs, drywall, screws, tape, and mud. They buy a new sink and toilet too. Pink, because it is on sale. Chris is surprised by Johnny's knowledge of wood and plumbing; it is as if Johnny were shining a light back onto himself and revealing secrets. One day he asks, "Where did you learn all this?"

"My father," Johnny says. "I just don't use it much. Lazy, I guess."

Chris likes working beside Johnny and having little diagrams drawn on the plywood floor. One time Johnny describes the guts of a toilet bowl; leans over and pencils the snake-like design. "There's an air trap right here," he says, tapping at the scribbles. "Very necessary, otherwise you'd get the perfume of the sewer coming back into the bathroom."

Chris learns to snap a line and lay out walls with sixteen-inch centres. Screwing the drywall is the hardest; Chris keeps missing the stud and the first sheet especially is riddled with holes. Johnny doesn't seem to mind, claims it can be patched. One Saturday they're running a vent from the sink up through the roof. Johnny is standing on a step ladder and Chris is down below so that when he looks up he can see the bottom of Johnny's boots and his crotch.

Johnny is talking, something he likes to do while he works. He calls down from his perch and says, "I was thinking last night, sitting around with the kids here, about what's important. I mean to those kids. To you." He pauses, looks down at Chris, and asks, "Could you say really?"

Chris is holding a hacksaw. The handle is made of wood and it's smooth. He knocks the hacksaw against the ladder and says, "I dunno."

"I figure it's feeling good," Johnny says. He climbs down, takes the saw, and cuts the PCV pipe to length. There is a slight smell of burning plastic. "Or fitting in. Or sex, maybe." Johnny looks at Chris and lifts an eyebrow. This is an invitation to speak, or confess, or share.

Chris doesn't answer. He wonders if Johnny masturbates.

Johnny is back on the ladder, sliding the pipe up through the hole in the ceiling. The pipe gets stuck. He sends Chris up into the attic to grab the pipe as it passes through. The attic is dark and stale. Chris takes care not to walk on the tiles; "Step on the trusses," Johnny warned.

Chris finds the pipe and pushes it up until it touches the planking of the roof. Shingle nails poke through and tear at his hands. Johnny's voice rises through the pipe, telling him to come down. Chris can hear another voice now, a girl's, talking to Johnny. When he comes down later, sweaty, his eyes itchy from the insulation, he sees Allison Dueck. She's holding a can of Pepsi and she's spinning around on an old piano stool, telling Johnny about her mother.

"She's got all these kids, see? Seven now, and I'm supposed to be the oldest. I am, that's true, but that doesn't mean I have to do everything for her. She's always pregnant. I don't even know what she looks like skinny." Allison sips her drink, sees Chris, and says, "Hi."

Chris nods. Rubs the itch with the back of his hand. He knows Allison; they're in the same class. She's sort of like Melody; feel-good. Only, Allison is run-down, poorer than Melody, and so doesn't have that same smooth disdain Melody has. Still, she's all right. She likes Johnny, that's obvious.

Allison wants to work. Johnny suggests she hold the drywall while Chris sets the screws. So they work together for about an hour, lifting the awkward sheets and hushing them against the studs. While Allison plants her back to the wall Chris fumbles with the gun and seeds the floor with screws, succeeding finally in setting the one screw which will hold the sheet.

Allison and Chris don't really talk, but Chris likes working with her; she has a nice rhythm, and when they face each other across a sheet of drywall, the tendons in her forearms stretch and Chris thinks of lying with her in the sun on a beach somewhere. One time she asks to try the gun, so Chris hands her the dark blue drill and it rests heavily in her small hand. He holds her elbow and helps her aim. Her mouth goes tight and thin and the drill zips and stops. "There," Chris says. "No problem."

Allison does a few more on her own, and Chris stands back and wipes at his damp hair. He watches Allison's elbows. Something safe about this girl, he thinks. Lighter than Melody, in a way. The week before in English class Allison had an unfinished assignment and so had to memorize a poem and recite it before the class. Chris doesn't remember the poem or the author, but he can recollect a phrase and he remembers this only because of the way Allison's hand went up and out as she spoke.

Chris says these words now, "witches' broth," watching the back of Allison's head. Allison groans and turns and says, "Oh, Jesus. And my mother thinks it's so neat because Frost is her favourite poet. I wonder if he wrote about babies?"

Chris goes, "Ha."

Then Johnny needs help with the tank on the toilet, so Chris does this. Allison goes to the front room; she's given up on drywalling. She is knocking pool balls around. Chris can hear the occasional scratch of chalk on the cue tip. He wonders what Allison's breasts look like.

Melody calls. She's got something to say, but not over the phone. "There's a party at the river tonight," she says. "Can I pick you up?"

"Sure," Chris says, though he's wondering if his mother will be alone tonight. It's still a while to her due date but Chris worries about her. He doesn't tell Melody this.

Driving out to the river, Chris sits in the passenger's seat and watches Melody's hands hold the wheel. Her knuckles are boxy, fingers square, nails chewed. Chris likes this. Her wrists are thin and her forearms have a light almost bluish covering of hair, as if an artist had shaded in the growth.

It's a cool night; Chris is wearing a warmer jacket, Melody has on this down vest and a flannel shirt, sleeves rolled up. Chris reaches out and touches Melody's elbow. Then takes her hand and holds it. They don't talk. He doesn't ask her what she has to say. He'll wait. She's far away tonight, pouty, maybe angry. She does what she does. Chris follows.

Melody slips a joint from the glove compartment and hands it to Chris. He lights it, draws, and gives it to Melody. Her fingers reach out and she takes her turn. The dim light from the dash makes her face ghostly.

Before they get out of the car Melody decides she wants to kiss. Chris slides his tongue over the roof of this girl's mouth, then down along her bottom gum. She smells good tonight. Like lilacs. He touches her vest, looking for what he loves. She grinds her lips on his and comes up wet, eyes shining. He waits. When she says, "Let's go," he opens the door.

Everybody's talking. Nobody's talking. Gary Wohlgemut, the oldest one present, brings the beer. He's nineteen but still hangs around at the centre and tries to squirm into the action. He's socially retarded. Nobody really likes him. He tries to date younger girls.

Walker, one of Chris's friends, raises a beer and says, "Hey."

"Hey," comes an echo.

Melody's sitting between Chris's legs. She's got her head against his chest. She's quiet and her eyes are closed. At one point she whispers, "I think I just saw someone holy walking through this big white door."

"You sad?" Chris asks. It's darker now and the wind has picked up. Sparks jump out at the group. Melody opens her eyes. Chris can see the whites and the flame from the fire reflected in them. She doesn't speak, just looks up at him while the chatter revolves around them. He takes his jacket, covers her, and slides his hands underneath and seeks out the warmth of her belly. She doesn't mind.

Then Wohlgemut says he wants to swim and he has his clothes off and he's standing there naked by the fire. He's a man, Chris can see that now, and it's frightening in a way. A lot of hair. Is that what girls like? Wohlgemut goes down to the riverbank and there's a splash and a shout from the group. Chris doesn't move, neither does Melody. Someone yells that he's gone and then there's another shout, something about the other side.

"If he hits the Red, he's finished," comes a voice.

Footsteps running across the bridge. Laughter. Shouts. The noise of trees breaking. Bushes. "Here he is."

"Fuck, you're stupid."

Melody and Chris move under the bridge, up against the cement supporting wall and out of the wind. They huddle there and Chris puts his mouth on Melody's but her teeth are chattering and they knock his. This is a bad sign, Chris thinks, and he is confused; he senses he may be losing Melody Krahn.

Finally, after listening to the scramble and flurry of Gary Wohlgemut being pulled out of the water, Melody says, "Your mom. Did she want that baby?"

"Yeah, I think so."

"I mean, did she say to herself beforehand, I'm gonna lie with Johnny Fehr and we're gonna have a baby?"

Chris laughs, "Lie with Johnny, that's great."

"What's so funny?"

"Huh? Sorry. Jesus, Melody."

Melody pushes away from Chris's lap and hugs her knees. "It's the grass maybe. I'm blue." Together they watch Gary Wohlgemut pull on his clothes near the fire. His body is shaking and he's hopping on one foot, then the other. He's talking, and kids are actually listening.

"What a hero," Chris says.

"*We* lie together," Melody says.

Chris looks at her but can only see the back of her head. Her hair is long and has a bit of a wave. If he runs his fingers through it he comes up with strands that twist and float and fall to the ground.

"I'm not saying anything," Melody continues. "It's more like *What if?* and *Now what?*"

"You're scaring me," Chris says. And it's true, there's a pain in him that only Melody can produce. Like she has this long spike and whenever she likes she drives it through Chris's palm, or foot, or gut.

"Sorry."

She doesn't mean it. Doesn't care. She laughs and says, turning to him, offering shadows and her too-sweet breath, "Wouldn't that be fun, lying with someone who's fat and big like your mother?"

Yes, Chris wants to say, *it is lovely.* Melody can't know that though. It's impossible. He doesn't understand. "I like you, Melody," he says.

A quick toss of her head. Perhaps disgust for him. Impatience. "Little boy," she says, and gets up and goes over to the fire.

Later, he follows and sits across from her and, through the flames, watches her drink and drink and then she's beside Gary and holding on to him, fool, and by the end of the evening she's in his lap and at one point she looks across the fire and smiles at Chris and his heart leaps. He smiles back.

And then Walker brings up forms of torture. "There's this one," he says, "called the skull crusher. An iron cap is fastened onto the head by a metal chin strap. As it tightens the teeth are forced right out of the jaw."

Someone laughs.

"Pol Pot," he continues, "killed the educated. People with glasses, teachers, intellectuals."

"Who the fuck was he?"

"I guess that'd make you dead, hey, Walker?"

"I'll take that as a compliment," Walker says. "There was this guy in France who had his tongue pierced and attached to his cheek with an iron pin. Then he was burned alive."

Chris is listening to all of this and watching Melody. Wohlgemut has pulled her in really close. His mouth is on her neck and she's not resisting. Her eyes are closed.

"Or," Walker says, "ram a glass rod up a guy's penis and then break it into small pieces."

"What, the penis?"

"No, dildo, the glass."

"Water torture," someone offers. "Funnel water down the throat and almost drown the guy. Let him come up for air and then hit him again."

"Use boiling water."

"You're sick," one of the girls says.

"The mind," Walker continues. "That would be the worst. To have someone play with your mind."

Wohlgemut's trying to touch Melody's breasts. It's so obvious. She's not really stopping him but Chris has figured out by now that she's drunk and dazed. He sees that he will have to save Melody. It is only right. And so later, as the crowd disperses and Gary pulls Melody towards his car, Chris intercepts them.

"Whaddya want, tiny boy?" Melody giggles. She wavers, teeters towards Gary who wraps an arm around her and pulls her in. Gary is not terribly confident and Chris realizes this. In fact, the older boy seems dizzy with all this attention tonight and is probably already planning another cold swim at the next party. It was just last year that Roger Emery attacked Gary Wohlgemut. Pulled him from his car and pummelled him, left him mangled, his face battered, body propped against the curb. Gary's father, manager of the Credit Union, had the police charge Roger, who scoffed and claimed he had every right to beat on any guy who lusted after his ass. And so, Chris, remembering this, looks up at the older boy.

"She's gotta get her dad's car home," he says. "She's late. Come here, Melody."

Gary hesitates. He has a dumb way of staring.

"Come," Chris says and takes Melody's arm. This touch seems to awaken something at Melody's core, a brief flicker of light, and she falls towards him. But just as quickly the light dims and she pushes him away.

"Groovy," she says.

"I'll take her," Gary says.

"Fuck you," Chris says. "Just fuck off." He would like to hit the faggot. Mush his face.

Gary moves off. Melody has her head on Chris's shoulder. He can't hold her much longer. She's a dead animal in his arms. "Come with me," Chris whispers.

Melody chirps as he drags her to the car and lays her in the passenger's seat. He drives her home, stopping once to allow her to throw up on the side of the road. He pulls into the Krahns' driveway, headlights out, and wakes Melody.

"Quietly," he says, "quietly."

He deposits her inside the front door. Hands her the car key. She clutches at him. Noses his neck. "Fuck," she says, too loudly. Then, "Something. Something to tell you." Chris pushes away, listening for the wrath of Mr. Krahn. The house is a tomb. Chris covers her mouth; her tongue pushes against his palm.

"Not now," he whispers. His lips are on her ear. He wishes her good luck and kisses her, catching a whiff of vomit as she stabs at him with her head. Then he is gone. And he runs. Through the south end of town, past the Mennonite church, up towards Main Street and past the centre and Chuck's, and out of town past OK Feeds. It's quiet, there are no vehicles. No people. The world is a deserted and empty place. Just Chris and the moon. And then he's out on the highway walking along the shoulder and he feels awfully big. And small. He slows down and walks the five miles to his house.

On the gravel road a mile from home he stops to pee. Finished, he looks up at the sky and shouts, "I love Melody Krahn." He says this again and then keeps walking. He reaches the house just as the sky is lightening at the edges. He looks into his mother's room. She is sleeping, her left arm thrown back against the pillow. He tiptoes in and stands over her. Her fingers jump. In the dark like this, she looks foreign, Mexican maybe. He leaves her and climbs the stairs to his own small room. As he undresses he looks out of his bedroom window and sees Johnny trudging across the yard to the house. Chris crawls into bed. Before he falls asleep he pictures himself being roasted on a huge spit and, turning the spit, at either end, their elbows swinging in and out and in and out, are Melody and his mother.

BABIES

It is, to Johnny's mind, a perfect spring. Though the farmers complain of too little rain, Johnny likes the occasional cloudburst followed by days of endless sunshine, producing the gradual greening of the shrubs and grass and trees. The leaves appear slowly at first, little brilliant tongues that slip out of hiding and then quickly, violently, become full grown. The birds are wild, drunk, out of control. They twitter and chant and wake Johnny in the early morning with their clatter.

The world is pregnant. Everywhere Johnny goes he sees the possibility of birth. He is especially aware of pregnant women. He sees them on the streets of Lesser in various stages of development. Farmers' wives open their doors to his knocks and stand swollen and huge, fingers splayed over their abdomens, their faces round and full of promise. He talks to them first of feed, output, and prices, but in the end, the conversation comes back to babies and he lowers his voice, whispering of his own wife who is soon due. These are relative strangers, people from other places who don't know of the town of Lesser and its secrets.

"Yes, it's my first," Johnny says, and he smiles and endears himself by speaking of morning sickness and false labour and of Loraine, his lovely wife, who can no longer sleep on her stomach.

In the late afternoon of these spring days, he returns to Loraine and finds her at the kitchen sink, or in the egg room, or simply feet-up by the TV, and he kisses her cheek and brushes his hand like a feather across her belly.

She still comes to him at night, though not as frequently. The last few weeks she has not wanted him inside her. "It's a phase." she says, "I remember this with Chris, suddenly needing privacy, as if preparing myself for something that was all my own. I should warn you, this continues for at least six months after the birth."

Johnny mumbles something. He is nuzzling her rump, unable to get too worried; he can't think beyond tomorrow. And besides, there are other ways, like using her leg, or spilling himself into the crack of her bum, *here*, sliding himself along that tuck of flesh.

She pulls him up so they are nose to nose. While he touches her, a fumbling attempt to communicate his need, she speaks of breathing methods and how, this time, she would like to stand for the labour. "That midwife I met at Claire's. She suggested there was less work involved if you stand. Claire would have to hold me up though and I don't know if she's strong enough."

"You want me there, then?" Johnny asks. He is pleased. His hands have found her ears.

She smiles; a hair is stuck on her upper lip. One leg is thrown over Johnny's. His own belly touches her bigness; a circle of heat. "Yes," she says, "that would be nice, I think."

Johnny pulls the strand away. Curls it behind her ear. Kisses her lobe. "Thank you," he says. "I need to learn to breathe."

"I'll teach you," she says. "We'll practise. Starting tomorrow." Her arm jumps. She is sleeping.

But, tomorrow, a Friday, is not a day for breathing lessons. In the calm of the early evening it is revealed to Johnny that his life still teeters between light and shadow. In fact, he wonders if there are other people out there who shuttle between heaven and earth, never finding that comfortable and safe middle space. He questions too whether he has, in some way, more affection for darkness, for the coarse and obscene, represented so fittingly by the apricot-orange of Loraine's anus which, when seen from above, produces an ache in his chest: the sphincter drawn tight, the puckered kiss and his desire to return that kiss, holding all the while Loraine's tight fists as she shudders and drives against his face.

He is at the drop-in centre. Before he opens for the evening he goes to the back room and, leaning towards the rust-edged mirror that hangs over the tiny sink, flosses his teeth. He's thinking and humming to himself when he straightens. The back of his head itches. Someone is here. He turns, the floss still twisted around his fingers, and discovers Melody Krahn standing in the doorway. She's leaning against the jamb. Her hair is wet at the edges as if she's just showered. Her fingers worry at a wooden beaded necklace.

Johnny's working with his tongue at a stubborn piece of food. His cheek bulges and he is comically aware that he could be an animal in a zoo and Melody the keeper. Her eyes are sharp tonight, as if she had just walked beneath a fall of light and soaked up the brilliance there. Her hands fall to her sides. Johnny turns, rinses his mouth, and swivels back. "Hi," he says.

"Hi." She walks over to a chair and sits. She crosses her legs. It has been an unusually warm day and she's wearing jean shorts; the frayed ends lie on her thighs. She swings a foot and looks right at Johnny.

"I gotta ask you for a favour," she says. Her voice is sure and clear, almost too determined, as if she were acting, projecting to an audience.

Johnny notes for the first time that her hands are shaking. He pulls up his own chair; close enough to maintain intimacy, far enough away for decorum. He'd have to stretch slightly to touch her shiny, bare, and rounded knee. "Okay," he says.

"I'm pregnant," she says, and her hand flicks up to her throat and drops back to her lap.

Johnny waits. He looks into her eyes because this is the easiest; there's a safety in their polish. They are marbles sitting in the sun. He waits some more.

"What I want, see, is an abortion and you can help me," Melody says. She tips her tongue at her teeth and continues before Johnny can interrupt. "I've gotta go across to the States, Fargo. Winnipeg's too close, I want the distance. Also, you'd have to be my father."

"Your father?"

"Yeah."

"Huh." Johnny snorts out through his nose. This girl is amazing. She's evoking all kinds of emotion in Johnny. He's feeling fiercely protective. He pities her, considers her stupid for getting pregnant, admires her bravado no matter how false it is. She reminds him of Loraine; in the way Loraine juts out her little breasts and says, "So." Johnny, try as he might to fight it, finds Melody's swinging foot provocative. He clears his throat. Finally breaks this long gaze he's held with Melody and says, "You're asking the wrong person."

"No, I'm not."

"Do your parents know?"

Melody presses a finger down on her bare thigh so that it leaves a white mark. "Of course not."

Johnny's shaking his head. "I can't do that," he says.

Melody's chin jerks up and then down. She licks her lips and looks around the room. "Okay, fine," she says. She stands and turns. The hard edge of the chair has left red creases on the backs of her thighs.

"Wait," Johnny says. "Sit."

Melody turns and the lift of her chubby bell-shaped upper lip tells Johnny that she thinks she has won. He is so easily taken, he thinks.

"Why me?" he asks, implying that there are others more likely than him: the school counsellor, Melody's older sister, even Loraine. But even as he asks this he knows what the answer should be. He is, despite his penchant for a grasping faith and a desire to appear clean, a wanderer, a tumble weed who sticks to no one and no thing. He is easy; a likable and gullible fool.

"You're so moral," Melody says. This is unexpected and Johnny wants to laugh. Instead, he says, "Really?"

Melody is sincere. She has her hand on his leg. With this touch she has claimed him and he senses how perverse her perception is, because her square fingers with the boxy black nails both beckon and warn. He wants to gather her in his arms; she is a fallen bird, one wing broken, mouth open in a silent squawk. He could so easily reach out and palm her tummy. He pulls back.

"How many weeks?" he asks.

Melody removes her hand and says, "Ten."

"So?"

"So, we'd have to go next week."

"Don't you, like, I mean, isn't any sort of counselling required?"

"No."

"That easy?"

"Yes."

"And no one else knows?"

"Only Carrie Klassen. I would be over at her house for a sleep-over. You know. That night."

Again, Johnny is amazed by the efficiency of all this, as if he'd been picked long ago, in another life perhaps, to play a role in this young girl's preordained drama.

"And Chris?"

"Not a clue."

"Why not?"

"He's a little boy."

Johnny sees how males are essentially useless. Dicks that rise and fall. "You could give the baby up," he says.

"Neat," Melody answers. Her eyes tell him this is a stupid suggestion. In this way, too, Melody is surprising. In Johnny's limited experience with pregnant teenage girls, the majority want to have their babies and keep them. This little girl's cold calculating heart is frightening.

Johnny decides to hit her where it hurts. "And money? It'll cost."

This works, because now Melody is quiet. A slight drop of her head, and then a coy touch on his knee. Slut, he thinks.

"Could you make me a loan?" she asks.

"How much?"

"Five hundred. I'll work it off."

Johnny doesn't answer. He's thinking how easily Loraine got pregnant. She simply had to nod her head at him and think about it. The expanding belly then became a force of sorts, pushing him away from Charlene. It was true, Charlene knew it too.

"You can have the money," Johnny says. And then he tells her to go, and after she has left he washes his face with cold water and holds the towel against his eyes for a long time and takes comfort in the darkness there.

Johnny's life is not his own. There are forces greater than himself that pull him to and fro. He is wind-tossed, driven by the gusts of desire and greed and needs of others. And he accepts this. In one of his dreams Melody appears to take his hand and guide him through a maze whose walls he takes for the inside of a hive. Melody's voice is low and calm, her fingers on his palm are clever and insistent. She refuses to let him go. She has sprouted wings and he can see through the webbed gossamer to the backs of her arms which are white and smooth. Her body is immature, perhaps underdeveloped, lacking a spine. She undulates as she walks. As they near the centre of the maze Melody turns to Johnny and smiles. Like a newborn infant, she has no teeth.

Johnny believes that messages are sent through dreams. He wakes and imagines Melody as a harmless bumblebee on the verge of splattering herself against a car's windshield. He lies in the dusty morning light of his little room. The window is open; birds are busy.

Over breakfast he considers telling Loraine. He watches her slide into her seat, her hair unwashed, her housecoat tied tightly around the bulge that is his child. She has grown to enormous proportions in just the last week. Her mood is protective. These days she ignores Johnny and Chris, pays them the same attention she would one of her chickens. Even though it is still three weeks to her due date, her body seems ripe, ready to burst. Johnny butters an English muffin and says that last night was a good one at the centre.

"Hmm," says Loraine.

"Chris was there, Melody too. Last weekend the kids had a party. Gary Wohlgemut went swimming in the river. Fool. Could've drowned. I don't know why he still hangs out with the younger kids."

"That was the night Chris got in at six?" Loraine asks.

"Yeah." Johnny's remembering last night. Watching Melody and how she was with Chris. She'd been distracted. Sat with Chris and then moved away. She was a cat on the prowl. Went out for a smoke and then came back in and rubbed up against the boy. Then back outside. She and Chris had left together at some point, Johnny hadn't noticed until later, and then he asked and some kid said they'd gone to Melody's.

He'd waited for her to come back, his thoughts returning to the up-and-down measure of her bare leg. It was like a deep and unsatisfactory affection for this girl who wanted to turn his world upside-down. By midnight, when the centre was cleared and Melody hadn't returned, he'd made up his mind. But, this morning, after the dream and then suffering the brooding of Loraine, Johnny understands what will happen.

He holds his coffee and says to Loraine, "Next week sometime, I have quite a few customers out near Sprague and beyond. I'll probably try to fit it all into a couple of days. Stay overnight somewhere. Maybe sleep in the car."

Loraine's eyelids are puffy. Her fingers chubbier. At this moment her thumb is pressing down on her bare calf. She's looking for water retention. She seems unconcerned by Johnny's intentions. They have a back-up plan, Mrs. Godwin, the neighbour, if Johnny's not around. "Okay," she says, whispering it would seem, to her leg.

Johnny experiences a small lift of jealousy. He has become a familiar and unimportant object at the edge of Loraine's life. She is lost in her own rapture. So be it, he thinks.

Which is perhaps why, when Michael Barry calls late Saturday night and asks Johnny if he wants to go baiting bear early next morning, he says yes. Michael picks Johnny up at six in the morning. Johnny's arranged for Chris to gather eggs today as Loraine's ankles are swollen. It's a warm morning and Johnny, dressed in work boots, jeans, a T-shirt, and plaid jacket, sits on the front steps, drinks coffee and smokes. Loraine is still sleeping; he listened for her but the house was silent, so he left a note on the kitchen counter.

Michael drives up in an old Fairlane station wagon. He's pulling a trailer with an ATV. He hops from the car, rubs his hands together and says, "Let's go."

Driving down through Steinbach and La Broquerie and into the Sandilands Provincial Park, Michael talks. He recalls last year's baiting. "A bear came after me," he says. "Right up the tree, mouth frothing, claws scrabbling. I fired a shot into the air and she stopped and slid back down and bulked off down her path. They all have their own path. They're scrupulous about stepping on the same track in the same way. A bear will approach the bait, sniff, go up on her haunches, swivel, and retrace her exact tracks."

"You say *she*," Johnny says. "You shoot females?"

"No. If I see cubs, I don't shoot. In fact, these last years I haven't shot anything. I seem to be going soft. I get a kick out of chaining myself high in a tree and just waiting and watching. It's wonderful to observe the approach. The delicate swagger, the nose high up. God, they have lovely noses, what an instrument." Unconsciously, Michael lifts his own nose and seems to sniff the air. "I hunt with a bow these days," he says. "It's a bigger challenge. More humane too. Shoot a bear with an arrow it'll run twenty yards and drop dead. Shoot that same bear in the same spot with a .308 and it'll run one to two hundred yards."

Johnny feels obliged to ask why. Michael is excited. He's pulling at his beard, shifting his chin down towards his chest as if focusing on a distant target. He answers, "You see, a .308 shell stops inside the bear somewhere, messes things up horribly, but doesn't kill immediately. An arrow, on the other hand, goes right through. Zip. The bear bleeds to death, just like that." Michael smacks his hands.

They're deep into the park now and the road is lined with pine and birch and poplar. The car picks up stones from the gravel road and knocks them off the wheel wells. Michael points at a skunk beside the road. They see a buck with big eyes at the edge of the forest. Its head kicks up at the sound of the car and then he's gone.

Michael was here last week and he takes a familiar sandy side road, a trail with two narrow tracks, up to the edge of a gully where he stops and says, "We'll go by ATV from here, I've got a series of sites about three miles further on. There's bog and all kinds of shit we'll have to wade through."

They off-load the ATV and an hour of rough driving takes them to the first baiting site where Michael builds a fire and fires up some bacon. Johnny sucks on a rasher. He's leaning against a stump, looking up at the sky, listening to the fire and the ticking of the small engine as it cools.

Michael takes an old sock from a bag and throws it in the frying pan. He stirs it, soaks up the grease, drops a good-sized stone down the opening of the sock, ties a long rope to the sock, and heaves the whole bundle at a fairly tallish tree in the clearing. Holding one end of the rope he drags the greasy sock through the limbs of the tree and finally leaves it dangling, halfway up.

Johnny watches from his stump. All this fooling around with nature strikes him as phoney, as if creation were a toy to be banged about.

Michael toes the ground. "In a week," he says, "if a bear finds this place, we'll come back and those drippings from the sock will have soaked the ground, and the bear will have ripped a four-foot hole in the earth. It's a fact." He looks up at the sock as if it's a beautiful and intricate invention.

"Where do you get all this stuff from?" Johnny asks. He's feeling slightly sleepy, slightly curious, locked in this sunny spot here in the middle of the woods.

"You pick it up." Michael sits down close to Johnny. He asks for a cigarette and Johnny gives him one. "Like how to hunt for moose. When you come across a trail, head downwind. The thing is with a moose, he'll loop back and come around like he's making a U, so you don't follow his trail, you cut across to meet him, knowing he's going to circle with the wind. The last thing to know, and this is the most important, is that if he senses you he'll spook. And when he spooks he'll run for one to two hundred yards and then stop to piss. So you have to run like hell and catch him as he's pissing, because once he's started he can't just cut if off. You could walk right up and kiss him."

Johnny is searching out the sense of this. "You shoot him while he's pissing," he says.

"Yeah."

"Huh. You've done this?"

"No. Just seen it."

They sit for a while longer. Johnny thinks maybe he dozes because when he opens his eyes Michael is stroking his bow, sliding his hairy hands over the cord and wheels and risers. Johnny sees it as a dirty instrument, hard and dangerous. Michael obviously adores the weapon. He polishes the shaft, fits an arrow in the rest. Draws. If Michael turned slightly, he could pass the arrow through Johnny's chest. A bizarre thought, Johnny thinks, but he waits and watches, breathing slowly. He has to pee. Michael finally stores the bow back in its black kit and Johnny opens his eyes and yawns.

They eat salami sandwiches as they bump and jolt to the next site. Arriving, they scatter donuts and Frosted Flakes. It is late afternoon by the time they retrieve the car and load up the ATV. Driving later, the wind filling his eyes, Michael calls out to Johnny, "How's the baby? Loraine, I mean."

"Okay," Johnny says. He'd forgotten her the last few hours. Forgotten, too, Melody, and the trip south he will be taking. He looks over at Michael who is pulling on an Orange Crush. When he lowers the can to his thigh, his upper lip has an orange rim that makes him look comical, more approachable. "Babies," Johnny says, and then he asks, "You ever wanted one?"

"How do you know I haven't got one?" Michael laughs. "Or more?"

Johnny laughs, waiting, but that's all the other man offers.

"I've been thinking about things," Johnny says. "About this war that goes on inside of everyone."

"Does it?" Michael asks.

"Yeah, take Lesser for instance. You've lived there a year now and do you have any better idea than me, who is evil and who is good?"

"Everyone," Michael says. "It's a curious place, Lesser. There's this above-the-surface cordiality and kindness, like life is fine and good and clean, and evil is something others suffer from. I don't believe in evil, by the way, not in the Judeo-Christian sense. If there is such a thing, it constantly changes, I mean it evolves, in the same way our brains evolve. Neanderthals, who did not write Elizabethan sonnets, were also probably incapable of ingenious methods of torture."

Johnny is trying to work his head around the bullshit. He fans a hand at the air. "Whoa, there. You're saying this massacre, these beheadings taking place in Africa right now, are not evil?"

"Forget that," Michael says. "That's out there. What about Johnny Fehr? Is he bad?"

Johnny ponders. Nods his head. "Sure," he says. "Sometimes."

"Which means you're always looking for salvation."

"Yes."

"There's this theory which I find quite possible. Claims that Jesus was gay. You know, homosexual."

"Ahhh, piss off."

"No, seriously. I mean, why didn't the man have any women? Think of it, twelve disciples, all men. Thing is, this theory states — and this is based on good research — Jesus and Judas were lovers. And if you accept that, how much greater the betrayal?"

Johnny's smiling and cracking at his knuckles. "You're unbelievable."

"You people don't admit to other possibilities. Narrow little views of salvation. What if I were to say that seeking out redemption in itself is evil; this idea that the world revolves around me. You know, *my* salvation, *my* soul, *my* wish to live forever."

Johnny says, and believes this very strongly, "No, I don't want to live forever. It would tire me out. I fear death, yes, but I'd rather burn brightly. What I'm doing, when I dig around in these ideas of salvation, is thinking of myself, of course. But why not? You don't think about yourself?"

Michael doesn't answer directly. He says, "Nobody is free to become a Christian: one is not 'converted' to Christianity — one has to be sick enough for it."

Johnny chuckles. He doesn't quite grasp what Michael's getting at but he does feel, at his centre, this idea of sickness. He wants to say yes, but instead he laughs. Michael, encouraged by Johnny's response, taps at the steering wheel with the tips of his thick fingers and growls, "The rancour of the sick."

But Johnny is no longer chuckling. A thought has come to him like an offering from above; a brief pleasant memory of Loraine slipping into his arms in the middle of a cold December night and laying her wet mouth on his chest and telling him that he was good. Good. Johnny's body trills.

He stops listening to Michael and Michael, sensing this, becomes reflective and quiet. It is dark when they arrive back in Lesser. After the Fairlane rattles down the driveway and back onto the gravel road, Johnny stands in the middle of the yard and looks up at the sky. There's a bit of a wind coming in off the neighbour's field, bringing with it the smell of rain. Johnny listens to the wind. He closes his eyes, then opens them again. He stares up into the sky and waits.

Melody phones Johnny at work on Monday morning and says, "I've got an appointment for tomorrow night at eight. That means I could leave after school and be back at Carrie's house by just after midnight. It's up to you now." She pauses. Up to this point her voice has been matter-of-fact, almost too aggressive, but now she says, with a breathiness that reminds Johnny of her pudgy lips, "So?"

"Yes," Johnny says. As he speaks he experiences a dizziness that forces him to sift through his brain for a balance. Melody's voice rights him.

"It would be best to pick me up away from school. I'll be at the Tot-Lot on the south end of town. 'Bout four o'clock, okay?"

Johnny, after hanging up, is grateful for Melody's precautions. He himself, in his haste to get this done, would simply have risked picking her up at school. She's intelligent, this one, Johnny thinks. Almost too.

The next day, he finds her where she says she'd be. Crawling up in his Olds, Johnny sees her first. She's straddling a swing, rocking it side to side and kicking at the sand. She's wearing jeans and a thick green sweater and big black boots. An overnight bag squats at her feet. The park is empty save for two other kids. They're about eight or nine, wrapped up in a game by the climbing structure. Johnny, not wanting to attract attention, waits till Melody sees him, and when she does she's off the swing and clutching her bag and walking towards him. She almost runs; not quite.

Johnny leans back and watches. Her youth is a perfect disguise for what she's about to embark on. Melody settles into the smoothness of the car; she sighs and slides low.

The leather seat squeaks.

"Don't worry," Johnny says, "the windows are tinted." He drives up the 75 through Morris and keeps going directly to the border. The fields are brimming with water and in some of these lakes there are geese and ducks foraging, or resting, or swimming in circles. It's a cool day, there's a possibility of rain. Johnny has the heat on, Melody's feet are tucked underneath her. The darkness of the swift clouds, the hum of the engine, the wheel in his palms, Melody beside him, all of this evokes in Johnny a sense of both comfort and approaching loss.

Just beyond Morris, Melody pulls out a joint and asks, "This okay?"

"Shit, Melody," Johnny says, "we're crossing an international border and you're carrying dope."

"It's my last," Melody says. "Should I toss it?" She's sly, because even as she says this, she lights up and adds, "It'll help me be brave."

Johnny watches the road and sniffs the air. His palms tingle.

"Here," Melody pokes the joint at his face.

"Aw, girl. You're corrupting me." He takes it, another tiny step down these stairs he's descending, and pulls twice, hard. He holds his breath, exhales into the glass of the windshield and says, his voice shifting to a whine, "You won't tell?"

"Uh-uh." Melody cozies herself into the seat. The two of them pass the joint back and forth like a popsicle two children must share. Johnny is surprised by the wetness at the tip, as if Melody's mouth were full of water, or she'd gathered her lips and kissed it. Loraine gives wet kisses. Even the simple goodbye ones.

"Do your folks know who you are?" Johnny asks.

"Huh? Waddya mean?"

"Like, do you hide everything from them?"

Melody's voice is low, hard to hear. "That's how we do it in our family. Keep our secrets. Don't make trouble. Like my mom at the supper table will say to my sister and me, 'There was this man I used to love, and then I met your father.' And my father, well, he'll sit there and say, 'No one is sinless.'"

"Do you like your father?"

"Does any teenage girl like her father?"

"A lot do, I would think. Yes. Lots." Johnny sees that Melody is, above all, unhappy.

"I feel sorry for him," she says. "Everyone thinks my mother is all beaten up and stuff like that, like under his thumb. No way. She's king-shit. At home. It's just around the town, in church, etc., etc., that she puts on this oh-I'm-so-pathetic look."

"You hate *her* then?"

"Do I?" Melody giggles.

Johnny smiles. Grunts with sudden contentment.

The border arrives quickly. Johnny opens the window to clear the odour, his head. He concentrates on this red flashing light beyond the windshield. He's got it then, *snap*, it's gone.

"Where'd you get that shit?" Johnny asks. He's swinging now.

Melody answers but Johnny doesn't attend. Her voice is a mosquito trying to land in his ear. He swats it away, readying himself for the border. "I hope it's busy," he mutters.

It isn't. The officer leaning into the window is older, trained to sniff out lies and fear. Johnny, close to the man's mouth, sees sharp teeth. Johnny jabbers, "My daughter and I are going to Fargo for a day. Do some shopping."

"It's evening," the man says.

"Yes?" Johnny waits, not quite getting it.

"You gonna stay overnight?"

"Sure, officer, yes."

The man leans in further, nostrils moving. "How old is your daughter?"

"Sixteen."

"Anything in the trunk? Firearms? Alcohol? Tobacco?"

"No sir."

"Fine." The teeth disappear and all Johnny can see now is a pudgy hand waving him on. He coaxes the Olds forward and regains the highway. "Let's not do that again," he says.

Melody asks for a cigarette. Her hands are shaking as she lights it.

"My father hated Americans," Johnny says. "No real reason, just found them contrary and pushy. He refused to cross the border."

Melody doesn't answer. She's staring out her window. She lights a second cigarette.

"You blaming anyone for this?" Johnny asks finally. Melody's abrupt silence worries him.

She doesn't answer. She concentrates on her cigarette, finishes, and flips her butt out the window. There's a gasp and a sucking noise as the glass slides down and up.

"No," she says finally. "No one." She hesitates and then adds, "It's just a fact. Nobody to blame."

"I drove Chris to school today," Johnny says. "He told me you'd stopped talking to him."

"What's to say?"

"Okay," Johnny answers.

It is only later, about an hour from Fargo, when they've stopped for a bathroom break and they're sitting at a counter drinking coffee and a Coke, that Melody appears to exhale the breath she's been holding for the last hour. She says, "Chris wouldn't understand. He wouldn't know what to say. I remember, it was months ago, when we were just getting to know each other, and I was gaga. He's so fine, I thought. But I don't need *fine* right now. You see?"

Johnny nods. It is odd to be labelled in this backhanded way. What does Melody see in him, he wonders.

They both smoke then. These shared times with cigarettes have become both intimate and illicit, a devoted few moments making them equals, both deftly touching their ash into a common dish, the tips glowing, the smoke they exhale mingling and drifting upward: the love they feel for this thin cylinder. Better than drugs, Johnny thinks.

Melody laughs, her first real sign of spunk in a while. She says, "Yesterday I was sitting in my room and this wasp came out of nowhere. Buzzed around like it was lost. Circled my head, landed on my window, went bang bang against the glass. Should've still been hibernating, I figure, if that's what wasps do, but somehow it got out of the hive and ended up in my room." She stops. Puts her finger against her nose.

Johnny reaches out and touches her head. Runs his hand down her hair and then pats her back.

Johnny doesn't know much about abortion. He has heard murmurings of a suction hose, like a miniature vacuum, yanking the fetus from the uterus wall. There is a pill you can take, he thinks, that aborts the baby. Scraping? He's not sure. He's never been terribly adamant one way or the other about abortion. He's not big into rights and issues, though he does figure a woman's got a right.

Johnny huddles in the waiting room of the clinic and reflects on the situation. Melody has already been ushered through the swinging door, on the arm of a crisp small black nurse with large calves. "My name's Laverna," she said, and offered Melody her hand. Johnny was ignored. He was a pariah of sorts, a dirty-deed man; necessary but filthy.

He wonders what they do with the fetuses. What they look like. If he feels any guilt, it has to do with the perception of other people. The people of Lesser. Inevitably, this escapade over the border will come to light and when it does both Melody and Johnny will suffer. Johnny especially, but that doesn't concern him. There's a fierce need in him to snub the zealots. In obvious ways the people of Lesser could ruin him, but he gives this little thought. He's still buzzing. Listening for the voice of Melody. Wondering if she'll cry out. He thinks he would have made an excellent soldier. Simply for the rush, the sense that death is close by, nipping behind him, not much to lose.

He steps outside and stands on the sidewalk and smokes. The clinic is located in a residential area, on the main floor of an older two-storey house with a wide outdoor porch. Everything about it is comforting. Like those hospices for AIDS patients Johnny saw on a documentary one night: cozy rooms in a homey atmosphere. Like coming home to Mom's to die — or lose your baby. Perhaps we need to lie to ourselves, hide our garbage, our deaths, our sicknesses, Johnny surmises. He dislikes the falseness of it yet allows that he too finds solace in the belly of the building he has just exited.

In the car, driving through the middle of Grand Forks, Johnny had handed Melody the money. Five bills. Hundreds. A thin sheaf that she quickly pocketed, sliding her hand into the narrowness of her jeans pocket, lifting a hip with a slight pelvic thrust that Johnny registered in the recesses of his mind, the sexual synapses back there lying dormant, repressed, activating and making his tongue burn. She didn't say thank you. Didn't respond. Just took his money.

Across the street from the abortion clinic is a little restaurant with a patio bar. Johnny crosses over and picks a spot where he can observe the entrance of the clinic. He checks his watch. It's been almost two hours.

He is served by a young girl who looks slightly older than Melody. In many ways she is very much like Melody. She chatters to Johnny, about the menu, where he's from — she knows he's Canadian by the accent.

"Don't get many of you down here these days. The exchange rate's lousy," she says. "You here on business?"

"Yup," Johnny answers. "Feed. Grain." He orders Sangria and sips slowly, sucking on the ice. He smokes Camels and savours their bite.

Then Melody appears, stepping gingerly out onto the cobbled sidewalk, reaching down a toe off the sill as if testing the water in a swimming pool. She stands in the evening shade of a huge elm, her arms hugging her purse, her head shifting slowly, hunting down Johnny. He stands and waves. Calls her over. She sees him and lifts her hand. Drops it. She walks towards him and Johnny assumes that she is a little dismayed, moved by the simplicity of the act she has had performed on her. If he were a woman, he would stand and hold her. But as it is he takes her elbow, helps her sit and says, "You okay?"

"Yeah." She laughs weakly. Asks for a cigarette. She avoids him. Eyes everywhere but on his. "I'm hungry," she says. Her face is pale.

"Wanna eat here?" Johnny asks. "Someplace else?"

Melody gives a mock shudder. "Not across from there," she says and throws a hand carelessly backwards over her shoulder, at the place she's just left. After Johnny pays for his barely touched drink, they drive out past strip malls and gas bars and pull in at a Pizza Hut where Melody bows before a large Pepperoni and a jug of Pepsi.

After she's eaten her mood becomes euphoric. Hands flit like little angel wings at her shoulders. She chatters, allowing him now to see her black pupils, round islands surrounded by blue.

"The doctor was a woman," she says. "She was nice. Her hands were warm. Her gloves, I should say. She gave me a local, froze me down there. It's tickling right now, kinda like the dentist and getting your feeling back in your gums. Anyways, it didn't hurt. The doctor explained exactly what she was doing. 'I'm going to use this instrument here,' she said, 'It's called a vacurette.' And she showed me this tiny piece of white plastic like a miniature vacuum nozzle, the kind you use for hard-to-get places, you know?"

Johnny nods. It is strange to have these intimacies explained to him. She's just blabbing. In fact, the Pizza Hut waitress with her little eyebrow ring would do just as fine.

Melody natters, "Anyway, I didn't feel it. 'We have to dilate you slightly,' the doctor says. 'Dilate?' I ask. 'Open you up,' she answers, and all I could think of was going fishing with my father and prying open the fish's mouth to find the hook. Still, it didn't hurt. The oddest thing though was feeling it wasn't me. Kinda like it was someone else lying there, not Melody Krahn. *That* was creepy."

"You still feel that way?" Johnny asks.

"No. This is me." And she slithers another piece of pizza onto her plate and burps loudly.

Johnny doesn't know if it's the grass she smoked still seeping around in her brain, or the anesthetic, or just the relief, but Melody appears to want to show her gratitude because she says, "Thank you, Johnny," several times and touches his hand, his forearm, leaving tiny cool spots there.

Melody, when she's finished her meal, says, "You're going to be a father soon, aren't you?"

Johnny runs an eye down Melody's nose, past her belled mouth, her chin, along the veins of her throat, the bones at her collar, to her breasts which are small and hidden by the mass of her sweater. "Three weeks," he says, and he remembers as a child, the feel of a wishbone in his fingers, not quite dried, springy like this girl's body.

Since he left Lesser with Melody at his side he's experienced a sense of freedom and risk. His life lately has been encircled by work and eggs and Loraine and the centre. This wonder he has been feeling with Melody — a breathless, wrong-headed, and lovely need to run — has been absent from his life. He is relieved that Melody is not blubbering and all broken up. That could have been awful, a scene full of panic and accusations. Instead she sits, her thin wrists crossed, her chin brave. The two of them could be anywhere, be anybody. Up to this point Melody has been like a lover. In the dark and unacknowledged corners of Johnny's mind, it is as if Melody has cornered him, touched his chin with a fingertip, and whispered in his ear, *Come here, Johnny.*

And so the mention of this inevitable baby is like a quick sharp tug, as if Johnny were a kite being hauled back into captivity. One side of his mouth goes up. "Funny," he says, and he points at Melody and then back at himself and the word comes out with an effeminate lilt, so that he has this image, seen through the eyes of Melody, of a man who is hiding his true identity. He laughs. Waits for Melody to join in. She doesn't.

"You wanted that baby?" she asks.

"Of course."

"And you're a Christian, right? Like, born again?"

"Many times."

"At what point does that become a joke?"

Johnny is solemn now. He cares deeply for this subject. "I'm beyond that," he says. "Really, Melody, I'm lost. I have no chances left."

There is, Johnny believes, a brief shadow of fear in Melody's eyes. Her voice is hard though. "You're joking."

"Unfortunately, no."

"I'm confused, really. I've been raised on the shit you're talking about. It's a mind-fuck. I heard someone say once, and he was a lot older than me, that we have to stop looking outside ourselves for salvation. In fact, he cursed salvation. Called it fake. What we need is awareness, you see?"

"Sounds mystical," Johnny says. "Airy-fairy."

Melody takes a cigarette and sucks on it deeply, as if thinking that were she to let go it would disappear. Johnny is smitten by this girl's intelligence, her ability to argue, to speak. She's smooth: a beautiful girl full of doubt and cynicism who laughs, Ha, Ha, from deep in her throat and then lifts her eyebrows as if to ask, *Who laughed?*

"We should go," Johnny says. They do.

It's past eleven. The night is colder now. In the distance, across the prairie, an April storm is approaching.

"Smells like rain," Melody says, hand on the passenger door.

And then they're driving and Melody sleeps a bit, jumping awake at the border, then trying to sleep again but not succeeding. Melody and Johnny don't talk much. The barriers that fell away as they headed south are now fitting back into place as Lesser approaches. Johnny breathes with great difficulty. He whistles something, then stops. Melody finds an FM station and they listen together.

The lights of Winnipeg begin to glow. Johnny eats an Oh Henry: The King of Candyland, the wrapper says. He dislodges a peanut from his tooth and says, trying to crowd out the music, "Sweet Marie just doesn't match up to Oh Henry. This one's bigger, chewier."

Melody turns and stares at him. She is weary.

Johnny takes the St. Adolphe bridge, planning to circle back along the gravel roads, following the river and then up the 312 and into town. Through the back door. He is listless now, aware of a bitter taste in his mouth, left there by overexcitement, too many cigarettes, sexual fatigue. Crossing the river into St. Adolphe, the lights of the bridge slip by. Johnny looks over at Melody. She has her eyes closed. Her neck lies back against the leather headrest. She is frightfully young. A pain, like a sharp needle, passes through Johnny's temple and out his eye. He pulls at a fistful of hair, trying to relieve the smarting.

Close to town Johnny shuts off the air-conditioning and opens his window. The smell of Lesser, a mixture of diesel and grain, clover and rain, wet dust and a sour hint of garbage, floats into the car. Melody sits up, alert.

"To Carrie's," she says.

Johnny obeys. They sigh through a silent sleeping town. Carrie's house is located at the south end, in Lesser's only real suburb tucked away behind the high school. Johnny stops the car a block from the house. An upstairs light glows.

"That's Carrie's bedroom. I'm supposed to throw a rock at the window." Melody has the door open, one foot already on the street before she thinks of something and stops. She tosses her head. "Hey, Mr. Fehr. Thanks." She stretches across the seat and pecks Johnny on the cheek, her bottom lip the tiniest bit wet.

"Yeah, well . . ." Johnny begins, but she's gone. The car door slams and then there she is, outside, cutting across lawns, legs twinkling, a soft shadow slipping under the moon. Johnny imagines he can see her in the darkness along the edge of Carrie's house, though he is not sure. The side door finally opens. A strip of light. A figure slipping in. The door closes.

In the morning, after spending the rest of the night at the centre, Johnny eats breakfast at Chuck's. He arrives early and sits in a booth by himself. His head aches this morning. He should call Loraine but hasn't quite found the courage. He's not sure if he wants to rediscover her yet. He's poking at an egg when Eric Godwin, Loraine's neighbour, finds Johnny, points a finger at him, and bellows, "You little son of a bitch you. Hok-ey. Goddamn. Congratulations."

Johnny studies the grinning fool.

Godwin's voice gets louder. "What? Where've you been? Out all night? Wow. You're a father, Johnny Fehr. Wife tells me it was a girl. Blue eyes. Everything's great. Good God, man. Home with you."

But Godwin needn't have offered this advice. Johnny's already out the door. He's gone, his Olds a black arrow carrying him back to the nest he left a day earlier, out on a mission that would eventually bring him, sullied and older, back to the bedside of Loraine, his lover, the mother of his child. And when he arrives, Loraine smiles a radiant and tired smile, lofty, and holds out the little prune for Johnny to see. "Here," she says. "Ours."

And Johnny takes that infant, and he weeps.

IN

On the May long weekend Loraine asks Johnny if he wants to move in. He's sitting at the kitchen table, gnawing at a rib of celery. Loraine's spinning her lettuce in the clothes washer; a tip she got from a cookbook: *If salad greens are wet and you need them right away, place in a clean pillowcase and spin dry on gentle cycle in your automatic washing machine for a few seconds. This hint is especially good to know if you are serving salad to a large crowd!* Johnny, Chris, and her, not a large crowd but the idea appeals to Loraine.

Johnny's hard to read. He doesn't speak, just nods. Strange, how the thrill of being near this man still touches at Loraine, like a warm breeze across the skin.

"I talked with Chris and he didn't seem to be against it," Loraine says. "He's preoccupied these days. Melody still."

"A woman'll do that," Johnny says.

Loraine swivels, hands on hips. "A woman'll do that," she mimics. She stops and for some reason remembers the morning after the birth. She asks, "You still mine?"

Johnny snorts, touches his ear, "Naww," he says. He stands and backs her into him so Loraine can feel his belt buckle, the metal pressing through her shirt. He touches the flab on her belly.

"Fat," Loraine says.

"Ummm."

"You'll get less sleep, you know, sleeping with me." She senses a certain direction in his thoughts and corrects him. "Rebecca, she's up three, four times a night."

"Oh."

"So, you can fetch her. Bring her to me."

The baby's upstairs now. Sleeping. Really, her motivation for asking Johnny to move in is fear. She has felt, since the birth of Rebecca, a slipping away of this man, as if they all were on ice and playing Crack the Whip and Johnny was at the end, spinning wildly, going faster and faster. One of these days he's going to lose his grip and fly away. She wants him close. Wants to hold him, tie him up.

"Silly," he says now. "In the washer."

"But see," Loraine answers, holding up a leaf to his cheek, "perfect." She smells his neck and vows that one of these days he will hear all about the birth. She will tell him everything.

It was a Tuesday morning and Loraine was thinking that this was the day the baby would come. Not that she'd been experiencing any unusual movements or pain or spotting. The baby had been quiet for several days, pressing down on her pelvic floor.

Lying in bed, listening to Johnny leave — he didn't say goodbye to her which was surprising and disconcerting; even this lack of affection on his part struck Loraine as a sign — she thought she should call Claire just to make sure she stayed available that night. She didn't call though and by noon had dismissed the notion of an early birth. Still three weeks left. Don't be foolish, she cautioned herself.

Before supper she hung out in the barn with Chris. She counted flats and he delivered carts stacked with eggs. Chris was brooding, silent. Later, while they lifted flats and counted, Loraine tried to talk to him.

"How's school?"

"All right."

"Homework tonight?"

"Uh-uh."

"You still seeing Melody?"

Chris's eyes went up to the ceiling. He attempted indifference but his face fell apart. He pushed his chin into his far shoulder and hid. His crying was quick and hard, his neck moving like a dog who was bolting food.

Loraine didn't speak. Didn't touch him. She kept counting, lost track, then started again. She would have liked to wring her hands. Pat his shoulder. See, she said to herself, didn't I predict this?

She tried the obvious. "You broke up."

Chris's shoulders hunched and dropped. Loraine wanted to throttle Melody. Call her up right then, make her ears ring. Little princess.

"I don't know," Chris said. His face was less twisted now; a quick spurt of grief. He cradled an egg. "She won't talk to me."

"Won't? You tried talking to her?"

"Aw, Mom, forget it. Doesn't matter anyway. I'm only fifteen. It doesn't matter shit."

"Maybe she's pregnant."

"Yeah. Sure."

"It's happened."

"We don't sleep together any more."

"Really." Loraine was pleased. In fact, the idea that Chris would no longer spend time with Melody filled Loraine with hope. The girl was both sweet and cold, as if all that religion she'd suffered had split her heart in half: one side sunny, the other full of gloom. "Since when?" she asked.

Chris watched her, no answer. His look was curious. Sometimes when Loraine caught him staring like this at her she felt her son was far away, perhaps in another house across the way from hers, and he was staring with binoculars out a window, searching for her. She was uncomfortable then, acutely aware of her own body and of what she was wearing, of how she sat, and the way her chest rose as she breathed. Loraine shivered now, lifted a hand. Chris's eyes widened and dropped.

"You're young," Loraine said, heaving herself from the stool.

"That's what *I* just said," Chris responded. He turned away. Loraine, walking back to the house, wondered if it was possible for a son to lust after his mother. Funny thought. Sick.

Loraine's water broke in the kitchen. She was experiencing what she thought was a minor tightening of the uterus; a Braxton Hicks, she thought, they'd been playing with her all week. But then, with a whoosh, just as she was sinking her hands into hot water, a massive contraction clawed at her, forcing her elbows to the counter and wobbling her knees. She gasped, moaned, closed her eyes, and breathed through her mouth, fire dancing along the spine of her belly. Then, somewhere below her, there was a faint pop: a cupful of warm water had been poured between Loraine's thighs. "Oh shit," she said. She put her hand inside her panties, pulled it away wet, and eyed her fingers. The liquid was clear. "Good," she said. She straightened and looked at the clock. Seven. Chris was still in the barn.

Loraine panicked slightly, aware of how quickly she laboured, of her distance from the hospital. She resented — it was like a slight stitch in her side — Johnny's absence. And then as another contraction bent her earthward she understood that she would have this baby alone. Johnny would be off meandering the countryside, chatting it up with farmers and their wives, sipping tenderly at bitter coffee while she, Loraine, braced herself for the passage of their baby.

She moaned lightly, thinking how like the wind she sounded. Finally, at rest, she picked up the phone. The Godwins didn't answer. Loraine, breathing loudly, tried the neighbours further west, the Loepkys. No answer. She would have to call 911. Her body was folding back into itself. According to the clock the contractions were coming every three minutes. Too fast. Too furious. Through the kitchen window she could see Chris walking across the yard to the house. She closed her eyes, her cheeks expanded. Chris was behind her, standing in the doorway. "I'm having the baby." She was talking into her breasts.

"No," he said. "It's not time."

"I'm having it now," Loraine said. She checked the clock. "My water broke already," she announced. "I tried Mrs. Godwin and Mrs. Loepky. No answer. I'm going to go upstairs. You listen for me, meanwhile try to call Claire and tell her. Ask her if she can come here."

"Here?" Chris was circling Loraine, pulling at his fingers.

"I'm not driving anywhere," Loraine said. "St. Pierre, the closest, is too far." She lurched left, moaned, and lassoed her son's neck. She yanked him close and laid her face on his neck. One of her fists burrowed into and pulled at his hair. In the distance, like a dull echo, Loraine heard, "Mom, that hurts."

She leaned hard into Chris's body. He stumbled, then held her. "Like that," she said, and it was oddly comforting to smell the boy, to inhale him. She felt safe. Finally Loraine straightened and let out old air.

"I'm scaring you," she said.

Chris shook his head. Loraine left him by the phone and made her way up the stairs to the bedroom. She took off her clothes, methodically, ecstatically: blouse, sweatpants, bra, panties, socks. She went to the bathroom and stood there naked, muttering her way through another contraction. In the mirror, when she opened her eyes at one point, she observed the shape of her belly as it squeezed the baby downwards: the roundness disappeared and her stomach shuddered into a misshapen oval, like a rubber ball pressed between two large hands.

She ran a hot bath and sank into the water. Chris appeared at the door, hesitant, eyes slipping sideways towards the wall, saying that Claire was on her way. She would also call Dr. Pitt.

"Fine," Loraine murmured. "Get a pitcher, would you? Don't be shy."

The boy reappeared and Loraine, arms propped at the edge of the tub, advised him to pour bathwater over her stomach during the contractions. She had read about this in one of those books, about it making you relax.

"How do I know when?" he asked. He was kneeling beside the tub, head bowed.

"You'll know," Loraine gasped.

Chris dipped and poured, dipped and poured. Loraine dug her nails into his free wrist. "I wanna push," she said.

"Shouldn't you?" he asked.

"I don't know." She felt again with her hand on the other side of the hill and said, "I don't know if I'm fully dilated." She paused, wiped at her face with a washcloth, and said, "You're a brave boy, Chris. You'll help me do this, won't you?"

"Sure," Chris said. He was afraid.

Loraine, after several more hard contractions, wanted to exit the tub. "To the bed," she said, taking Chris's arm. Between the contractions, when the baby was like a sliver fluttering just above her body, she seemed clear-headed and hopeful. Her manner was even jokesy, as if she and Chris were lovers come together for an afternoon tryst.

"I'm sorry about all this," she said to Chris, tipping a hand at her body and then back at him. "I guess I should cover up but I can't stand the feel of cloth on my skin. Good education for you," she grinned, and the grin seared down into a grimace.

She attempted lying on her side on the bed. "This," she said, her mouth full of the rough grain of the bedspread, "is too uncomfortable." Next, she stood, her hands turned inward, pressing down onto the dresser. She directed Chris to stand behind and support her. "Your arms here," she said, and brought his biceps under her own arms and locked his hands at her chest, just above the gap between her breasts. He held her then and she groaned and ground downwards. For some reason, she wanted to be good at this, to be full of grace. This was a test, she thought, and if she passed, she would have a long and beautiful life. Her baby would be healthy. Johnny would stay with her.

Though Chris was not touching her now, she could sense him behind her. He carried on his body the odour of ten thousand chickens, of all those eggs. An egg had a scent which reminded Loraine of the bottom of a china teacup. Chris's fingers were smooth at the tips, the heels of his hands had minute ridges, so imperceptible as to be only discovered by microscope. To Loraine's mind, these ridges were like deep gouges. They pressed her skin, heightened her pain, distracted her. During the last flow she pushed Chris back so that he stumbled. Loraine fell to her hands and knees, the knot of her hanging low. She howled.

It was only later, perhaps the next morning, that she recalled that pushing-off moment as if Chris were land and she the boat. And she remembered too the texture of the rug like hot wax on her knees, her black panties crumpled on the floor, three holes — how odd, and, Oh, yes, she thought, for two legs and a waist. Mine. She saw, stuck in the matting of the rug just at the edge of the box spring, a toothpick, and remembered a time long ago when her husband still lived, and they had eaten pasta and salad on the bedroom floor and Jim chewed a toothpick and later they had made love on the rug, which was a novelty for Jim. Still, he said, he preferred the bed. Loraine, a week after the birth, thought of that toothpick and crawled over the floor looking for that shard of wood. But she did not find it.

Chris was hurt. He sat on the bed and observed his mother as she lifted her head and looked behind her. "I'm sorry," she said. She could say no more. Chris's feelings were unimportant now. "I'm going to start pushing," Loraine said. "You'll have to catch the baby."

Loraine knelt by the bed, her head on the mattress. She directed Chris to take up a position behind her. "Don't be frightened," she said again. "Look at me as a machine."

Chris nodded, all obedience. Loraine, during the next drawing together of her uterus, cried out as she sometimes did when she was with Johnny, only this cry was harder to understand; it grew from some place that she could not call her own and when she spit it out the walls shuddered and she cared not a bit that she was pouting her rear end at her son's face and bellowing at the ceiling.

The knot loosened. It always did. One of the women at Claire's party had suggested to Loraine, "When you're having this baby, imagine yourself floating on water, travelling from one place to another. See it as a passage."

Loraine couldn't quite manage this image. Instead, her body felt as if it were a tangle of rope that, in order to be freed, required a certain trick. She sensed that she had little say in this process. Her body was being turned inside out and she was flagging, weary.

She reached down between her legs and touched. She held her air and her head swelled. Chris called to her from the far shore. And then quickly the baby was born and with the tearing of her body Loraine sensed that she had both lost and found something. She looked back over her shoulder. Chris was holding the child as if it were a precious glass vase. Loraine pushed herself off the bed. Delicately, slowly, she lifted her left leg up and over the baby's head and lowered herself to the floor. She sat, legs spread, and, "Oh my," she said. "Oh my sweet sweet thing."

The purple baby offered a vacant O for a mouth and finally croaked and then wailed. "Look at her," Loraine whispered. "Are you cold, little girl? Oh my, Chris, it is a girl, isn't it?" A rooting then, mouth grasping, and then the first pull at her nipple.

Chris crouched beside his mother. Loraine became aware of her bare shoulders, the coolness of the room, her son at her side. She asked for a blanket and, later, she cried out several times before standing and delivering the placenta on her own, hating that part, the unrewarding pain.

Perhaps she slept then, she was not sure, but suddenly the doctor was present, prodding and poking, taking the baby from her. Claire was there too, beautiful and shiny behind the doctor's shoulder. Loraine was so proud; of herself, of Chris.

Johnny arrived at her side later in the morning, about nine. He appeared with an open mouth, wide eyes. He absolutely filled the room. Took up the space, swallowed all the oxygen so that Loraine had to breathe more quickly, greedily, as she confronted the father of the baby. Johnny was rumpled, his hair tangled and dirty. He bent to kiss her and his taste was of the leather in his car, cigarettes, eggs, and something else hidden there, the hint of another woman. Loraine stored this information, saved it for another day. She pulled the baby, its mouth surprised, from her breast, and handed the bundle to Johnny.

"See?" Loraine said.

Johnny's eyes were wet. He was blubbering. Loraine's chest heaved and fluttered.

Loraine loves her fingernails. Works hard at keeping them perfect. When she planted the garden she observed the advice offered in her cookbook: *Stuff small pieces of absorbent cotton in the fingers of your gardening gloves to prevent fingernail damage!* Loraine is impatient with Johnny and Chris, who nibble at their nails and spit the shards onto the floor.

Her fingers, the tips of her nails, smooth down Johnny's clothes now as she lays them in the dresser drawers and hangs them in the closet. She's given him the top two drawers: underwear and socks in one, T-shirts and jeans in the other. It's already the Wednesday after the long weekend and Loraine's had to finally go out to the little room beside the barn, pack up Johnny's stuff, and haul it in boxes across the yard and up the stairs to the bedroom.

"Chicken shit," she mutters. He's frightened of what this all means. But, finally, it means nothing. He can always leave again. Loraine's not like Charlene; she won't kill herself, burn the house down. Not for Johnny.

Johnny's got three extra pair of cowboy boots. Loraine tries on a black pair with white stitching. She stands by the full-length mirror and walks like a duck. Claire hollers from downstairs; she's come out from the city. Light footsteps and then she's in the doorway, laughing at Loraine.

"Did you ever imagine," Claire asks, "having a guy who wears those?"

"They're not so bad," Loraine says. She swivels. Kicks up a heel.

Claire sees the open drawers.

"I'm moving him in," Loraine says.

Claire is disappointed. She doesn't understand who Johnny is.

"He's got it too easy out there," Loraine continues. "Comes knocking for love, then leaves. Ha. Time he got to know his baby."

The baby squeals and Claire scoops her up and noses her brow. Kisses her ears. "Wonderful," she says. "So fresh." Then, "I've got some soup and bread downstairs. Homemade jam."

Over lunch Claire asks if Loraine's been for a check-up yet.

"Why?" Loraine asks. "I feel good. What can a doctor tell me?"

"True. Every time I went for a check-up after a birth," Claire says, "the doctor wanted to know if I'd had sex yet. I always lied and said yes."

Loraine's got some soup on her chin. She dabs it away. "I haven't allowed Johnny yet. He's disappointed. But I'm not ready."

Claire laughs, "Men are always disappointed."

Loraine remembers those winter nights. Running, violent with desire, across the yard, snow bright with moon, falling all over Johnny, and then returning, her body sore, to her own bed. She wonders if Claire has known that kind of desperation. If it matters.

"When Johnny's not here," Loraine says, "when he's left for work, I think about him. I try to remember his face, his mouth, the soft underarm skin. I do that and then I get desperate and want to see him."

Claire offers a brief, humouring smile.

Loraine blushes. This preoccupation with the body that she has. Claire is blessed, always has been; even as a child she was favoured by uncles and aunts. Bounced on knees, offered candies, while Loraine sat quietly on the sidelines. Loraine doesn't resent this, simply wonders at the forces that shaped their lives. Claire doesn't understand. Never has. Like way back, Claire was interested in the cellophane-wrapped peppermint while

Loraine was fascinated by the up-and-down movement of the uncle's knee on Claire's tiny bum. Loraine, remembering this, experiences a glow of guilt, a quick watering at the edges of her tongue. She butters more bread.

Johnny doesn't like this new arrangement. Loraine's not sure if she does either because Johnny sleeps right through Rebecca's cries. Loraine ends up elbowing and pushing at his big body until he grumbles and groans and thumps to the crib and returns, spilling the squalling baby into her arms.

Rebecca feeds for twenty minutes on each breast while Johnny snores, one hot leg touching Loraine's hip. By morning the bedroom is littered with dirty diapers, breast pads and burp rags coated with dried milk. Loraine listens to Johnny tread that messy maze and then the shower erupts and Loraine sleeps a delicious late-morning sleep, Rebecca a light bundle at her side, having found her way to the bed sometime during the night, Johnny being too tired to return her to the crib.

She and the baby awake together. A stirring, a squeak, and Loraine opens her eyes to discover the milky blue of Rebecca's stare. She misses Johnny then and wonders where he is, whose farmhouse he's sitting in, what long thin highway he's coasting down. He is not a happy man these days. He helps her with the eggs, the feed. Even organized Chris's friends to empty the barns of the old chickens one night. Then brought in the new batch and helped stuff them in their little cages, three to a wire house; clean white new layers all set for a year of producing. Still, he's a dog scratching at the door, waiting to be set loose. She tries to hold him back, rubs his neck in the evening and says that this is a phase. "This too shall pass," she whispers.

He disappears some evenings. Takes his car and just goes. Not a word. These silent departures touch Loraine in a deep way. It seems, on those particular evenings, that Rebecca is colicky and demanding. So, Loraine rocks her and watches TV or she paces the bedroom, shushing her child. There are things she should be doing, she thinks, a garden to tend, ironing, laundry, or a simple act like showering and washing her hair. Impossible. So, she rocks. Rebecca squirms and cries. Loraine cries too, her face hot and wet, until, finally, the child sleeps.

Two days after the birth, when Loraine's breasts were as hard as the rocks that lay beside her fallow garden, Johnny sat at the edge of her bed and asked her about names.

"How about Rebecca?" Loraine said.

Johnny stroked the baby's head. "Well, it's *your* baby," he said.

"I asked Chris," Loraine said. "He said okay." She paused, then added, "It's *our* baby. I had an aunt named Rebecca. I liked her. Everyone called her Becky."

"It's old. Solid," Johnny said. He smiled and cupped Loraine's bare breast.

"Don't." She pushed him away. "We'll call her Rebecca."

"Fine."

Loraine watched Johnny's eyes, saw in them a disappointment, in her, the baby. As if he were accusing her of grinding him into the earth, giving him roots. She roused herself, hard breasts knocking, leaving Johnny with the baby. She showered, expressing milk that rolled down her belly and between her legs. She returned to find Johnny treading the green rug, a tiny head laid in the crook of his arm. Loraine towelled her hair, conscious of Johnny studying her bum, her loose stomach, her blue-veined breasts. She ignored him and dressed in loose pants and a large T-shirt.

Later, after the baby was sleeping and they were in the kitchen, Johnny wanted to hold her. She let him. Felt him play at her hair, her neck, her ears. His hips were hard. He'd lost weight.

She patted him away, sat down, and said, "You've never asked about the birth."

"Hasn't been time," he answered.

He had no idea. None. He claimed to be looking for miracles but he'd never find one; he was blind. Still, Loraine wanted to talk to him, explain how helpful Chris was, how the baby arrived, as if she'd just knocked on the door one night and demanded entry. Loraine wanted to speak of the peace she felt as the baby crowned, of the immense pleasure of leaning on Chris's shoulders, of the boy's particular fragrance, the pressure of his shirt buttons on her bare skin, the lack of shame in her nakedness and how that was a revelation to her, as if from then on she would never again be ashamed of her body.

Listen to me, Johnny, Loraine wanted to say. But she didn't. Instead, she claimed the bitterness Johnny was offering her and said, "You like to kill things, don't you?"

Against her own wishes, Loraine finds herself doing her grocery shopping in Lesser; the baby is too demanding to travel all the way to Winnipeg. She shops at the Solo Store, picks up her mail at the post office, even has her hair done at Agnes's. She usually ends up talking to someone about the baby and the birth. This she does without haste, with a particular joy. It's her story and most people seem willing to listen.

One morning she meets Avi Heath just outside the entrance to Bill's Hardware. Loraine's going out, holding a brown bag of washers, Avi's entering. They stand off to the side, in the shade of the awning. The baby is sleeping in the stroller and Loraine has an irrational fear of something unnamed; that her breasts are leaking through her shirt, or that Avi is that shadowy woman she tasted on Johnny the morning after the birth.

Avi, long shiny legs in shorts, has a youngish manner, though Loraine notices her neck, when tanned, looks older than it should.

"I'm on a break for four months," Avi says. "I'm being awfully decadent. Travelled out to the East Coast and up to Cape Breton. Michael and I plan to spend the last three weeks of August in Europe."

Loraine nods, smiles. Europe. For a second she has a glimpse of Avi lying topless on a European beach. Avi's breasts, which are quite heavy and sack-like, would flop sideways if she were on her back. Loraine wonders if Avi likes the tickle of Michael's beard on her nipples. Michael must be hairy all over; like sleeping with a baboon.

"Michael doesn't really want to go," Avi's saying, "but I told him he'd be back for hunting season." Her eyes roll. Avi stoops to the baby now, almost touching Rebecca's brow.

"Lovely," she says. She stands, rising above Loraine. "In fall," she says, "we're continuing our book club. Perhaps you'd like to come."

Loraine feels she has been offered something both precious and poisonous. "I don't read much," she says.

"That's okay," Avi responds. "We're doing *Madame Bovary* the first month. If you're interested, I'll get you a copy."

Loraine wonders what it would be like to replace a dead woman; as if she would have to somehow assume Charlene's role. She wonders who Madame Bovary is. There's a speckling of sweat on Avi's nose; Loraine would like to reach out and dab at it. "Maybe," she says. And then adds, "So, you're enjoying Lesser."

Avi's forehead pushes up searching out an important thought. "What *I* wanted when I moved out here was a sense of village, of ritual. Meaning. The city is full of indifference. Lesser isn't."

"Exactly," Loraine says.

"You'd like to escape?" Avi asks.

"My husband, Jim, chose this place. The farm. Ever since his death I've considered moving." It is obvious to Loraine that Avi is in love with the sensations of Lesser. "Wait for the Lesser Fair," Loraine says. "The parade itself is a wonder. Tractors, Model Ts, kids on bicycles. And the contests. Best pie, bread, jam. Even best eggs." She laughs, remembering her own participation one summer, long ago. Her perfect white eggs laid out in a basket, a clean white tea-towel beneath them.

"Best eggs?" Avi says. "Based on what?"

"Oh, texture, colour, weight, size. Health of the yolk."

"See," cries Avi. Her eyes gleam.

Avi's not really a part of this life, Loraine thinks. She's just playing, an outsider trying to lap up the good things, sifting through all the rubble and hoarding the gems. Loraine is annoyed by Avi's pleasure. Annoyed too by her loping body, by the fact she has time to chat.

"I had the baby at home," Loraine says as Rebecca purls and stirs.

"I heard. Must have been frightening."

"Not at all. Dogs, pigs, horses, cats. They all manage. Why not us? Another form of village life."

Avi's neck stretches. Her eyes widen. She doesn't respond.

This angers Loraine, flusters her. She bends to pick up the baby. Uses the child as a shield. "I'm bursting," she says. "Gotta get home and feed the baby."

But she doesn't make it home. She has to stop the half-ton, pull over onto an unused driveway, unbuckle Rebecca and offer her the breast. The window is half down and across the field comes the mumbling of a tractor pulling a seeder. The earth all around is black, newly turned. Rebecca slurps. Loraine thinks about Avi's thighs clamping Johnny's head.

SUMMER

TONGUES

For the summer Johnny has managed to find Chris work as a 'gofer' at OK Feeds; Johnny drives Chris to and from work. They don't talk much. Usually the windows are wide open and the air claps at their ears and cheeks and makes speech pointless. However, one morning in mid-July it is raining and cool; the car is sealed and musty. Johnny turns on the air-conditioning and asks, his voice dropping from the sky, if Melody is still around. "Haven't seen her at the centre lately," he says.

Chris is working his nails, fingers at his mouth. "Oh," he says, "you'd like this. She's gone charismatic. Hangs out with Barkman's group. She's living there."

"Really?" A small squeeze of panic in his stomach encourages Johnny to reach for a cigarette. He lights up and asks, "Where?"

"At Phil's. With his family."

"She told you this?"

"Early June. Last time I talked to her." Bile in Chris's voice here.

"Does that make sense?" Johnny asks. "I mean, to you. The religion, living with Phil and Eleanor?"

"Sure," Chris says. "I don't know. Why not?"

Yeah, why not? Johnny thinks.

Chris continues, "I'd go too, if Melody didn't detest me. What you lookin' at?"

Johnny swivels back, watching the road again. He feels sorry for Chris. The private knowledge Johnny has burns at him when he lets it. Sometimes when he's alone and driving through Morris, he remembers that night and how it was with Melody and he understands why Chris would suffer deeply; her wild frayed edges stick like burrs. But this revelation of Chris's is confusing.

Johnny wags his head. "Thought she had a mind of her own."

"Huh?"

"Nothing." Then, "A woman can kill you. Beat you up, not?"

Chris twists the side of his mouth. Loraine there; the lips, the thin angled nostrils. Chris doesn't quite get it, hasn't reached that cynical point. And, in any case, Johnny might be talking about his mother.

All that day Johnny ponders this news about Melody. She must be suffering and, like Johnny when he suffers in some acute way, has managed to seek solace in the hands of Phil Barkman. Hard, he thinks, for a sixteen-year-old to harbour this loss, tuck it away, pretend it never happened. Still, she wanted it. He wonders how much Phil has yanked out of her; he's good at that.

He has lunch at Chuck's, sits with the Penner boys, stalwart charismatics, and tries to glean some information about Melody. But first, the boys ask, with genuine concern, how Johnny's doing.

"Are you praying?" Glen asks, and after Johnny nods, guiltily lying, Gordie pursues, "Are you right?"

"Sometimes," Johnny says, and he smiles widely, hating the stink of self-righteousness in the booth. But these fellows really aren't self-righteous. They are, Johnny realizes later, very sincere. They nurture a huge love for Johnny's soul.

The men discuss fame then and Gordie says everybody wants to be famous, to be known in some way, and Johnny considers a little and then agrees, though he's never really thought about it.

Glen says that he and his wife Judy are working on their relationship.

"We watch too much TV," he says. "Come home, she makes supper, eat in front of the TV, do a few chores, watch the day's taping of Oprah, and then go to bed. It's not terrible but neither is it healthy. Maybe because we don't have kids. We should be setting more time aside for Bible study and prayer. Just the two of us. 'Cause that's when we talk to each other. Prayer is really just a therapy of sorts. Another way of talking to your partner. Makes us closer but it's hard to do."

"That's logical," Johnny says. He tried to get Loraine to pray once but she was full of titters and lust, wouldn't concentrate.

Gordie, who is the younger brother and has three kids, says that the less time you have to yourself the more disciplined you have to be. He says, "Me and Marion, after the kids are in bed, which is usually ten o'clock, have to fit everything in: laundry, dishes, talking, sex, prayer." His mouth opens and he brays. Delighted. He dunks a plastic creamer into his coffee.

Johnny watches him and wonders at how easily this man fits everything together. Johnny has never considered before that laundry and sex are on the same level. He wonders if that's truly possible.

Still aware of his goal here, Johnny brings the conversation around to Barkman's house and the meetings. He says, "I hear Melody Krahn is attending."

"Yeah, regularly," Gordie says. "Spoke in tongues last week."

Johnny burns his tongue on the coffee. Slops onto the saucer. "Really?"

"Funny thing," Gordie continues. "I've practically begged God for that gift but he won't touch me with it. Some get discernment, some charity, some ministering. Melody walked in one night, sat down, and halfway through the meeting she broke down in tears. Too much weight."

"Did she talk?" Johnny wants to know. Panic sits in his throat like a bubble.

"Not much. Phil prayed over her and oomph" — here Gordie snaps his fingers — "she headed off on a wonderful singsong piece. Face shining. Was beautiful. You should come again. We've missed you."

"Yeah, I should," Johnny says. His soul is dark. "And she's living there," he slips in.

The men don't seem to find this odd. They nod and Gordie says, "She was lost. On the verge of running. Phil and Eleanor have big hearts."

Johnny, listening to Gordie, understands that there are better people in the world than him, and this does not surprise him.

After breakfast, Johnny steps out into the sunshine and climbs into his car. He drives out past the sport complex — arena and curling rink — and circles around inside the little housing development which holds Phil and Eleanor's house. He parks behind a clump of bushes, in a semi-islolated spot, with a good view of the side, back, and front. There is a look of disorder to the place, of *almost*. The house is half-painted. Swings in the front yard. A tractor mower is parked on a bit of lawn. Lots of dirt and sandpiles. A stack of shrivelled sod. There's a kid wandering around in the yard, throwing clumps of dirt in the air. The house looks quiet; Phil must be off hanging stucco wire. It's a part-time job for him; supplements the donations he gets from his followers.

Eleanor steps onto the back porch and hangs laundry. Diapers. Toddlers' clothes. Johnny wonders if Melody is washing her own clothes. Then, there she is, standing beside Eleanor. She still has a way of moving that reminds Johnny of someone squirming from a hole. Her shoulders are strapped by a tank top. Thin neck and arms. She's holding Eleanor's youngest, hipping him and spooning food from a bowl into his greedy mouth. Melody twirls at one point, clutching the child. Happy. The flash of a spoon against the child's back makes Johnny's heart jump for some reason. Johnny leans forward, a hint of tobacco rising from his front pocket. He waits till Melody disappears inside the house, her hand flicking out behind her in gesture to Eleanor, and then Johnny lights a cigarette. He feels like a pervert. He goes.

And then, two days later he's driving west out of town when he passes Melody on her bicycle going into town. Johnny swings the car about and, idling up to Melody's pumping legs, pulls even, hums down the passenger's window, and calls out, "Hey."

Melody falters and brakes. Hops on one foot and straddles her bike. It's a mauve mountain bike; her fingers curl on the rubber handles.

"Hello, Johnny," she says. Her voice is the same, Johnny thinks. It's her eyes that have changed; they're not as quick, not as shiny.

"Got a minute? Can we talk a bit?" Johnny asks.

"I have nothing to say."

"Haven't seen you at the centre," Johnny says, sliding into the passenger seat, leaning his arm on the door.

"Been busy."

"Yeah? You okay?"

"Sure, why not?"

"You angry?"

"No, Johnny, Jesus," and her mouth almost lifts up in a half-grin, like it used to. But she pushes it back down.

"People say you're holy now."

"Yeah, just like you." Her foot goes up to the pedal. She wants to leave. Get away from him. Strange how a saviour turns to shit later. Johnny can feel her tightness, it's there in her haunches, the way she shifts her bum on the saddle. Her tendons move in her neck.

"I saw you holding that kid the other day," Johnny says. "On the back porch."

"You been watching me?"

"I was passing by. Looking for Phil. I saw you."

Melody doesn't believe Johnny. Still, she says, "That was Kirby, he just turned one. Real sweet."

"So, you babysit?"

"I help out. It's my board."

"You're staying then?"

"I dunno. I suppose. I'm not unhappy, you know. Not now. For a while, at home, I was wrecked, sure. Couldn't stand the sound of my mother chewing her food. But then I ran into Phil." She drops her head. "He was so good to me. I didn't tell him anything. He just held me. Eleanor too." She taps at her chest here and says, "So."

Johnny thinks maybe he's looking into a mirror. It's so painful. "Congratulations," he says. "My wife, Charlene, used to say that to me. She's dead." Then, before Melody can think about this, Johnny says, "Phil's a good man. A good man."

Melody simply nods. Smiles too, but this seems forced and colourless.

"Hey," Johnny says again, forcing her to turn and pay attention. "You want to talk about your abortion, about that night, you go ahead. Don't worry about me. If you need to get rid of all that, then just do it."

"I've got nothing to tell." Her hand moves to her thigh, then her ear. Johnny looks for love and beauty and grace and forgiveness in her eyes. It is possible, he thinks. She leans and touches his elbow.

"Well," Johnny says, letting her hand rest there. His eyes hurt. Pain for this girl. "You're a good kid." And then he adds, "I heard something you'd like. On the radio. It seems that the number of people living now outnumber the dead. Huh."

Melody smiles. Blinks. "Bye," she says.

Johnny watches her go, is mesmerized by her thin feet strapped into sandals. He lights a cigarette, blows a draft out the open window, and thinks that this town is not good for him. Some day, he will have to leave.

Friday night Johnny opens the centre late. What with holidays and all he doesn't expect too many kids on a summer evening. He's right, three youngish boys show up and play ping-pong for a bit and then they scatter. It's quiet till midnight. No one. On Saturday, instead of wasting his time in front of the TV at the centre, he detours out towards Phil Barkman's. Pulls in behind Gordie Penner's new snub-nosed Dodge half-ton. Lots of cars tonight. This makes Johnny nervous. Still, the thought of Melody lifting her pale face skyward and jabbering drags him up to the front door. His knuckles hurt on the metal door. Eleanor lets him in. She's holding a cranky Kirby. Her manner is unhurried though; gentle and generous. She offers Johnny her home, her husband, her time. Gives him coffee and says, "We're in the front room."

About forty people sit in a half-circle. Johnny finds himself beside Melissa Emery. He has not seen her since his baptism last fall. With gratitude and warmth he recalls her presence there. She falls towards him now and smiles. Melissa is a little naive. Perhaps not too smart, Johnny thinks. She's careless with her hands, touches his knee, breathes in his ear, "Welcome."

Johnny's scalp tickles. He smooths a hand up his brow and pushes at his hair. Then he sees Melody. She's sitting at the other edge of the semi-circle, across from him. She's staring at him. He smiles but she doesn't respond. It's as if she were contemplating an important event taking place somewhere behind him.

Phil Barkman approaches the lectern and prays. His prayer meanders all over, touching the lives of Lesser, of Canada, the world, and finally coming back to the specific needs of this group. Then, for a few minutes, Barkman dwells on the sin of lust and Johnny listens carefully to Phil's voice which is smooth and comforting and full of warning. Lust is a big issue, Johnny thinks. He wonders if Phil ever wants to sleep with someone other than his wife.

According to his watch it's about a fifteen-minute prayer. The last bit is an exhortation on the Spirit and this, Johnny knows, will get the mouths vibrating. In fact, he feels a heat emanating from Melissa Emery beside him. It's not unlike a sexual energy and he sneaks a look. Her hands pull at the padded shoulders of her sweater. Her head sways. She pants lightly and Johnny, sitting so close, feels a slight swelling in his crotch. He is amazed. Not at all cynical. He admires those who manage to find deep within themselves this fury that can spill out in a torrent of lovely babble.

Phil Barkman, also feeling the energy in the room, shifts his voice and says, "As we sense the moving of the Spirit, let's respect each other's voices. As much as possible, let us listen to one before another starts. In this way the interpreter will have a much easier time of it."

This advice is so structured and so against the prevailing joy felt in the room that Johnny wants to laugh. But, by now, Melissa Emery is speaking. Her brow is damp, one hand clutches her knee. What she says makes no sense to Johnny but he doesn't care. He closes his eyes and allows her voice to carry him. It is beautiful. Melissa Emery is beautiful. Grace lifts Johnny's soul upwards.

When she is done, Eli Doerksen interprets. He stands, shuffles his feet, and quickly, with a look of surprise on his face, says, "There is a false presence here tonight. Something harmful. Perhaps it is a thought, a resentment, perhaps it is the burdened mind of one of our own. But it is a disturbing presence." He pauses, and concludes, "These were the words of Melissa Emery."

A poor interpretation, Johnny thinks. Completely off. He looks at Melissa to see what she thinks of Eli Doerksen's foolishness but she hasn't heard. She's being held by Phil Barkman's wife. They're in a tight embrace and Eleanor is kissing the sweat from Melissa's forehead and whispering in her ear.

The mood in the room has changed. Eyes shift. Johnny experiences a quick descent, a coolness in his chest now. Fear. Guilt. And later, when Melody rises, is drawn slowly upward as if lifted by a silent pulley, Johnny is overwhelmed by a desire to stand also, to join her and sing a duet, quell his shaking body, hold her hands and squeeze.

Melody's language is foreign, but at its core is an oozing of familiarity, as if Johnny's heard this story before. Or lived it. Her voice is the same one he heard that evening in Fargo, lilting, then crawling, then tippling upwards, her tone telling him to draw closer.

Now, talking to this group, she sways. Her body pushes out, first at Phil Barkman, then at Gordie Penner, who sits beside her, all eyes. Her hips grind. She moans. Johnny thinks that all of this is quite embarrassing but rapt faces around him seem to accept this sexual act, this tease, not as physical but as a form of cleansing.

Then, her voice slows and the words become common and legible and, This is no longer tongues, Johnny thinks. Melody is describing an act, an intimate and extreme act. And quickly, before Johnny can grasp what is happening, Melody is entertaining the bunch with a tale of drugs and driving and a dead baby. The whole story is told.

Johnny is watching Melissa Emery's knuckles. Chapped a little. Then Melody's face. Full of peace. He himself is experiencing tremendous confusion. When Melody sits, is in fact caught by Gordie and cradled briefly in his arms and then released, Johnny is on his feet, willing to offer what he hopes will be seen as a faithful interpretation. His head is bowed. Surprisingly, people wait. Melody is gasping; real tears, Johnny hopes.

Johnny stutters. Tries again. He has an audience, something he's always liked. His voice is surer now, his mind slipping down that long black tunnel to the place he wants it to go. "Jesus Christ was a fag," he says. "There is this theory which is quite possible. Claims that Jesus was gay. You know, homosexual." Johnny grabs a quick breath here and forges on, knowing that any little pause now will allow for a stifling of his voice. "Seriously. I mean, why didn't the man have any women? Think of it, twelve disciples, all men. Thing is, this theory states — and this is based on good research — Jesus and Judas were lovers. And if you accept that, how much greater the betrayal?"

Johnny's smiling now. "You're all unbelievable," he says. "You people don't admit to other possibilities. Narrow little views of salvation. What if I were to say that seeking out redemption in itself is evil; this idea that the world revolves around me. You know, *my* salvation, *my* soul, *my* wish to live forever. And besides that, Apostle Paul was a fag too. Especially liked little boys. Imagine, him giving us advice on marriage."

Johnny shrugs his shoulders. A terrible lightness there. People muttering. Rumbling. The beginnings of a storm. A stoning perhaps. Johnny backs away towards the front door. Phil Barkman is stretching out his arms, eyes begging. What a handsome man, Johnny thinks. Little hooded blue penis. A good man. Melody is in the background, a wan ghost who listened to his voice. Good for her.

Johnny turns now and runs, out to his long black car. Gravel sprays, the faint ping of stones on Gordie's Dodge. He drives too quickly across the washboardy gravel along the road to Loraine's house where he finds her in bed with the baby and a book. The baby sleeps.

"Are you okay?" she inquires, staring up into his wild face.

Johnny is touched by this question. So simple. She makes room for him on the short side and he touches her hip; the flow of her skin on his fingertips. The abandoned book takes flight at their feet. The roll of the mattress stirs the baby; Loraine hushes from above and finally giggles and gasps as she comes in his mouth. And then his quick efficiency, easing into her for the first time since the birth of Rebecca, and rocking slowly, his nose on the bone of her shoulder. The insanity of the evening dissolves and he concentrates on her, no one else; just this woman he loves, who lives out here above the black earth, a bright and vital star. His, for now.

OUT

In the days that follow Melody's revelation, Johnny holds his breath and closes his eyes. What he has, this life with Loraine, hovers delicately in a cold blue sky so that Johnny begins to see himself as a bird; a bird like that raven Noah set loose upon a watery world, the one which never returned. Johnny, like the bird, seeks a place to rest; a rock, a piece of earth, a tree, but he finds nothing. There is no peace. One night Johnny wakes and has an urgent need to use the bathroom. He creeps from the bed and feels his way through the shadows to the toilet. He sits, eyes closed, and senses that he is ghost-like. His body is weak and flimsy, the weight and size of a scab barely clinging to its base. Johnny pulls at his chin and pinches hard at his thigh. The pain restores his faith and he shuffles back to bed and rediscovers his hollow beside Loraine and, before falling asleep again, smells her head twice.

And then one day Loraine phones Johnny at work. Her mouth is full of something, pain maybe.

"Johnny," she says, "you should come home."

"Yeah? Why?"

"We have to talk." A little pull of air through her teeth now, as if the baby were feeding and biting her nipple. "Chris just told me about Melody."

"I thought Chris was sick," Johnny answers. "Couldn't move, eat, or talk this morning. He should be working."

"Is it true?" Loraine says.

Johnny won't give in so easily. He distrusts the veins of gossip in Lesser; they become clogged and twisted so that what enters as fact at first exits as story, something made up: interesting, like the poetry Charlene used to read, but completely wrong — nonsense. "What did he tell you?" Johnny asks.

"That you were with Melody the night Rebecca was born. Down in Fargo. Helping her abort the baby."

"I didn't help her. I was the chauffeur, that's all. And it wasn't a baby yet. It was like eleven weeks."

Another pause and Johnny has to listen to Loraine's panic; her breathing is quicker, elevated. Then, "Oh, Johnny, I was hoping it was all wrong. Careless talk. But . . . shit, you took her down there?"

"What," Johnny says. "What." He can hear Chris talking in the background. His voice is high and strained, but Johnny can't get the context. Just drivel.

"That's it?" Loraine asks. "That's your explanation, an adolescent 'what'?"

"I've got nothing to hide. She asked for help. She came to me. There was no one else, she said."

Loraine laughs, a cracking squeal that hurts Johnny's ear. "You're so gullible," she says. Then her voice tightens into a dry whisper. "And you're not sorry, are you?"

"Why?" Johnny says. Sometimes Loraine's a mule. Puts her head down and won't budge. "I'm sorry I wasn't at Rebecca's birth, sure, but she wasn't exactly scheduled for that night, was she? I mean, I could have been hunting with Michael, or drinking in St. Adolphe. I just happened to be taking Melody down to Fargo to take care of a fetus that your son happened to be responsible for too. Only what would he have done? Married her? It's the coincidence that's killing you Loraine, admit it. I've done nothing wrong. It's just the timing was off."

"You're sick." The venom in Loraine's voice makes Johnny sit up and take notice. He switches the receiver to his right ear. His neck, if he were to look in a mirror, would beam out at him, red and patchy and hot.

Loraine's still talking. "Riding south with a teenage girl. Killing a baby. Huh. You probably wanted to fuck her." Horror slips in. "You didn't, did you?"

"Jesus, Loraine." Johnny's thinking about Chris, who's sitting near his mother, listening to her talk like this.

"You wanted to though, didn't you? Nice young cunt."

Johnny doesn't answer. He's listening to Loraine cry, thinking how her face looks when she gets like this — all old and ugly and loose. He's losing his patience. His tongue touches a sharp lower incisor; he lost a piece of it last week, biting into a steak. The rough edge makes the tip of his tongue hurt and swell.

"I'm sorry," he says.

"And then there's Chris. You should see him. He's *completely devastated*. Walking around in circles, mumbling. I had to yank this out of him. It's like he's been hit by a truck and managed to survive. Did you ever think?"

"Yes."

"So, it didn't matter."

"It wasn't the most important consideration at that point."

"You screwed up Melody too, I hope you know."

"Yeah," Johnny says, "I'm a pretty awful guy."

"It's the scope, you know. You understand? A decision like this pulls everyone down with you. You have no sense of the implications. You don't get it, do you?"

Johnny thinks that there is a relief in finally giving up and falling, spiralling downwards, aware by now that nothing and no one can save him.

"This isn't going to work," Loraine says. "This family thing. You're the odd one out, Johnny, you see? I certainly can't sleep beside you any more. I said you should come by. Don't bother. Your clothes will be out by the road."

Johnny flutters feebly; one last attempt at flight. "Oh my. A sad day. Leaving your bed. Don't fuck any more, anyway."

"That's everything to you, isn't it. Fucking. That little muscle you adore."

"You used to adore it."

"When I could find it."

This ought to be funny, Johnny thinks. He laughs, then realizes he shouldn't. He opens his mouth then and says what he knows will hurt. "That's fine. Just fine. I'm out. Now maybe there'll be room for Chris in your bed. He's been aching for you. Cozy and convenient. No problem."

There is a brief awful cry and then silence. Loraine has hung up.

That same day Phil Barkman comes to visit Johnny at OK Feeds. Phil seats himself and announces there is a movement afoot to close down the centre. Phil says this almost carelessly, as if he were speaking of the weather. He's wedged himself into a black vinyl chair and his fingers tap his thighs. Johnny knows Phil doesn't lie, he has no need. His carelessness is simply a mannerism — his eyes show concern, not glee.

"Melody's dad came to see me," Phil says.

Johnny ducks his head.

"He says he'll talk to the mayor and the councillors and he'll start a petition," Phil adds. "He figures he can have you shut down by next week."

Johnny sighs. "It's not a bad thing," he says. "The centre. Nothing evil there. Not even me."

"I know that," Phil says.

"The kids'll miss it."

"Sure they will."

"How's Melody?" Johnny asks.

"She's a strong girl. Eleanor talks to her. Has set up a little prayer time with her. She's full of forgiveness. She's living with us. We made a little arrangement with her parents for the summer." Phil says all this quietly, as if it were private or liable to break Johnny in some way.

But Johnny ignores the soft tone and says, "Yes." He thinks he should apologize for the other night and as he considers this the words just turn up on their own, as if Phil were pulling them out on a rope. "Sorry," he says. "You know. That night. I was lost. Confused. Don't believe at all what I said. I heard it somewhere and it came in handy. Or I thought."

"Sure," Phil says. "Hey." His face is calm and joyful. Johnny feels an urge to hug him but now Phil is lifting his hands to the ceiling as if begging for a blessing. "Like I said. Melody, who could have been devastated by your comments, seemed the least critical."

"I'm a noisy gong," Johnny says. Phil always makes him feel contrite.

"All of us, sometimes," Phil says. "It's a good verse to remember: 'If I speak with the tongues of men and of angels, but do not have love, I have become a noisy gong or a clanging cymbal.' Keeps us honest. You're unhappy, aren't you?"

Johnny thinks about this. Looks inside himself, considers, and discovers he is incapable of finding any sadness there. "I live on faith, hope, and love," Johnny says. "I love Loraine." He closes his eyes. Opens them. Phil is still there.

"Of course you do," Phil says. "You're a lover of women."

Johnny stares at Phil. He's got a small head, big eyes. Strange, to be called "a lover of women." Makes Johnny feel good. Sometimes, Phil's perceptions are perfect.

"How do you separate feeling from doing?" Johnny asks.

"I don't always."

"You suffer from weak flesh?" Johnny asks.

"Sometimes," Phil answers.

Johnny wonders what that means for someone like Phil Barkman. Probably something to do with Eleanor, who had a look about her, touching Melissa that night. Then Melody. A glow; like it was lovely to minister to a woman's skin.

"Pride's a bigger one for me," Phil says. Then, shaking his head as if surprised at this conversation, he asks, "What are you going to do?"

Johnny thinks he's never had trouble with pride. Selfishness, yes, but never pride.

"Close it down," he says. "That's what I'll do."

That evening Johnny lets himself into the centre and stands in the middle of the main room and listens. The tap is dripping in the back. The Pepsi machine hums. Several flies buzz and bang against the front window. Johnny picks up a swatter and kills them. It's fly season in the country. He remembers when he was young and how the cows tightened their assholes so flies wouldn't get in. Johnny can feel his own body tightening, closing up, keeping out the vermin of Lesser. A protection of sorts, but dangerous too; nothing good can come of it.

He finds a piece of paper and a purple felt pen. He writes "Closed" on the paper and tapes it on the big window facing Main Street. He takes his few belongings from his desk, drops them in a paper bag, locks the front door, and leaves. Johnny stops at Bill's Hardware and buys a pup tent, Coleman stove, sleeping bag and a frying pan and camping dishes. The girl who serves him is new in town. She's unfamiliar with the cash register and fights with it. She's got an empty hole in her nose, no stud, and no other jewellery. Her shoulders are bare, she's tanned.

"New job?" Johnny asks. He knows all the teenagers of Lesser.

The girl nods. "I'm here for the summer. From Abbotsford. Bill's my uncle."

"Oh." Johnny watches her fingers touch the merchandise. "You like Lesser, then?"

Her nose wrinkles. "You going camping?" she asks.

"Sure," Johnny says, sliding his credit card back into the wallet. "Sort of."

Johnny knows where he's headed, but before he goes there he drives by Michael's land out by the river. Johnny has never been here before, though he's driven past and caught glimpses of the one-and-a-half storey house. One light glows from the big room facing the road. Johnny knocks, waits, knocks again, and then Avi is there with her big head and long neck, a book in one hand.

"Michael's not here," she says. "He went fishing. Left this afternoon." Avi is watching Johnny's face, as if she knows about him. Has already caught the smell of his sin drifting on the wind, which all day has blown from the east. She lets him in, though not happily it seems. Johnny surmises she wants to spend the evening reading and drinking. Still he slips past her; she has aroused in him a memory of big, rangy, Charlene. Perhaps it's the alcohol, or the smooth fall of Avi's shoulders. He feels a need in his gut.

Johnny stands beyond Avi and takes in the room. Everything's open. The walls have been removed and big beams run along the ceiling. Mounted animals everywhere. Birds in a potted tree by the window. Butterflies pinned on cork. Bear rugs on the floor. Moose head on the wall. There's a stand of guns over by the bookcase. Johnny turns now, thinks he should leave.

"You all right?" Avi asks.

"Sure," Johnny says. "Why not?" He is certain now that she knows.

"Here," Avi says, lightly pushing Johnny's elbow. "Sit. I'll get you a drink."

She brings him a whisky. No ice. He works at this slowly while Avi settles herself in a low chair. She seems smaller now; Johnny is still standing, looking down at her.

Avi says, "Michael was at Chuck's this morning. News is you've been trying out the role of Good Samaritan."

"I don't think people see it that way."

"Well, it probably goes beyond their sense of goodness." She pauses, rubs a finger lightly over one eyebrow, and says, "I'm surprised."

"Yeah?" Johnny likes the feel of this house, even though it is a bit Michael-heavy. Avi leans to lick at her half-full snifter of rum. Each of her little sips softens Johnny so that he begins to see her as an accomplice. Here is a woman, he believes, who understands him.

"Yeah," she echoes. "Michael said people were upset."

"A little," Johnny says. He watches Avi's hand run over a bare leg. Her skirt slid up when she sat and Johnny can see a bit of ripple in her thigh. The beginning of fat. He likes that, likes what it says about Avi Heath; that she eats well and likes to put sweet things in her mouth and doesn't mind the look of herself in the mirror. Her fingers are long. Nails are chipped. That too is exciting, especially after the perfection of Loraine's tiny hands. Avi's movements are slow and sleepy. She's been drinking for a while. Being here is like resurrecting Charlene. Johnny's throat is on fire. He stands now and tiptoes the edges of the room, touching delicately at the animals.

"Michael doesn't let me touch," Avi says. "Just the rugs."

Johnny ignores her. Strokes the head of what he thinks is a whisky-jack. He touches the neck of a Canada goose. "I quit my job," he says. This is not true but Johnny thinks that it could be a possibility. Especially now that he's said it.

"Oh." She's standing beside him now, also touching the goose. Her voice is in his ear. A whisper. "That's my bird. Michael convinced me to go hunting that fall."

Johnny wonders why she had it mounted. He turns and is looking at her jaw. Her hair is pulled behind her ear. She is turning grey.

He thinks that Avi would simply have to turn and then it would be Johnny and Avi all over the place, tearing up the rugs, knocking over delicate birds. But Avi keeps looking at the goose. She says, "You're a strange man, Johnny Fehr. I didn't like you at first. Despised you for the death of Charlene. But that's not fair, is it? Not fair to Charlene, who had her own mind, her own furies. Do you ever miss her?"

"Now," Johnny says. "Right now I do."

Avi pulls back. Her mouth parts and her glass goes up. "More?" she asks, taking his glass, tearing away, moving towards the kitchen.

Johnny experiences both regret and relief. He has a memory of Loraine, way back, in the egg room. He'd never even kissed her before and they'd been talking when Loraine stood and walked over to Johnny and fell into his arms. Or he fell into Loraine's. It was never quite clear. They kissed, long and hard. After, they were more pleased than surprised. Then, Loraine pushed him away and backstepped. "That's enough," she said. "I want you to come back."

Johnny, hearing Avi clink bottles now in the other room, is despondent. He has the urge to go, to leave this house and this woman. He sits. Waits for his drink.

Coming back to him, the amber liquid waving in the glass, a plate of crackers balanced in one hand, Avi is more distant, more clear-headed. "You make foolish decisions, Johnny. You never should have taken Melody to the States. Realistically, you could be arrested."

"She's sixteen," Johnny responds.

"Ah, but if it were pushed by her father, he'd have a point. You probably pretended to be this girl's father, right?"

Johnny nods, tired now of Avi's presumptions. Thinks she knows everything.

"You should have passed her on," Avi continues. "To a counsellor. Her mother."

"That's what you would have done?" Johnny asks.

Avi smiles. She reaches for the Saltines. Eats them greedily. "How about Loraine? This must have been a shock to her."

"She detests me," Johnny answers.

Avi doesn't respond to this confession. She licks the top of a cracker. Her long tongue repulses Johnny.

"I gotta go," he says.

"I'll tell Michael you came," Avi says. She kisses him at the front door, sweet rum passing onto his lips. But Johnny is cured by now. He's remembering Loraine, and right now, walking away from Avi, he thinks she'd be pleased, proud of him.

He goes back to his land. To the farm where only rubble remains. In the dark he pitches the pup tent alongside the row of spruces lining the driveway, unzips his sleeping bag and crawls in. The grass beneath the tent is uncut and so is high and soft. He sleeps deeply, waking once during the night to the sound of a small animal, perhaps a skunk, scuffling on the other side of the nylon. The animal leaves. The wind pushes at the trees. The night is dark, no moon. He sleeps again and rises in the early light, hungry. But he has no food. Poor planning.

He drives to Île des Chênes, taking the gravel road past Loraine's farm, casting a longing eye at the stillness of her house. He stops at her driveway and retrieves the boxes of clothes she has dumped beside the ditch. Rising from the depths of his trunk he hesitates and listens, hoping for the sound of the screen door slamming, the dog barking, the pad of her rubber boots. But everyone's still sleeping.

He has toast and coffee at a small restaurant and then wanders the countryside. This is Saturday. He follows a similar routine on Sunday: out past Loraine's, breakfast in a foreign town, rolling up and down the country roads. Near the end of the day he pulls into Lesser and stops at Chuck's for cigarettes. He considers having coffee as well. He steps into the restaurant and discovers Melissa Emery sitting in a booth touching shoulders with Eleanor and across from them are Melody and Phil. All four are leaning forward and almost knocking heads. They don't see Johnny, so he pays and leaves, but not without first seeing Melody's hand go up to Phil's shoulder and Phil turning and looking at her, his face astonished.

The following day, Monday, is a holiday, the August long weekend. The roads are empty. People are resting. By midafternoon Johnny finds himself puttering along the river road west of Lesser away from St. Adolphe, towards the Rat River bridge, the same bridge he smashed into last fall. He remembers this accident ruefully, touching now at his jaw, the tiny scar on his cheek. There is a gathering at the river today. On the east side. Hundreds of cars. Johnny, curious, parks his Olds and steps down a newly made path between scrubby oaks to the rear of a crowd of people. Johnny wonders if this is a baptism, just like the old days before the invention of indoor tanks. It isn't.

A man is speaking to the crowd. He talks of Mennonites and settlers. And then a younger man with a blue-and-red tie takes over and he explains how the first eighty or so families of Mennonites arrived here by riverboat in 1874 from Fargo. Came up the Red River and decided to settle here.

Johnny realizes that his grandfather could have been on that boat. Or a later one. He's not at all sure but the possibility excites him. He thinks how beliefs, or greed, or bad or good luck, or the simple meandering of life, brought people to these banks and those people had children and the children had children and Johnny might be one of the offspring. He realizes he's happy to have his own child. Rebecca. Odd. History has never excited Johnny but it moves him now.

He circles the edge of the crowd. He knows a few people, not many. He stands beside an older couple. The man has grey hair, a large nose. Johnny recognizes him as his old high school principal. Johnny used to be good friends with this man's son. The man turns as Johnny attempts to sidle away.

"Johnny Fehr?"

Johnny nods and grins. Shakes hands with the couple and then the salesman side of him takes over. He's good at this. Chats comfortably with his old principal, who must remember him as a scoundrel, a poor student. There is a vague memory of kicking the headlights out on this man's car. Those were angry times.

Johnny asks about their son, recalling that he was a bit of a writer. He mentions this and the older man laughs politely, dismissing the fact. Says his son is a teacher. Has four children. Then Johnny talks about himself, about the youth centre he runs, his new baby, his job at OK Feeds. He gives the impression that his life is solid and for a moment he believes it himself. Believes that when he goes home tonight he will find Loraine and Rebecca and Chris waiting for him.

Later, driving away from the gathering, he feels full of goodwill.

A week passes. During this time Johnny does not hear from Loraine. Chris is absent from work; he just stops coming. Johnny drives by Loraine's late one night and catches a glimpse of someone standing in the light by the window. He thinks maybe it's Loraine holding Rebecca but he can't be sure. He drives to his land and fires up the stove. Heats up a can of noodle soup. Eats it out of the pot. He has discovered the water from the old well that stands beside the machine shed. The pump was rusty and unused but a few shots of oil eliminated the squeaks and after several gushes of brown the water flowed clear and cold. He goes now to clean the pot. The night is humid. He strips and puts his head under the pump. Washes his hair. Soaps his armpits, his chest, his crotch. He stands naked, swatting mosquitoes, towelling himself dry with a clean T-shirt. Lightning dangles in the west. Muffled thunder.

The storm hits after midnight. Johnny wakes, his fingers and toes rigid. The lightning and thunder are inside his tent. The wind and rain flatten him. Within fifteen minutes he is lying in a pool of water. He scrambles out into the rain and runs to his car. He finds shelter there, though it is stuffy and the windows fog up. He removes his wet T-shirt and underwear. His clean clothes are in the car trunk, so he must huddle on the seat, shivering. He idles the car and blows heat around until his head drops and he sleeps. He wakes an hour later with a sore neck and an erection. He was dreaming of Loraine and Chris; they were making love and Johnny was watching.

Johnny believes that Loraine will come looking for him. And when she does he will neither gloat nor mock her. There is a lot of room inside Johnny for everyone's foibles. He is a trusting man; he feels full of luck. Love too. He used to lie beside Loraine at night and listen to her sleep and he would offer thanks for her, touching lightly at her knuckles, her toes, her knees, her hipbones, her belly, her ribs, the mole on her neck. "Thanks," he would whisper and his body would tremble with impatience and delight.

He realized that this had little to do with sex. If she never again allowed him to enter her, he would still worship her. He imagined her as a vessel full of seeds, a ripe and lovely fruit perhaps, and many times he opened his wide mouth and tried to fit her head, her hands, her feet, inside him. During those moments his body ached.

Johnny finds that his waking hours follow the pattern of the sun. He is beginning to enjoy this: the early rising, the priming of the stove, the blisters produced by the work with the pump and the axe, the small fires before bedtime, and even the digging of a latrine, a hole deep enough to bury his own shit. Everything is simplified and labour-filled. There is no shortage of time. He goes to work, avoids the office, stays out of the way of Lesser and its awful pity. Does his shopping in other towns. He fancies himself a settler of sorts, though he misses TV.

And then, on a Wednesday night, ten days after she asked him to leave, Loraine comes to find Johnny. Though the daylight has barely disappeared, Johnny has already taken shelter in his tent. He hears a car pull up. A door opens. Footsteps, and someone is standing on the other side of the thin nylon.

"Johnny?" A whisper.

Johnny unzips the flap and sees Loraine and the baby. Rebecca is sleeping; a log in her arms. "Climb in," Johnny says. The hair rises on his arms as Loraine crouches past him and brushes up against his waist. She sits cross-legged at the far end where Johnny usually lays his head. She's a shadow. Johnny lights a cigarette and for a few seconds the warmth of the flame becomes a common focus. The flare also offers Johnny a view of Loraine's face; fatigue there, dark eyes, heaviness. Is this the woman he loves? He leans closer as if to identify her. He perceives grief. The match goes out.

"Welcome," Johnny says.

"Chris is gone," Loraine responds. Her mouth is slow, full of rocks.

Johnny realizes now that her grief has little to do with him. A tug of disappointment. Resentment towards Chris. And then, as Loraine sobs and snuffles, Johnny begins to understand that children can kill you. He reaches out, takes the sleeping Rebecca. His daughter. She's a foreign object. Has so little to do with who he is, his own private anguish. He wonders at Loraine's lack of self these days, at how consumed she is by Chris and Rebecca. The baby arcs her back and opens her mouth. A lazy yawn, a grasping of paws. Johnny pats her and shushes softly.

"He left a week ago," Loraine says. "None of his friends are talking. The police think I'm an idiot. Kids that age often run, they say. Then they come back. They always come back. I went to Winnipeg last night. Drove for hours around downtown, hoping to see Chris. Nothing. Rebecca screamed and hollered. I hollered back until finally the little thing slept."

Johnny kisses the baby's head. Again.

"I keep thinking he's dead," Loraine says. "Can you help?"

Johnny wishes he were as tiny as Rebecca right now. Then he could lie in Loraine's arms. Burrow beneath her shirt and come up weary from excess.

"Can you go find him?" she asks.

"Okay," Johnny says. He reaches out a hand in the dark and finds Loraine's face. Touches lightly at her eyebrows and cheeks. Traces her mouth and trails his fingers down her neck. Her breathing is more relaxed now. Relief reveals itself in the settling of her shoulders, the push of her head against his hand.

"You poor thing," she whispers. "You shouldn't have to live like this."

"It's good for me," Johnny says. "I'm spoiled."

In that small space they lean into each other, press noses on necks, and feel the baby stir at their bellies. It is a good thing, Johnny thinks. This. Then Loraine gathers up Rebecca and before she goes, kisses Johnny on the cheek; a moist spot there. Johnny listens to Loraine leave and tries to settle in. The ground is hard beneath him. He turns, seeking a hollow for his hip. The wind blows. The trees move. A car passes on the gravel road, spitting stones into the ditch.

History, for Johnny, is what he can remember. And he always remembers most vividly just before sliding into sleep. Tonight though he keeps shifting between what is real and what is dream and it requires all his attention to separate the two. There is Phil Barkman's hooded blue penis, shrivelled and cute. Melody, pregnant again. Baby Rebecca, talking in tongues. Charlene, swimming in a pool of Hiram Walker, face down, a pickled pig. Himself, a field mouse being attacked by a small nighthawk — he scurries into a hole. And finally, there is Loraine, standing far off across a barren field, beckoning to him. He crosses the field but the going is slow, the land is rough and full of clumps and furrows. Burned stubble appears here and there. His shoes turn black. He fears that by the time he reaches the far edge, Loraine will have disappeared. Still, he presses on.